THE BIOGRAPHER

By

Kent Ostby

For Kradan and the kids, who have always given me the time, space, and encouragement to pursue my dreams.

November 2014

Chapter 1

Why me?

Sebastian Fox pushed the question out of his mind for the hundredth time that day.

He stared at the clown in the mirror and continued to apply whiteface. A couple of strokes to accentuate his eyes and lips, a rainbow colored wig, and a purple press-on nose instead of the standard red one.

Why Charlie? It was a better question. Sebastian checked his pockets, making sure they contained all of his tricks.

A knock on the door interrupted him.

"Everybody's here, Sebastian," Petey said through the door.

"Go ahead and crack it," Sebastian replied.

Sebastian put his hands on the floor and flipped his oversized feet into the air.

"Okay."

Petey pushed the door wide open then headed into the living room to gather the kids around her. Petey and Sebastian had done fifty of these events over the years they worked together, giving sick children a chance to have a big birthday event. *Kids with Cancer* matched up families with volunteers, and Sebastian loved the way giving up an afternoon could change a child's perspective on life.

He creaked as loudly as possible across the floor boards of the raised hall, until he was teetering on the single step that led into the Hudson's living room. The horn on his costume sounded, and the kids turned with a shriek.

Charlie, the baldheaded birthday boy, loved clowns and when he saw Sebastian, his face lit up with a huge smile. Several of the boys charged toward Sebastian, but Petey intercepted them. Sebastian's arms ached as he made the trek to where Charlie sat.

"Mom, it's a clown," Charlie said.

Betty Hudson beamed as she drank in her son's excitement.

"Your nose is the wrong color."

Sebastian, still on his hands, spun around to see whose nose Charlie was talking about. As he rotated in a circle, candy fell from his pockets and most of it landed on Charlie's lap, but enough made it to the other children to keep them happy.

"You're silly," Charlie said, pushing his finger into Sebastian's chest.

Charlie giggled, and Sebastian drew strength from the laugh. His self-pity disappeared below the surface, and all of his senses focused on Charlie.

Petey cleared a landing spot, and Sebastian righted himself. Once settled, he pulled balloons out from Charlie's ear.

"I hear that you like," Sebastian lowered his voice to a conspiratorial whisper, "dragons."

Charlie's family attended several fairs over the summer, but none of those clowns could make a decent dragon. Forewarned, Sebastian's pockets were stuffed with red for fire, green for the body, and a pale yellow balloon for the wings. A few deft movements of Sebastian's hands, and a ferocious dragon appeared.

"That's awesome!" yelled one of the kids.

Charlie beamed.

Petey, who worked for Sebastian, moved in behind the clown so she could lavish Charlie with attention, while Sebastian moved through the crowd. Dogs, cats, penguins, and even a unicorn leapt from his fingers, but he steadfastly refused to duplicate the birthday boy's creature.

When once balloon creations filled every child's hands, Sebastian rounded everyone up and led them to the backyard.

"Since Charlie tamed the dragon, there must be a dragon's treasure nearby."

A couple of volunteers made a chair with their hands for Charlie to ride in, like kings of old. Sebastian declared himself Charlie's guide, and they emerged from the house in search of a royal treasure. Charlie pointed at a small chest nestled in the long grass, but Sebastian turned his nose up at it.

"'Tis not fit for your majesty," Sebastian said pompously.

With a slight nod of his head, Sebastian directed the volunteers carrying Charlie in the direction of a much larger chest full of football cards and Charlie's favorite candy.

Once Charlie claimed his chest, Sebastian turned to back to Petey.

"Release the others," Sebastian bellowed and, with a roar, the yard filled with kids looking for their own treasure chests.

Mrs. Hudson took the chest from Charlie as Sebastian led him back inside.

"Mom, my leg hurts," Charlie said to her.

Sebastian settled Charlie back into his favorite chair while Charlie's mom, Betty, prepared his medicine. The other parents looked concerned, but the children continued to babble excitedly about their treasure chests.

Betty Hudson pushed her way next to Charlie, and Petey began to read the story that she had written for him. An astronaut named Charlie starred in the illustrated book as he visited all of the planets, met friendly aliens and learned the secrets of the galaxy.

Sebastian noticed Charlie's father, Dick, stayed in the kitchen as though his feet were nailed to the linoleum.

When Petey finished Charlie's book, everyone clapped. She passed it over to Betty Hudson who tucked it away for safekeeping. Petey pulled a colorful book out of her bag and slowly read *Pickle Chiffon Pie* to the assembled kids. The book reminded Petey of her childhood, and she loved to pass it's magic on to others. Sebastian drifted through the crowd with the camera, ensuring that every kid was captured at least once. Charlie nodded off to sleep during the story, and the party concluded with cake and ice cream, but no birthday boy.

Sebastian attempted to engage Charlie's dad in a conversation, but the man simply slammed his beer can down hard on the kitchen counter and headed outside through a side door. Moments later Sebastian heard the engine of a truck roar to life and tires squeal, as it took off down the street.

Sebastian cleaned off his makeup and changed back into jeans and a sweatshirt. Betty Hudson caught up with him as he entered the kitchen to help Petey clean up.

"I'm so sorry," she said. "Dick doesn't know how to handle all of this."

Sebastian stopped.

"It's okay. No one has any tools for dealing with this kind of tragedy."

Betty closed in on him, the fingers of her right hand playing down the sleeve of his sweatshirt. Unfortunately, grieving parents were not a new phenomenon for Sebastian so he turned slightly and offered his side for the inevitable hug which arrived fifteen seconds later. His eyes danced towards Petey who saw his predicament and rescued him. Petey put an arm around Betty Hudson, and the woman sagged her weight onto Petey and off of Sebastian.

"I hope Charlie really enjoyed today," Petey said.

The hug turned into a chokehold as the woman fought for control of her emotions.

"We needed this so much," Betty said. "He's always the sick kid or the kid with Leukemia. Never just Charlie. And you made him a dragon. I couldn't have designed a more perfect day."

Betty lost her composure and cried silently against Petey's shoulder until she stopped suddenly and looked embarrassed. The three of them stood there awkwardly for several moments until Betty relinquished her hold on Petey. No more words were said as the two visitors slipped out the front door.

Sebastian ignored Petey's attempts to start up a conversation on the 45 minute drive home. Mixed emotions flowed through his veins as he contemplated this day and the week that preceded it.

4

"You don't have to do the parties anymore," said Petey.

Sebastian bit his lip, not trusting his voice. Finally, he looked at her for a second.

"Do you think Charlie enjoyed today?" he asked

"Of course he did. Maybe the first good time that he's experienced in a year," said Petey.

Sebastian remained silent, and Petey knew that there would be more parties in their future, however long it might last.

The early spring annually held additional responsibilities for Sebastian, which is why a few days after Charlie's party, he was standing looking closely at the cropped lawn in the cemetery on the other side of Georgia.

"So that's how things are, Mom and Dad," he said to two faded green markers.

He had been there for half an hour, about the same amount of time he usually stayed. There was no sign of the old man. Most years when Sebastian visited his parents's graves, Duke visited his wife Winnie's grave as well.

Sebastian generally used the flexibility of his self-employed schedule to assuage the loneliness of the old man, often talking for an hour or more to just sit and listen. He wondered if Duke had died. It would happen one of these years.

The sound of weeping drifted over the humid air coming from the direction of Winnie's grave. Sebastian craned his neck and caught a glimpse of a red dress nearby, perhaps another relative. He decided to respect the woman's privacy and turned to go to his car.

Sebastian turned to go, winding his way between the stones. Whoever was in the cemetery had parked her shiny Mercedes-Benz behind Sebastian's late model Mustang. Through the cracked driver side window, the yapping of a small dog assaulted Sebastian's ears.

"Hey puppy," he said.

The dog barked and growled as he walked past to the Mustang. As Sebastian opened his door, his eyes fell on the flowers that he had meant to leave at his mother's grave that morning. He made the long trek back up the hill and placed them carefully the base of the marker.

On the way down, his path intersected with the woman whose crying he had heard earlier. She walked hastily toward her car, not noticing or at least not acknowledging Sebastian's presence, until she opened her car door. Her eyes flickered and noticed his license plate.

"I WRITE," it proclaimed.

Glancing back in response to Sebastian's footsteps sounding on the pavement, she made eye contact.

"Oh. You're the writer that my dad told me about."

From a distance, Lilith Roberts was beautiful in that work-out-body and perfect-makeup kind of way. Sebastian stretched out his hand, and she barely took it, exchanging a finger shake rather than a handshake. Up close, the makeup barely hid the lines and a few gray hairs hid amongst bottle-blond hair.

"Sebastian Fox," he said.

"Lilith Roberts," she said. "Duke Farmington is my father."

Sebastian hesitated unsure of how to phrase his next question.

"Is Duke ..." he trailed off.

"No, no," she laughed stiffly. "He's sick but not dead, too sick to make it out to Mom's grave today. He had his third heart attack a couple of months ago. Those cigars will kill him one of these days."

She paused for a heartbeat or two.

"Listen, I'd really like for you to do a story about him. Money is no object I've got plenty of that, but I'm running out of time."

"I'm sorry, Lilith. I'm actually taking some time off right now trying to work in a little bit of vacation while I have the chance."

"Please," she begged him. "There are some things about Duke that I really need to know. Just tell me your terms. I don't know how long he has left."

Her weight shifted just a little, closing the space between them. Sebastian fought the urge to look her up and down from the new angle and, in doing so, made the mistake of locking eyes with her.

6

"Well, I guess I could do one more story, but there might be some interruptions to accommodate my travel."

"Thank you! Thank you!"

She almost jumped up and down.

Sebastian handed her a business card with his website address and phone number. Lilith promised to set up time for Sebastian and Duke the following weekend.

"Not ten days from now but this weekend," she said.

"Okay," Sebastian said weakly.

The best laid plans would have to wait. Now that she had his card, he could tell that he wasn't going to get out of this assignment without a fight. A small bit of hesitation gripped him. The biographies were always a little bit trickier when the main subject wasn't paying. Before he could change his mind, she had driven off.

Petey couldn't believe it when he told her later that night.

"What about your trips? What about that special dinner with that special girl?"

"I still have time to work those out. The concert isn't for a couple of months so I can worry about that later."

She disappeared out to the guesthouse behind Sebastian's place and checked to make sure that Pops was sleeping for the night. When she got back, they figured out her hours for the week, and Sebastian wrote her a check.

"How is Pops doing?"

"He's an old man, who lived off of beer for thirty years. How do you think he's doing?"

"Besides that?" he said.

Pops had been a career alcoholic before Sebastian took him in.

"Fine. I checked his pulse and blood pressure yesterday. He won't live forever, but getting him off the streets like you did will certainly add a few years."

"It already has added a few years. And you're still fine with our arrangement? You'll take care of him after I leave?"

Petey nodded her head.

"Steady job, good pay, not a problem," she said quickly.

One more loose end wrapped up.

As Sebastian fell asleep later, he thought suddenly of Duke and wondered if the old man fell asleep thinking about loose ends.

Chapter 2

Duke Farmington lay on top of the comforter on his old four-poster bed. He smelled the humidity through the open window and heard the buzz of hundreds of bugs whose presence reflected the wet winter and brought promise for the birds who would soon feast on them.

Winnie's presence still dominated the room. The only change he'd made since he lost her all those years ago was to donate her clothes to charity. Her picture had been on his nightstand for years. As the afternoon wore on, his gaze moved from it to the curtains that stirred in the breeze of the open window.

The old phonograph wore its way through the record of Italian love songs, the only incongruent aspect of the otherwise country style ranch. Seating himself on the edge of the bed, his eyes flicked between the small wooden clock and the framed picture of his wife.

"Your daughter is sure a pain in the butt," Duke said to Winnie.

The picture made no sound, but the expression in Winnie's eyes brought a few tears to Dukes eyes which he wiped away with a large paw.

Time ticked off on the clock, and he hoped that Lilith would leave during his nap. He rarely slept, but at least he avoided her constant haranguing. Most of his naptime had been taken up by the constant recollection of an old man, who lived too much in his youth and not enough in his old age.

Today, Lilith presented a special inconvenience. He had mentioned in passing an author whom he met whenever he went to visit Winnie's grave. Lilith had hired Fox to write a biography of Duke and that put Duke in an uncomfortable position. He liked Fox. The kid always looked Duke in the eye instead of making him feel like a waste of time. In fact, Duke would have loved to have traded Fox for Lilith's cell-phone-checking husband except that Duke would never conscribe Fox to a punishment of misery as great as being married to Lilith.

Duke's problem with Sebastian Fox was simple. A man in Sebastian Fox's profession pried stories out of curmudgeons like Duke. The old man had no lack of faith in his own ability to stonewall, but he didn't usually have to go up against a professional.

Still, Duke thought, it would be nice to have a listening ear from time to time other than Lilith.

Duke heard the crunch of gravel as the writer trekked up to the house. Peeking from behind a curtain Duke could see a green car at the bottom of the drive. Lilith's heels sounded on the outside stairs, and Duke eavesdropped on their chatting.

"Mr. Fox, thank you for coming on such short notice. My father is rather moody, and I wanted you to get up here before he could talk you or me out of this somehow."

"That's something I want to talk to about," said Sebastian. "I've worked with a lot of people in the past, and things don't always turn out the way everyone expects."

"Oh, I know," she said. "But I'm sure you'll be able to get him to talk. After we met this week, I looked at your website and recognized Sarah Rausch's name. I went to college with her so I called her up this week. She said that you had done a fabulous job on her dad's book."

Sebastian remembered Scott Rausch.

"I'll do what I can Miss Roberts. Mr. Rausch loved telling his stories and felt genuinely excited about having a book written about him. An unwilling subject isn't usually fertile ground for transparency."

She handed him a check for ten thousand dollars.

"I only need five-thousand up front," Sebastian protested. "The rest isn't due until I've completed my work, and who knows how long that will be if Duke's not inclined to cooperate."

10

"This is easier for me," she said. "Why don't we go sit on the porch? Duke is sleeping right now so he doesn't have to talk to me. He's gotten more difficult as he's aged."

Duke took all of this in through the window, but when they moved to the side porch, he could no longer hear them clearly so he slunk into the living room and listened from there instead.

"I know a little bit about Duke from our talks at the cemetery, but what can you tell me about your mom?" Sebastian asked.

"My mom? Why? Oh, I guess for background and stuff. Her name was Winifred. She loved Dad and dancing although I never saw them dance together. When mom would teach us to dance in the living room, Dad would just sit there and tap along to the beat. I don't know how she put up with so much grief from Duke through the years, but she still loved him when she passed away."

Duke bristled at the description, but remained hidden where he was.

"Okay," Sebastian said. "I can talk to Duke more about the two of them also. Now what do you want the biography to focus on? I'm assuming that you'd wanted to cover most of his life."

"Maybe. Although, it's really the war that I'm interested in. He'd never talk about it, but it always seemed like the problems and arguments boiled back down to that."

"Did your mother known him then?"

"Yes. They met during the war. She used to tell us stories about Dad and how he had changed during the war, but I don't know if she ever knew the details of what happened over there. He laughed less and seemed agitated when they were off the ranch. They'd go out for a walk in town, and when he came to the corner, he'd poke his head around and then jerk back. She'd laugh at him when he'd overreact like that. I never saw him do that so he must have grown out of it after a while."

Duke felt his face flush and wondered if this was how it would feel to go to your own funeral.

11

"Another time," Lilith was saying, "Antonio snuck up on Dad out in the woods. When Antonio lunged out of the bushes, Dad flipped Antonio onto his back and dropped down on top of him. Antonio was only nine. You can imagine how scared he felt. He jumped up, and ran crying to Mom. My folks yelled about it for hours. Finally, Dad came back and apologized. In fact, I can't ever remember another time that I ever saw him apologize."

Duke cringed at the revelation, given so freely to a stranger.

"Where did he fight during the war?"

"Europe I think. Hang on."

She moved into the house, and Duke could hear her heels clacking against the floor. He stood as still as possible willing her to stay out of the living room and she did, walking past the doorway and over to the kitchen wall where she slid a picture off the wall with a scrape. Her retreat sounded and then the screen door opened and closed behind her.

"I know he served in Italy. Here's a picture he keeps from back then."

Duke knew which picture it was, of course. Four young friends, loaded down with all sort of weapons were standing in front of a huge plane. Behind the men in the picture, an airplane loomed, adorned with the words "Rome or Bust" with the word "Bust" leading up to the ample bosom of a woman who had also been painted on the plane.

"Let me see. The one on the left is Tony, then dad, then Herman, and in this last one I always forget his name. Tony, Duke, Herman, and..."

Duke strode quietly until he was right next to the door that led out onto the porch.

"Jake. The last one is Jake," he said in his unusually deep bass voice.

"Dad!" Lilith exclaimed. "You're up."

"When you machine-gunned across the floor with your heels a minute ago, I almost tried to duck and cover before I remembered that I couldn't move that fast anymore."

Duke stepped out onto the porch and extended a firm handshake to Sebastian. The writer took it, held his own, but backed down soon enough for it to be considered a draw.

"Well, I'll just be going," Lilith said.

"Your car's over there," said Duke.

Lilith's eyes returned fire, but she held her tongue and retreated to her vehicle.

Once he was certain that she had cleared out, Duke settled himself into one of the rocking chairs so Sebastian followed suit. The old man lit up a cigar and offered Sebastian one, but the writer politely declined. The porch overlooked a couple of acres of Duke's ranch. A creek flowed through the property, and the trees were celebrating early spring.

"Beautiful isn't it?" said Duke, breaking the silence.

"It's a view I could live with," Sebastian said.

"It's the view I'll die with, you know."

Sebastian nodded.

"Did Lilith tell you what I'm dying from?" Duke asked.

"She said you'd had a couple of heart attacks."

"My heart is deteriorating, thanks to my beloved cigars. She wants me to give them up. Do you think I should?"

"I might have a couple of years ago. Now, I think the dying have a right to go out in whatever way they choose."

Duke made some sound of agreement in his throat.

"Do you know why I'll die with a cigar in my hand? Because they help me remember the good times."

They sat that way for a few minutes, drinking in the morning. Suddenly, the old man jumped to his feet.

"I've got something I want you to try. Stay right here."

He banged through the screen door and returned carrying two Mason jars of a clear liquid on a tray along with a plate of biscuits, some butter, and some jelly.

"The biscuits are fresh. My dad's recipe. What do you want on yours?" asked Duke.

"Butter and jelly will be fine," Sebastian said

Duke made up three of the biscuits setting each on the arm of Sebastian's rocking chair as he went. He adorned a few for himself cradling them in one huge hand. Sebastian took a bite and pushed the rest of the first biscuit into his mouth.

The writer picked up the Mason jar and paused, smelling a sweet odor wafting up from the drink. When he had swallowed his first biscuit, he took a sip of the liquid.

"Moonshine?" Sebastian asked.

"Honey mead. Another family recipe. You won't find anything else to match it."

Sebastian drank some more mead, and Duke thought the writer's eyes might roll back in his head.

"I won't be able to write if I drink very much of this."

"Better than codeine for pain, and it helps with the forgetting," said Duke

More silence followed, and eventually, Duke gave in and restarted the conversation.

"So do we just sit here all day?"

"We can if you'd like. Lilith already paid me so I'm on the job."

"And what is the job?"

"My contract with your daughter is one of my standard ones. I spend twenty hours with you and the family then write up a biography covering any part of your life. I'll put in pictures and make an individualized cover. You get ten copies, and I keep one. In exchange I give up several weeks of my life, and you give up ten thousand dollars. Or in this case, Lilith does."

"And Lilith paid you the ten grand already?"

"Yes. I usually only take half up front, but she insisted on paying the whole amount."

"That's because," said Duke, "she doesn't want to be bothered by talking to you again. It might interfere with her trips to the tanning bed. I mostly agreed to talk to you because I knew it would cost her money, and that's the only way I can get back at her for blaming all of her problems on me."

Duke glanced at Sebastian expecting the writer to question him about the relationship, but Sebastian had heard everything in his years of writing and just let the comment pass. Instead, Sebastian opened his briefcase and passed over a sample biography for Duke to look through.

After a few minutes, Duke guffawed at a new thought.

"What if I don't want you to tell Lilith everything?"

"Once I cash her check, I'll be working for her, and we'll have a binding contract."

"I'll make you a deal, Fox. Tear up Lilith's check. Tell her that I wouldn't talk to you. I'll write you a check of my own, and you can come back next week. If you stay with me drink for drink, I'll tell you my whole story."

Sebastian shook his head, aware that he was mired in the middle of a longstanding feud. After a minute, he looked back at the old man and shrugged.

"Okay, but I don't think Lilith is going to be very happy about your idea."

"That just makes it a better idea," said Duke.

The old man passed the biography back to Sebastian and as he did so, a ticket fluttered to the ground.

Duke picked it up and stared

"Who's Adria Rider?" He asked.

"An actress and singer," said Sebastian. "Thanks for finding my concert ticket. I thought it disappeared for good."

15

Chapter 3

Adria Rider slammed out a rock tune, easily the loudest song in her repertoire. Halfway through the pounding number, a disembodied voice cut her off.

Calibrating the transition to *Crazy Calypso* from the soulful ballads that dominated her work demanded the trickiest adjustments of the night for the hack that ran her sound board. Verifying those fluctuations in each new venue also marked the end of the band's pre-concert ritual.

"That should be all we need," said a faceless voice over the PA.

"Way to pick it up, Dave," Adria said to the drummer.

Dave waved a stick back at her. Dave had been struggling with the transitions since he had joined the group a few weeks back. Adria checked her watch.

"Okay. Everyone, be back here in four hours. We're doing the first show at 9:30 and another at 11:30."

One of the band members suggested going to a pub for a few drinks.

"Just make sure you're sober enough to play tonight, guys," said a grinning Adria.

She hated playing mother, father, and caretaker for the entire band. Her ten year age gap over the rest of the band made total connectedness an impossibility, but in her faded memories, she remembered being much more mature than this group.

The sound check had started early today, because her publicist, Guy Davies, was in town. She glanced at her watch and realized that he'd probably arrived at the hotel already. The band dropped her off at the Holiday Inn. When she made movies, Adria commanded half a million dollars per appearance and a nice place to stay, but now that she had turned back to her first love of music, she was paying the bills. Holiday Inn topped the list of what she could afford, no matter how much the band complained.

Guy was sitting in the lobby, typing on his computer, when she walked in. She waved and bounced up to him. He looked exasperated with her even after a faux Hollywood hug.

"Adria, I've got a flight out of here in two hours. You've got to be on time."

She looked at Guy's balding head, a horseshoe of salt-and-pepper hair surrounding a bright sheen in the center. She laughed when she saw the deadly serious look on his face.

"If you don't want me to make you late then plan an overnighter when you come to see me or just email me."

Davies hated email. He felt it took away from the personal touch.

"Adria, you know we need the face time."

"Well here I am, Guy, but I need a shower. Once you get your computer put away, come and talk to me in 212."

She handed him her spare room key.

Warm water sprayed down her body and the grime wound down the drain. They had rode in the van all day to get here – then it had been time to set up the stage. If you were in the band, you were part of the road crew too, even her.

She leaned back, stretched, and then touched her toes, letting the heat seep down her back. The water brought refreshment to Adria. By the time she heard Guy enter her room, she was standing in front of the mirror with the bathroom door closed. She ran her brush through her long brunette hair.

17

"Adria?"

"Just talk to me through the door. I'll be out in a minute."

"Adria!" Guy said with obvious exasperation in his voice. "You know that Karlie is going to ask me if we were together in your room. And if that's not bad enough, you're not even dressed."

"Guy, you and I aren't even together in my room. I'm in the bathroom, and how do you know I'm not dressed?"

A sigh escaped Guy's lips.

"You wouldn't have the door locked if you were dressed and if you were dressed, you'd probably get undressed just to irritate me. You were in the shower and ... Oh forget it. We need to talk about your schedule, and I've got a packet of fan mail. Sarah pulled out the interesting stuff."

Sarah worked for Guy, and she took the first pass at Adria's mail.

"Didn't we just go over the calendar two weeks ago?"

"We did, but the shooting for *Crocodile Dreams* slipped again. We may need to move a concert or two."

She looked at the mirror and pulled out the ponytail holder she had used to keep her hair dry. She brushed frantically, her blood pressure rising.

"Can't producers keep anything on schedule, Guy? I can't reschedule concerts all the time if I'm going to make any headway in the music business."

"I know Adria. The schedule flowed better last year when you focused on acting instead of mixing the two businesses."

When she had rubbed the apricot scrub onto her face, she turned the sink water as hot as she could stand and dipped the washcloth under the flow. Why had she even taken that movie?

18

"Well, they are going to have to work around the concerts."

After the scrub had been on for two minutes, she rubbed it off, swearing at the painful heat. Every night, she vowed would be her last, but nothing else kept her complexion this clear.

Adria pulled on her bra and a white shirt. She turned to see how her figure looked in the mirror. Satisfied, she yanked open the door and Guy toppled into the bathroom. He had been leaning on the door to hear Adria over the water.

Adria laughed.

"Trying out for a part as a jack in the box?"

His face turned crimson as he pulled himself off Adria's arm.

"Steady, Guy," she said smiling.

"You're impossible," he said back to her, but he was smiling too.

They walked into the main room, and Guy piled three folders on her table.

"Two scripts plus the fan mail," he said, anticipating her question. "One of the scripts has some promise. The other is too small a part for you, but you'll like it."

Guy had been with her for a long time. They had even tried dating once which explained Karlie's jealousy. She definitely was going to freak out about their meeting in Adria's room. Guy knew Adria's styles and what she was willing to do. He didn't always approve, but he didn't try to run her world.

"There sent another musical, but I left it out."

"I get a musical every month now that I've actually sold a few CDs. You should have sent it along, though. One of these days, I'll get one worth doing."

"Nobody goes to musicals these days, Adria. Not unless they are adapted from the stage."

"That's because the scripts for the musicals are 'boring,'" she said, sing-songing the last word.

They sat down and began going over her calendar. She fumed as he went over the changes. They had a few options and worked through them until they came back to the same starting point that Guy had suggested when they first sat down. Guy wasn't the best in the business. She couldn't afford the best in the business, but Guy understood her and what she wanted in a career. No matter the subject, they always came around to Guy's suggestions. She knew that they would, but she wanted to control what was going on with her life.

After he left, she sat on the bed, flipping through mundane TV channels filled with reruns. She flipped open the script with the small part and agreed with Guy. The part might earn her a Best Supporting Actress nomination, if she played it well. Given how early the character died in the script, she might be able to squeeze it into her concert schedule for the following year.

Fan mail was another part of the job, and Guy's assistant Sarah had developed a system that worked well for his clients. Sarah did the first pass of Adria's mail. If it involved an appearance, Sarah gave it to Guy and he made the decision. There were just too many requests and charitable causes out there for Adria's soft heart to handle. Sarah would send out autographed photos and pass along anything else interesting to Adria. Sometimes, for a young fan, Adria would respond with a personal note of encouragement.

Leaning back against the headboard, she penned a few half-hearted responses then crammed the rest of the mail back into the folder. Most of the new scripts she read were shallow, the concerts chaotic, and the men she met all the same. Adria was at the nexus of scripts, concerts, and men, and she was beginning to think that she was the problem. She had run through every kind of boyfriend she could imagine, and none of them were a good fit. Her sister had even said that Adria was searching for her lost soul when she had restarted her music career.

The loneliness of the road made her wish she could at least figure out what she wanted in a man. She stood and walked around the room wondering what she wanted in a man.

"A man who can make me laugh."

Adria tossed the manila envelope onto the desk. One letter fell to the ground. It had a red "X" through it. She had seen Sarah mark correspondence with that before. Usually, they went straight to the trash and never made it to Adria. This one must have gotten put into her packet by mistake. She flipped it open, wondering what made the letter bad enough to rate Sarah's red X.

"Adria," she read aloud, "I want you. You are so hot. Call me. My cell is ..."

She tossed the letter into the trash can.

"Ah. Why do I even bother? I'm not going to find Prince Charming in a letter. Married to the road, since I can't find anyone else to marry," she said to nobody at all, as usual.

The dissatisfaction ate at her and threatened to swallow her whole when the phone rang.

"You want to grab some dinner with us," Dave asked.

"Sure. Just let me grab my shoes, and I'll be ready to go."

Chapter 4

Sebastian watched as Adria Rider, on the screen, tumbled through the air, flipped at the last second and landed on her feet. Gunshots sounded above her and her fellow spy Bruce. Bruce fell to the ground, a stain of red spreading across his shirt.

Adria ran to him, dragging his bleeding body out of the line of fire. She pulled him around the corner to safety. Peeking carefully around the rock, she saw the shooters began their descent on the wire. She unhooked the cable, and the pursuers plunged into the river and were swept away.

Turning back, Adria found the male lead holding a gun on her. Sebastian had suspected as much. Apparently, Adria's character had suspected it as well. She stood, now, in a Mexican standoff, a two-shot derringer in her right hand.

"Go ahead and shoot," she said.

"I wasn't going to hurt you, Sandra," the turncoat Bruce replied.

"Put your gun down and I'll put mine down. Then we can both walk away from here."

"Don't do it!" Sebastian yelled at the TV where the movie played.

"All right," said Bruce. He started to put his weapon down, but as Adria lowered hers, he whipped his hand back up, trying for a shot. She dove to the side and fired. Getting to her feet, Adria walked toward Bruce and kicked the gun away from his dying hand.

The camera angle of the film widened and spun away from Adria, panning the countryside as she stood and watched her former friend and lover dying because of his greed.

Sebastian made Petey watch all the special features. The interview with the actors had Sebastian studying Adria's face. At times, she acted playful and excited, but then he saw it again, a distant wistfulness. For just a second on the screen, her guard dropped, and Sebastian saw behind the mask.

When it ended, Petey looked at him, "And so ends another Adria-fest."

Sebastian blushed, "Don't you have somewhere to be?"

Petey laughed.

"I'll check on Pops on my way out. What time do you need me here in the morning?"

"Whenever you want."

He paused.

"I updated my website," he said, changing the subject.

"No longer accepting submissions for work?" she asked.

"Something like that. Sebastian Fox, biographer to the non-stars, is beginning a well-earned vacation, etcetera. I still have four biographies to finish up, but only a couple of them have any real work left in them."

"What are you going to do with your vacation?"

"Dream," he said.

"You're crazy, you know," Petey replied.

"Where are you headed now?"

"Oh, I'm meeting Cary and Sarah in Buckhead. They said ten o'clock so I've got plenty of time. We'll hit *The Blue Spigot* and a few of the other usual places."

"Who's the designated driver?"

"Don't be such a worry wart, Sebastian."

"Petey."

"I'll make sure we take a cab from Sarah's, okay?"

"Okay."

Petey's face shifted from annoyed to amused.

"Sebastian Fox, you really need a life, or a date, or something."

The next morning, Sebastian sat in front of the computer willing the words to flow from his fingertips onto the screen in front of him. For a man who had written several books, it hardly seemed possible that he would struggle with a simple fan letter.

The events of the past months flooded through his mind again, swirling inspiration into action. His fingers tapped out the rest of the message. Tone was everything – a step beyond normal, but not scary. Eye catching, but mature. He worked it and reworked to perfection.

Adria probably received hundreds of letters a month asking for photographs and proposing marriage. He wondered if his medium request would appear odd.

Dear Adria,

My name is Sebastian Fox, biographer to the non-stars. I'm not writing you to do your biography since you're a star and that wouldn't fit in with my career plans.

Before I go on, I wanted to mention how much I've enjoyed your album, and the way the music compliments, rather than overpowers, who you are. Your live performances seem to have avoided the South, so I'm going to drive up to Columbus and see your show there.

While not wanting to change your life or become your biographer, I admit that there are times when I wonder what it would be like to share a nice meal with you.

Nothing exotic, of course. Nothing that smacks of Hollywood posh.

Perhaps when you sit surrounded by the Hollywood elite at some two-hundred dollar a plate restaurant; you

24

*wonder what it would be like to be just another woman
enjoying a nice meal and a few laughs with a normal guy.*

Perhaps you don't, but then again, perhaps you do.

*I come to Los Angeles several times a year. If you wish
to step out into the real world for a breath of fresh air, I will
have reservations for two at Angelino's in Fullerton on the
following dates this summer:*

*Wednesday, July 6, Friday, July 28, and Monday,
August 14.*

*If you can't make it, I will have some extra room for
my feet when I dine at my favorite restaurant.*

He autographed a photo of himself, added his website
address underneath his name, and placed it carefully into an
envelope.

Petey's car in the driveway reminded him that she was
watching Pops. Given that Sebastian had been in his own world
for the past five hours, her presence meant that Pops hadn't
been ignored for the entire morning. He walked to the mother-
in-law suite and poked his head in.

"I need to run a few errands, Petey. Do you have your
key to the house?"

Petey's purple streaked hair appeared around the corner
of the kitchenette. She ran her tongue over her lip ring while
Sebastian talked. He suppressed a smile, but she noticed.

"What?" she asked.

"Just that you've had that ring for three years, and
you're still not used to it."

"I know I've told you that you were like my older
brother, Sebastian, but you don't have to act like one all the
time."

She gave him a hug to prove she still loved him.

"And, yes, I have my key," she said.

"So is that it?" she said pointing at the envelope tucked
under his arm.

25

He blushed, but nodded.

"Got to take a chance while I got the time," he said.

"Taking a chance is asking the girl down the bar out on a date. What you're doing is wasting good paper and postage," Petey said.

"Probably," Sebastian said, "but what's the worst thing that could happen?"

"Oh, let's see. Humiliation, the FBI breathing down your neck, and did I mention humiliation?"

"Yes, you did," Sebastian said, smiling. "I'm sure the humiliation will be short lived. I'm not significant enough for people to humiliate me on an ongoing basis."

Petey laughed.

"Probably not," she said.

"Bye, Pops," Sebastian hollered toward the back room.

"He's asleep," said Petey.

"Okay. I'll be back in a couple of hours," he said.

Early spring was painting with the varying hues of green that had originally attracted Sebastian to the Atlanta area in the first place. The trees had shrugged into their shirts, covering their twisted and gnarled branches and restoring privacy between the second stories of houses positioned too closely together.

When Sebastian slid the envelope across the post office counter and asked for the postage on it, the clerk glanced at the address then back at him. A couple of dollars covered it. No FBI agents leapt from hidden passageways. The clerk stamped the envelope and tossed it into a waiting bin that moved down a conveyor belt like the sands of time.

As Sebastian watched it roll out of sight, his phone rang.

"Fox?" said a gravelly voice. "This is Duke. The bank says you cashed my check."

"That's right. I was going to call you and see when you wanted me to come up."

"Any time is fine with me. My schedule is open. Although to hear Lilith, you better come over right away before I croak."

Sebastian smiled at the sarcastic cynicism.

After a few minutes, they decided that Sebastian would drive up the following evening.

Chapter 5

Duke watched as darkness crept over his house and yard. The old man sat thinking about Sebastian and what to tell him. Drinking and forgetting was easier than remembering. He'd done the best he could, during the war and with his family. It hardly seemed fair that so many people hated him, but he couldn't really help that.

Duke heard the crunch of the gravel as Sebastian rolled up to the house. The smell of dust raised from the writer's arrival was as predictable as a sunrise for the man who'd spent nearly sixty years living on the shoe box ranch in rural northeastern Georgia.

Sebastian found Duke on the back porch whether by intuition, the smell of the cigar, or the round circle of fire that floated in the dark evening.

Duke handed him a Mason jar of the honey mead, an action that was destined to be repeated multiple times that night.

"Okay, here are my terms. I don't want ten copies of this. I only want two. One for you to keep, and one for you to send to this address. Send the biography and this letter."

Duke had paid a private eye to find the address in Italy. He'd kept it for years and dug it out of his desk the night before. So many years had passed that he wasn't even sure anyone would care anymore, but he still did so he'd figured that the family might.

Duke looked at Sebastian.

"I don't want that copy mailed until after my death. Both copies are your property, Fox. Not mine. That way they can't pass on to my kids."

"Lilith mentioned that you had a couple of boys," Sebastian said.

Duke took a long drag on the cigar and blew out the smoke.

"My oldest son, Antonio, was killed in Nam back in 1968. I named both of my boys after men I knew in the war. I don't suppose you were in Vietnam."

Duke paused, gauging Fox's age.

"Nah. You're too young to have been, I guess. I still remember when we got the news. Winnie just cried like a baby for days and days, and I just felt so helpless. You think dying is hard to deal with? It's nothing compared to putting your own son into the ground. When the funeral was over, my other boy, Daniel, and I stayed and filled in the grave. It took us a couple of hours you know. More and more of the casket disappeared with every shovelful of dirt,and I kept thinking that maybe if I could make the casket disappear then it would turn out to be just a dream."

Duke tried to shake the memories away with a flick of his head.

"Daniel left for Canada the next day. He was only a few days short of his eighteenth birthday. Winifred couldn't bear to lose him too."

His voice shook, and the emptiness echoed in his chest. The picture held his mind for a few moments. Another sip of liquid courage, and Duke felt indomitable again. In the distance, thunder called out a challenge.

"Do you ever see Daniel?" Sebastian's voice cracked the weary silence.

Duke stared straight ahead, not wavering to the left or the right. Duke licked his lips.

29

"The last time I saw him was the day after Winnie's funeral. It was a long time after President Carter gave amnesty to all the draft dodgers. He came down from Canada looking like Grizzly Adams from that old TV show. After the funeral, we stood there just like we had twenty years before and filled in the grave."

He was running low on mead so he sloshed it around in his jar before he drained it. Looking over at Sebastian, he said, "Drink up."

Fox did as he was ordered.

Satisfied, Farmington continued his story.

"We talked the next morning for a few hours. More words than I can ever remember tumbled out of Daniel's mouth. He was a handyman who had a place up in the mountains with lots of rivers nearby for fishing. When Daniel left, he told me he wouldn't be back again."

That was all Duke would say for a while.

Finally, Duke waved Sebastian into the house. Dusty pictures littered the walls. As they walked into the kitchen, Fox caught glimpses of the faded photos, black and whites of kids in various stages of childhood and a smattering of color photos when the kids were older. A framed flag and the picture of a fearless young man, preserved these four decades.

Farmington flipped on the light switch in the kitchen and refilled their mugs. Sebastian leaned against the kitchen counter while Duke rustled in the pantry.

"I like to make popcorn at night," Duke said.

Farmington took down a sauce pan and filled it about a quarter inch deep with cooking oil. To this, he added a few popcorn kernels. At Sebastian's look, he explained.

"I wait for these to pop then I know the oil's hot. Started doing it one night after I forgot about the pan and just about set the whole house on fire."

Farmington guffawed at the remembrance. The laughter took his breath away, and Fox looked concerned. Duke doubled over and finally managed a deep breath.

The first kernels came to life, and Duke dumped the rest of the popcorn into the pan. While it popped, he took out a wooden bowl, big enough for a potluck salad. In a separate sauce pan, he melted butter. The popping started all at once, and Duke quickly shook the pan from side to side while holding the lid just above the edge of the pan. As the popcorn bubbled up, he lifted the lid a couple of inches and dumped the popped kernels into the bowl. He repeated the process until the bowl was full and the pan was empty.

They walked through a doorway and Sebastian was staring at a long, narrow living room. Two faded couches covered in 70's green formed an L around the fireplace. A leather backed chair filled in the remaining gap and Duke, in turn, filled that chair.

"You can sit on the couch, Fox, that way when you pass out, I can just roll you over."

Sebastian had no doubt that Duke would be able to out drink him. The first jar of mead was already having its effect.

Duke munched popcorn while Sebastian checked his notes.

"You were telling me about your son Daniel."

"Right," Duke said with a nod of remembrance. "Daniel. I probably should write him again although I'm not sure that I have a good address for him. Last I knew he was up north."

"In Canada?"

"Hmm," said Duke through a mouthful of popcorn.

"You could look him up on the internet," Sebastian suggested.

Farmington looked across at Sebastian, straining to see him clearly through the near darkness pierced only by a single, dull lamp in the corner.

"I don't own a computer. Never have and never will. Still, I figure I should talk to him sometime. A man should know when his father's dying, just in case."

Duke didn't finish the thought, but stared into the vacant fireplace, cold like the life inside him. He tilted his head back as he drank.

"Drink up, Fox."

Sebastian obliged.

"Daniel, you know, he was always the steady one. Didn't attract too much attention. Probably couldn't with Antonio around. Antonio was the athlete of the family, the one that always seemed to come out smelling like roses. He was faster, smarter, and more determined than Daniel. If I was honest, I'd say that Antonio was my favorite, and Daniel was his mom's."

"What about Lilith?"

"Lilith was a pain in the butt from the day she was born. She was coddled by all of her relatives because she was the first Farmington girl in a couple of generations."

Duke watched Fox work, aware for the first time that this wasn't idle talk, but rather a friendly interrogation. Sebastian started to say something, stopped, and then started again.

"When I first met Lilith, she said you had a secret that drove her crazy. Said she'd pay anything to hear what it was."

Duke laughed, put off by the truth.

"The big secret. That's her shrink speaking. There isn't some big secret, Fox. Oh, some things happened, bad things happened."

Duke trailed off unwilling to say more. Instead, he raised the walls and turned the tables by asking about Sebastian's family.

"No family. My folks were killed in a car crash in Georgia when I was in college. Dad was already sick with COPD. They decided to take a drive through the South because they didn't know how much time he had before he'd be too sick to travel. The other driver was a college kid who'd driven all night to make it back to class on time after a long weekend. He died too. All of a sudden I was an orphan. An adult orphan, but an orphan nonetheless."

"That must have been hard," the old man said.

"Yeah. Everyone was gone. I was so angry at that kid that I was glad that he died. Later I wished he wasn't dead so I could scream at him. I wanted to tell him what he'd cost me. The guilt hit me later, guilt for wanting him dead, for wanting anyone dead."

"That's understandable," said Duke. "Would you have killed him?"

Sebastian shook his head, "No. I wouldn't kill anyone. I mean, maybe in the heat of battle, but I wouldn't hunt a man down and kill him."

Duke grunted. "Heat of battle. Now that's a term that's overused."

Sebastian thought for a minute.

"Very few people today know what the heat of battle really feels like," said Sebastian.

"It's like nothing that you can imagine," said Duke. "I've seen a bullet one time whip past my face and heard it hit the guy behind me. He'd just asked me a question and by the time the answer was out of my mouth, he was dead."

"That's hard to imagine."

"Not for me," said the old man.

He took a long drag on his cigar.

"Not for me," he repeated, "It's been sixty years, and all I need to do is close my eyes, and it all comes flooding back. Sometimes right before sleep, it comes to me unbidden."

"It's hard for me to remember all the details of the accident, but if I think about it too long, I feel so alone," said Sebastian.

Duke recognized the hurt in Sebastian's voice because he had lived with his own for a long time.

"I'm pretty much alone, too," said Duke.

At that point, they began to drink seriously. Conversation was optional and infrequent. Duke watched Sebastian trying to keep up with him, a casual drinker trying to drink another man's liquor. Sebastian really began to struggle when Duke gave him a fourth glass. He took a sip and tried to set it on the edge of the couch. The Mason jar teetered then spilled its contents onto the couch and Sebastian.

Duke chuckled to himself, and threw a blanket over the sleeping writer.

Chapter 6

The white and blue van bounced along Interstate 25, jostling Adria's hand as she attempted for the tenth time to autograph a picture. Last night's concert in Denver had been their third and final Colorado booking. Santa Fe was their destination for today, as they wound their way down the Rockies, for another show.

Their Rocky Mountain sendoff had been attended by a depressingly small crowd. Adria had missed some notes on a couple of her songs, and the drummer had decided on an extra chorus during their last song. Mistakes like that kept the critics from taking her seriously.

Adria felt like quitting.

It would be so much easier to go back to her Hollywood life. On set, she was a known acting commodity, and both her and guy understood the business. Best of all, if she quit, she wouldn't have a band to deal with.

A love triangle was the last thing that a band needed, but it was the whirlwind that had caught up with Adria earlier in the day. She had been aware that Darla and Jimmy were sleeping together occasionally so Adria had naturally stopped by Jimmy's room looking for Darla when she failed to answer her cellphone that morning. Only Darla wasn't in Jimmy's room. It turned out that Adria, and a worried Jimmy, had found her in Dave the drummer's room.

Dave and Jimmy had thrown a few punches before Adria separated them.

I need a band mom, she thought to herself as the van bumped along the freeway.

Jimmy, nursing a long bruise under his left eye, was driving the van. Occasionally he glared at Dave and Darla who were sitting in front of Adria. She watched their interplay in the mirror. Dave caught Jimmy's eye and grinned through swollen lips. Adria kicked his seat.

"Dave, I wouldn't start any trouble if I were you."

The insolent grin on Dave's face made Adria want to punch him.

"I'm cool, Adria. I'm cool. It was just a misunderstanding on Jimmy's part," Dave said.

Adria studied Dave for a moment.

"Really? Which part did he misunderstand? The part where you were pulling your pants on this morning? Or the part where Darla wrapped herself in a sheet?"

"Look, Adria," Darla poked her head over her seat, "who appointed you to the morality police? Jimmy and Dave don't belong to me, and I don't belong to either of them. I'll sleep with whoever I want."

"Fine, Darla. Sleep with whoever you want, but can you wait until this part of the tour is over. Before you ask, yes, it is my business. Everything in my band is my business including personnel trouble. Thanks to you, I've got people trading punches instead of working together."

Just about everyone was listening into the conversation now, except for Luke who was hooked into his iPod. Adria and Darla just stared at each other for a minute.

"You worry about the band, Adria. I'll figure out who to sleep with." Darla turned back and started talking to Dave.

"Way to stay classy, Darla," Adria muttered under her breath.

Adria let out a deep sigh and slammed her head back against the head rest. She looked up and saw Gary glancing over his shoulder in her direction.

"What are you staring at, Gary?"

Before he could answer, a loud, thumping sound pounded from outside the van. Jimmy swerved to control the vehicle.

"Flat tire," said several voices in unison.

"Ugh. Just what we needed," said Adria, closing her eyes again.

She tried to banish the nightmare that had invaded her morning. It took two more hours for them to change the tire since the van was not equipped with the proper tools. Finding a shop to get them a replacement pushed their window to arrive in New Mexico down to almost nothing.

Taco McGavern's was a one-of-a-kind establishment that came as close to ripping off *Taco Mac* with its menu, decor, and layout as the law would allow. Adria and the band were well-publicized, and the manager had set up changing rooms for them in the back.

"Darla, could you please try to be celibate for a few days, until this section of the tour is over? It's not like you are in love with any of these guys."

"Lay off, Adria. You people are getting too worked up over all of this. Besides, don't you ever want to be held at night? Or are you becoming an ice princess as well as a singer?"

Darla's tone pushed Adria over the edge.

"Look, Darla, I like you and you've done well, but you're not the only backup singer in the world."

"And you aren't the only act in the world, Adria"

Adria groaned inwardly. She had meant to appeal to Darla, but instead had set her off.

"Forget it, Darla. You play the skank."

Before Darla could reply, Adria walked out and slammed the door. She wanted a good, stiff drink.

Adria remembered back to her teenage years when she first sang at an open mic night. It had been so fun and simple. Just stand up and sing.

From there, she had built up a small reputation around Colorado Springs, and she had daydreamed about a singing career. Instead, acting had overrun all of that.

Her friends had talked her into auditioning for a play as a freshman in high school, and she'd landed a small part, but played it to excellence. The following year she started getting all of the leading roles, and that trend had carried her throughout high school.

Entering college, she had thought about picking music up again, but almost accidentally she had landed a part in a movie that had turned into the teen drama of the year.

It wasn't long before she started getting the lead role in films.

Adria snapped back to reality when Darla stormed past her. Shaking her head, Adria finally broke down, got a beer, and sat at the bar collecting her thoughts. Napkins became to-do lists and calendars.

A man wearing a brown sports coat sat down beside her.

"I think you're working too hard on whatever that is," he said. "This is a bar. You're supposed to have fun and relax a little. Drink some beer, make friends."

Several comebacks jumped to mind, but Adria bit her tongue. He was a nice enough sort, but she wasn't interested in hooking up with anyone from Santa Fe.

"Thanks. You're probably right," she said.

Adria dropped her pen on the bar and picked up her beer.

"See, that's not too hard, is it. I'm Carl. What's your name?"

"You really don't know my name?" she asked.

Handbills and photos of Adria's face were plastered on both front doors as well as several other locations in the bar advertising the night's entertainment.

"Now, how would I know your name when we just met?" Carl asked.

Adria took a couple of steps until she was standing in front of one of the posters. She screwed her face up to match the look on the poster.

"Oh, you're her. The singer for tonight, uh," he tried to read the name in the semi-darkness. "Allison."

Adria could take no more and started laughing. She held out her hand.

"I'm Adria Rider. Pleased to meet you, Carl. Now, I really have to go work."

The concert itself went well, better than it had any right to go, given the rest of the day. They got a curtain call. Jimmy was outstanding, reading her and the direction of the concert better than anyone else. Whatever decisions about the band she had been putting off had been forced upon her by the poor showing from the day before. Adria would tough out the next four days. After that, she was getting herself a new drummer and maybe a new backup singer too.

She might not be a superstar, but her movies made her famous enough that she should be able to pick up some good back-up talent. If she didn't, the band was going to run her instead of the other way around.

Back at the hotel, another bag of fan mail greeted her– a FedEx present from Guy. Too wired from the show to sleep, she started leafing through the packet of mail.

One item in the stack caught her eye. A thick beige piece of paper with navy writing stuck out because of its odd shape. It was a letter from a man named Sebastian.

"Well, you're quite the optimist, Sebastian Fox."

She saw that he had included an autographed head shot which made her laughed.

"Oh, that's very good. Sending me an autographed picture. That's a new one."

Beneath his signature, he had written his website address.

Adria grabbed her laptop. She brought up a web browser in a flash and found the website he had listed. Sebastian's picture appeared again along with his pitch for custom biographies.

He was a writer. If she didn't have a rule about not dating fans, she might just take him up on it. Of course, she also had a rule about not dating writers. Or actors. Or musicians. No wonder she hadn't been out with anyone for months.

Sebastian's web site had a link to his blog and a list of his favorite things. Adria clicked on this and found that he didn't list his favorite actress, and the film that he had listed wasn't one of hers. Maybe he wasn't much of a fan after all. On the other hand, if she had found the website packed with pictures and stories about her, she would have dismissed him completely as a stalker.

Adria liked his eyes. There was something trustworthy there, something solid.

She yawned and checked the clock.

"One A.M. Time for sleep."

Mister Fox would have to wait for another day.

Chapter 7

Sebastian Fox pulled into the Roadhouse Grill parking lot. He didn't really know where he was, other than somewhere in South Carolina. Lilith had called. Duke had told her that Sebastian was going to be writing his story any way. She was upset and wanted to talk.

Her Mercedes stuck out in the mostly empty parking lot. Sebastian eased into a spot a few feet away. The darkened restaurant made Sebastian blink a few times as his eyes adjusted. Lilith was there, decked out in a white blouse and a pair of black slacks. As she walked towards him, Sebastian noted that she kept herself in great shape. Workouts were a part of her routine as Duke had mentioned, but Sebastian realized that she either was genetically blessed with a good figure, or retrofitted for effect. The outfit enhanced her look as did the perfectly applied makeup. A continual chill in her eyes kept Sebastian's imagination from running away with him.

Lilith's eyes put her into the classification of a man-eater. A woman who liked to look good and tease, but didn't have any real interest beyond that. Lilith, he surmised, used her looks as a means to getting and maintaining power. He decided to focus on her eyes, not out of politeness, but as a reminder of what lay beneath.

"Good afternoon, Miss Roberts," said Sebastian.

"Mr. Fox," she said, as if deigning to speak to a servant.

Roadhouse Grill, with its raised ceilings and darkness, provided a perception of space even amongst the closely set tables and booths. The air conditioning was blowing full blast, even though there couldn't have been more than a half dozen people in the place at this time of day.

The hostess seated them and set a small bucket of peanuts and another, empty bucket for the shells on the table.

"My father always throws the shells on the floor when he comes here," said Lilith.

"Roadhouse used to encourage people to throw them on the floor. I guess the second bucket means they want to revise their image."

"It would take a lot more to revise their image than people not tossing their peanut shells on the floor," said Lilith, looking pointedly at a wall painting which showed a western outlaw sticking the barrel of his gun up the nose of the sheriff.

The waitress came, and Sebastian ordered water. Lilith ordered a Long Island iced tea.

"That is the reason, the only reason, I chose this place. They open earlier than anyone else who sells my kind of tea," she said.

"So you wanted to meet with me, Lilith? What did you have in mind?"

"You broke our agreement."

"No. The contract is only valid once I have deposited your check, which I didn't do."

The waitress interrupted their argument long enough to serve them their drinks. Lilith fairly inhaled hers. Sebastian was amazed at how little of an effect it had on her. After a bit, he noticed a bit of a glaze on her eyes, and she stopped clawing at the edge of the table.

"Lilith, Duke would have never agreed to it with your money."

"But he had. He told me that he'd talk to you. He promised."

Sebastian watched her morph into a little girl.

"He promised he'd tell his story. You promised. It's not fair," she repeated.

"I'm sorry, Lilith. I can't make your father talk to me."

"Now, he's going to get it off his chest, and I won't ever get to find out what really happened. He told me about your agreement. That he was going to tell you so it was written down, but that he's not going to let me know."

Sebastian silently cursed Duke for opening his mouth. An interruption from the waitress gave Sebastian a short respite. They ordered then got back into their conversation.

"Well, right now I'm focused on understanding everyone's point of view. Maybe if you cooperate with the story, I can convince him to let you read it."

"You're requesting a lot of faith on my part," Lilith said.

Her gaze deepened as if she was trying to understand if Sebastian really believed Duke would come around.

"Okay, what do you want to know?" Lilith said.

Sebastian led her through a series of the usual questions that he asked. Where did she grow up? Out on the ranch, as they called it. Making it through high school had been her goal, and after that, she had escaped. Each trip back renewed her hatred for the place. They talked about life on the ranch. Antonio's death and the war had cycled through every family interaction since that fateful day.

"I used to think that all of our problems started with Antonio's death. The problems got worse after that, for sure. Antonio was dead. Daniel was gone. Mom and Dad barely spoke for months."

She caught the surprised look on Sebastian's face.

"He didn't tell you that part, did he? No. He wouldn't. He'd want you to think that everything was great between him and Mom. Appearances were always important to him when it came to family. They fought after Daniel left. It was the first

43

time I saw Mom stand up to him. She tried to force Dad to apologize, but he just grew more aggressive about his feelings towards Daniel. She tolerated him when she had to, but for months, she refused to join him on the porch. Nothing could have been more insulting to Duke than that."

"You said that you used to think that all the problems centered on Antonio's death?"

"Twenty years of counseling led me in a different direction."

"World War Two?"

"World War Two? I guess. More simply, my father."

Sebastian looked at her, the question forming in his mind leaking through his face.

"No. Not like that. No sort of sexual or physical abuse. Control, domination, doing things the Farmington way. The boys had to stay together. If they split up for any reason, a swift rebuke followed. I consistently supervised for my own good. When I turned eighteen, I escaped to school where I met Calvin. Dad and I barely communicated until he got sick."

"Did Antonio and Daniel get along?"

"Sure. Duke pitted them against each other all of the time. They were always competing. Who can run the fastest? Who can throw the farthest? Who can catch the most fish?"

Jealousy crept into Sebastian's heart. His solitary upbringing revolved around books. There were times he'd longed for a brother to get into trouble with.

"Fishing was important?"

"It dominated everything we did. I can still tie a fly even now, and I haven't touched a rod in twenty years," she said.

"Do you ever have any contact with Daniel?" asked Sebastian.

"Christmas cards from time to time. He sends those tacky postcard picture Christmas cards. Calvin and I document

44

our year in a nice letter, and I add a personal note. I've invited him out a few times, but he just ignores it. Nothing would bring him this close to Duke. He's put on a lot of weight since he left. Probably too much beer and not enough exercise. There's not a lot of exercise in fishing."

"You think Daniel still fishes."

"Sure."

She dug around her purse for a minute.

"At the last minute, I decided to bring last year's card just in case Daniel came up. Proof. Take a look at that trout on the wall behind them."

Sebastian examined the photo noting the family resemblances.

"He could have bought it."

Lilith snorted in derision.

"A Farmington mounting a fish on the wall that he didn't catch? You've got a long way to go before you understand this family. I feel bad for him though. I think he resented me because when I came along he stopped being the baby. He got the squeeze."

"The squeeze?"

"The family tree squeeze. An athletic older brother who can do no wrong. A younger sister who gets a lot of attention because she's pretty. Plunked in the middle, you have a competent, average boy. How's he supposed to compete? He can't be the fastest or the strongest. He can't be the cutest."

"So what was he?" Sebastian asked.

"Unhappy. No, that's not true. He wasn't unhappy, not most of the time. He thought too much of Antonio to fight for my Dad's affection. Still, he wasn't completely who he could have been. He was rather shy and withdrawn."

Their conversation dwindled, and Lilith signaled for her check.

"So I can't talk you into letting me read what you write for Duke? I'd double the price that he's paying you."

"Thanks for the offer, Lilith, but all I can do is to ask Duke to let you read it."

She left unhappy, just the way she'd arrived.

Sebastian threw Adria's CD into the player and started the long drive home from South Carolina. The miles wound away as he lost himself in her sultry voice. His mind drifted, thinking of seeing her at the concert, having dinner with her, and spending time with her. Regardless of the unlikelihood of any of it coming to pass, it burned the time that he had to get home.

The only communication he was likely to get from Adria was a restraining order.

"At least she'll know who I am," he said aloud.

As he neared Duke's exit on I-85, he decided to stop by and visit the old man. Sebastian doubted that there was a lot of variation from Duke's porch sitting routine.

Duke was nowhere in sight, but, from nearby, Sebastian could hear the boom of a rifle. Sebastian skirted the house, calling out as he went along lest he become an unwitting target.

In a small clearing, he could see where some bales of hay had been set up against a small hill behind the house. Across the bales of hay was a series of targets littered with holes. Duke was stumbling around in a drunken stupor, his back erect, despite his unsure footing.

"Hey Duke," said Sebastian from thirty yards off.

The old man spun around. He wore no shirt, and Sebastian was shocked by the scars that covered his body.

"What are you doing here?" Duke demanded.

"I just stopped by to talk."

"Talk? War is no time to talk. I've got to find the rest of my unit. I've got to find Tony, and Herman. I've got to find Maria."

46

He turned back toward the bales of hay and fired at the targets, framed against the dirty brown bales. Two of them jerked, shot through the center. Duke turned toward Sebastian.

"Where's Tony?"

"Tony's not here."

"He's not here? Did he go back after Jake?"

"I don't know, but why don't we get something to eat?"

"Are you with the 509th?"

"Of course, how else would I have found you?" said Sebastian.

The old man lowered the rifle and the writer turned toward the house.

"Where are we going?" Duke asked.

"There's a place over here where we can get something to eat."

"I am hungry."

They walked to the house slowly. On the side board was a basket of biscuits.

"Why don't you have a seat, soldier, and I'll rustle us up some grub."

Duke set the rifle in the corner and wandered into the living room. The next thing Sebastian knew, the old man's snores were echoing throughout the room. Sebastian unloaded the gun and put it back in the rack over the mantle. He had driven halfway to Atlanta before his hands stopped shaking.

The scars. Duke had told him, but Sebastian had forgotten.

Tomorrow, Sebastian told himself, he would start Duke's story.

Chapter 8

Arizona Mountains. December 1941

Duke moved downhill against the frigid wind.

For the previous hour, he waited in the high meadow and hadn't seen a single deer. He knew all the meadows where deer might feed, and now, he angled down the hill to another area. The wind was cold, and he began to wonder if it would snow.

Miles now lay between him and the ranch which was much farther than he had planned on going this morning. His brother Chance had seen a ten-pointer the week before, and Duke intended to bag it. Chance should have been out here with him. They could have cornered it together, but Chance was still sleeping when Duke had saddled up. Last night they had both been a little drunk, but Duke held his liquor better than his older brother.

Duke smiled about that just as a flake settled onto his cheek. Glancing at the sky, he realized that he needed to hurry if he was going to find that buck. He had left his horse downstream in a little makeshift corral. Chance and Duke's parents had used the corral for years, whenever they left the ranch and rode into the hills.

Duke usually crossed Frog Creek farther to the north. There, a huge dead fall spanned the river, but the look of the clouds worried him, causing him to hurry. He'd crossed here once before during the dry months of high summer, but now the creek was swollen from three solid nights of rain. Securing his rifle in the long leather wrap on his backpack, he began to jump from rock to rock. Water washed over his boots a couple of times and his jump to the final rock nearly carried him into the swirling current.

At sixteen, Duke spent most of his free time hunting and fishing in these hills just south of the Colorado border. Duke ran into a stand of smaller trees packed around two large fallen giants of the forest. The trees blocked the path that he had mapped in his mind, and he so he backtracked, working his way to the other meadow in less time than planned. Settling down to wait, he pulled his rifle out again, letting it rest easily in his big, rawboned hands.

Duke grew cold waiting.

Perhaps he should look elsewhere, but this meadow often drew the deer. He sensed movement to his left. Using just his eyes, he scanned the woods until he saw her. A doe stood on the edge of the clearing, tail twitching.

Duke held his rifle casually, comfortably. Another doe followed the first one out into the meadow, and still he waited. The doe looked up, and Duke stilled even his breath, wanting nothing to attract unwanted attention.

Ever so slightly the deer drifted away from where he was hiding. Duke's eyes narrowed, sensing a problem. Perhaps his scent reached the hollow from where he hid. He scanned the edge of the forest just as the buck broke from cover. It came on a dead run. Duke threw the gun to his shoulder and fired, cursing a rare miss. The buck froze momentarily at the sound of the gun then bolted out of sight.

A different sound erupted into the cold winter morning. It came from behind Duke in the form of a huge black bear, bursting from its den, a dozen feet away. Duke instinctively fired at the bear, even though he knew better.

The shot struck the bear's shoulder. Whatever damage the shot caused, it seemed to embolden and outrage the bear, a huge male that must have weighed six hundred pounds. Before Duke could fire again, the bear reached him. Duke used the rifle like a shield, holding it in his outstretched hands to protect his head. When the collision with the bear finally came, the gun was ripped from Duke's hands, and he felt a painful tear in his side. The bear's charge carried it past Duke, and he was spun to the ground. As Duke looked at the world upside down, he saw the bear stumble as it turned for another attack.

Duke struggled to his feet and climbed to the top of the rocks that formed the bear's lair, trying desperately to escape. The bear attempted to follow, but was waylaid by his injured shoulder. Looking in all directions, Duke desperately searched for a way out, as the bear made another run at the rocks. Sooner or later the bear would go around to the side of the rock that was easier to climb, and Duke would be trapped.

For the first time, Duke noticed the pain across his stomach and saw that he was bleeding. The bear lunged for the top of the rock again with a tremendous roar, getting within a few inches of Duke.

Snow began to fall, not a few flakes but a steady fall, swirling in a wind that was starting to pick up. Taking his eyes off the snow, Duke noticed that the bear had disappeared; the teenager turned to see the monster ambling for the low side of his refuge.

Duke jumped off the far side and rolled into a heap, slamming his back into an aspen trunk. Pain shot through his wound from the jolt. He scrambled away on all fours and pushed through some thick brush hoping it might provide a screen of some sort.

A black bear won't usually attack a man, but Duke's first shot must have startled this one from his lair. Since Duke had stupidly wounded it, it had been driven beyond reason. Duke could hear the bear now even as Duke rose and started south, staggering like a drunken man. The bear crashed through the brush that Duke had falsely placed his hope in.

Fear like an ugly, black bile, rose in Duke's throat as he ran. No matter what anyone had told him about playing dead, this bear looked to be in no mood for possum games. The bear chased Duke on three good paws, dragging the other like a useless set of razor blades.

Duke grabbed at a couple of stout sticks as he ran, finally getting one on his third try. A wrong turn brought him up against a tall boulder, and he turned to face the dark nightmare that stalked him with murder in its eyes. He drew his knife from the scabbard at his side, wondering if he could make a miracle throw that would save his life.

The bear was on him in an instant, and Duke had just enough time to slam the stick into the bear's jaws before it bowled him over. Time slowed. The forest disappeared. Like a deadly cartoon, man and bear rolled round and round. Duke thrust his knife again and again, while the bear racked his body with teeth and claws. A scream tore from his mouth as the black rolled onto Duke's right leg, snapping it loudly. The bear reared up on his hind legs and started to come down on Duke again. He shoved with all his might, pushing the knife deep into the bear's chest. The bear pulled back, tearing the knife out of Duke's hand.

As the bear rolled onto its side, fighting for breath, Duke saw frothy blood on its muzzle. Duke began to crawl, fighting pain that emanated from every part of his body. The river's voice beckoned Duke, and he turned toward it. Behind him, Duke heard movement and saw the bear dragging itself forward. Whatever damage Duke might have done to the bear, it still had a massive set of working jaws. Grabbing for another stick, Duke pushed the weight off of his injured leg as another scream came from his lips. The snow was coming down in

51

torrents now as he limped toward the river and still the dark eyes drew closer to him.

Duke fought to stay conscious. The water swirled near the top of the bank, flowing hard and heavy as the snow disappeared into it. Duke turned and found that the bear was only ten feet from him. Suddenly, the black bear rushed, looking surreal with the haft of Duke's knife sticking from its chest. It came closer and closer.

With a last look, Duke stepped forward and was swept into the current.

The water took Duke where it would. Planning wasn't an option as the river tossed and twisted this way and that, pounding his injured leg against the rocks. Duke's cries were drowned out by the water as he was pushed down, down, down. He waited, feeling helpless despite his man-sized strength. How long he rode the aquatic bull, he had no idea, but eventually the creek took pity and tossed him onto a shallow sandy beach at the apex of a turn.

He grabbed onto a small tree, growing almost directly out of the side of the bank. Duke wanted to give up. A memory of his mother telling him to be careful wandered through his addled mind. It was a strange memory in the midst of all his pain, clinging to a tree root in a dark, cold forest.

He pulled.

Nothing happened at first. He pulled again and slid the rest of the way out of the water, his teeth chattering. The snow had stopped, and the wind had begun to blow again. Duke needed help. His body wanted to shut down, but he wasn't going to let that happen.

In the end, he crawled. He crawled because he had only one choice -- crawl or die.

With each painstaking inch of ground covered, he heard his father's voice. He didn't know where it was from, but the same words pounded repeatedly inside his head. "Farmingtons don't quit, Duke. Sometimes it's because we're too stupid to know we're licked, but no matter what we don't quit."

Duke crawled for what seemed forever. The ground changed, flattening out. He stopped and realized he had found the trail. Somewhere nearby was the corral which meant shelter and his horse. Crawling again, he came over the ridge and saw his father and Chance standing there.

He slumped into the snow. As he faded away, he saw the flash of lanterns bouncing up and down as they ran to meet him.

With only his father's sweet honey mead to act as a painkiller, Duke came in and out of consciousness as the doctor treated his leg, setting the bone and making sure there was no further damage. Each jar would send slivers of pain all through his body. When the final tightening of the splint occurred, Duke would have come off the table if his father and brother had not been there to hold him down.

Afterwards, he passed into a fitful and haunted sleep.

The bear was coming after him. Claws tore at his skin and the bear's bloody maw came closer, but Duke couldn't move. Paralyzed in his dreams, he waited for his end.

He flinched himself awake, jarring his leg painfully. The giant hand of his father touched his shoulder, and the heat from the pot belly stove filled him with the kindest warmth he had ever known. A candle burned behind him. Seconds passed, and as the spasm subsided, his father gave his shoulder a short squeeze before removing his hand.

"Is there anything I can get you, son?" said his dad's voice, a voice that was missing its usual gruffness.

"Water."

Boots tromped off to the kitchen then returned. His dad sat on the rough-hewn coffee table and helped Duke drink a little. He asked for some more alcohol to dull the pain, and his request was met without question.

As the pain eased, Duke slept again. When he woke the next time, his mother sat in the nearby rocking chair.

"Chance and your father went to get the horse and to see if they could find the bear."

Duke's intake of breath startled her.

"Rest easy, son. They both took shotguns, and they are going up there together. No bear will stand against them today. Where ever your rifle is, they intend to find it and finish off that bear if they get an opportunity."

"I didn't even tell them what happened."

"Yes, you did, several times."

Duke remembered none of that, but his mother's word was gospel. They were back in the late afternoon with the horse and the bear carcass.

"We didn't have to do much. You killed him, son. He must have died just after you went into the water for we found him right at the river's edge. Dead as a doornail. I can't believe you fought that beast with just your knife."

There was a tremble in his father's voice as he spoke. Charles Famington was a tough man who had raised tough sons. He had rarely been shaken by anything, but this was the first time they had come this close to death.

Duke's mom told him later that Chance was feeling guilty for leaving Duke alone.

"Oh, for Pete's sake, Chance. You didn't do anything wrong."

"I should've been with you."

"We wouldn't have been together even if we'd both gone out that day. You would have been over by Stoley's old cabin, and I probably would have been right where I was. Or you might have tried that meadow, and you'd be lying here instead of me."

Chance remained silent.

"The worst of it is that I missed that buck you saw the other day. I had a clean shot at him and missed," Duke said.

Chance laughed. "No kidding?"

"No kidding. If you want to help me out, you could set some targets up off the back porch. I might as well practice my aim so I won't miss that buck the next time."

For more than a month, Duke's routine never varied. His mom would fix him three eggs and four slices of bacon, and he would go out on the porch and shoot. Sitting on the porch on the last day of his mandated rest, Duke was enjoying the sunshine and the coolness of an Arizona winter when his father got home from town with news.

The Japanese had attacked Pearl Harbor, and Roosevelt had declared war.

Chapter 9

Ray's Shine had been a clearing house for up-and-coming musicians in Columbus for fifteen years. The main room held two hundred and fifty people. Larger shows were broadcast out into *Ray's* patio area on huge TVs, complete with surround sound.

An hour before the show, Adria Rider and her agent Guy sat talking about her schedule in a back room.

She paced across the floor.

"What about Memphis or Nashville?" Guy asked.

"I don't sing country music, Guy. And why would I want to go down to Nashville where there are already a million singers?"

"Your mix of ballads and love songs gives you some crossover appeal. Plus, exposure in the South gives you another audience option."

Guy's comment made her think again of Sebastian Fox. Mr. Fox had said that his reason for coming to Columbus to see her concert was because she had been avoiding the South. Just knowing that she had a potential stalker in the audience distressed her..

"What about Atlanta?" Guy asked.

"No," she said firmly.

Guy sighed and retreated a bit.

"How about Lexington or Louisville? Maybe with some follow up back into Virginia where you have had some of your best showings?"

She bit her lip and nodded.

"Don't mind me," she said, "I'm just preoccupied with the thought of that fan, Sebastian Fox. He's supposed to be here tonight."

"If he makes you nervous, we can have security keep an eye on him."

"No. He seems harmless enough."

After Guy and Adria had finished up their scheduling talk, Adria wandered over to the bar got a drink. She retreated to the sound booth to watch the open mic acts that preceded her performance.

"Mind if I hang out here for the first part of the show?" she asked the sound guys.

"No problem. You can sit over there," said the crew chief, pointing to an empty chair.

The first patron through the door was Sebastian Fox. Adria was nearly sure of it, although the distance kept her from being certain. He stood alone for a few minutes studying the layout. Finally, he moved to a table near the stage. She watched him until the lights went down.

For thirty minutes, the audience was subjected to open mic acts, where anyone who had signed up earlier could play for five minutes. A couple of the acts were downright dreadful to Adria's trained ear and, she imagined, to many untrained ears as well.

After a bit, she made her way quietly down to the lobby and headed toward the back so she could make sure the band was together. As Adria exited the stairs from the top level and came abreast of the lobby, she looked to her left.

The door from the main room was shutting slowly behind Sebastian Fox.

Adria locked eyes with Sebastian, and he smiled at her. It wasn't a wickedly dazzling smile, more like the smile of an old friend. After a second, he made a slight nod with his head in greeting. Curiosity replaced most of the fear she had felt earlier, and she almost waved in return. Instead, strangely blushing, she retreated backstage.

Fifteen minutes later, Adria walked on stage, with bigger things to worry about than the fan sitting at the second table back, third in from the left wall.

She sat on a stool, with an acoustic guitar on her hip.

Her rehearsed spiel came out, as she said hello to her fans in Columbus, and lauded the history of the venue. Adria hoped that she looked confident, but she felt tentative, the way she had when she had first started touring. Even though her eyes drifted to her right, she couldn't quite make out Sebastian with the house lights down.

She started with a simple melody on her acoustic and began to sing, letting the soulful notes of her headline song, *Halfway to Where You Are,* arch through the building.

"Thank you," Adria said to a big round of applause. "There are times when I think that no matter how much pain or loneliness we've seen that it's only a matter of time until we find that person who can change our life."

The band joined in on the second song, and together they ran through several songs from her CD. No one seemed in sync, and Adria did her best to cover her anger. Even still, she could barely contain herself when the drummer jumped in a measure early on one of the songs.

When the set was over, the band took a fifteen minute break.

"What was that? I don't think there was a single song where you all did what we've rehearsed?" Adria said, when they were barely off the stage.

No one made eye contact with her. Even the usually trustworthy Jimmy had been off on a couple of the songs.

"Give us a break, Adria. Nobody's perfect all of the time." Darla said.

"You're right, Darla. I'm going to give you a break for the rest of the night. Maybe a solo show will work better," Adria said.

They filed off with a mix of embarrassment and anger leaving Adria alone to regroup. She flicked tears away with a finger, watching them hit the stage floor while she tried to relax. Her partial meltdown was slowed as she took a few deep breaths. As she stood there, a thought came from nowhere.

Sebastian Fox did this.

She was angry at him for being here. The memory of his smile from earlier came to mind.

"So you like to laugh, Sebastian Fox. Well, let's see if you think this is funny."

Adria walked on stage alone. No explanation was given for the band's absence since she couldn't think of one that wouldn't reflect badly on her.

Her first song was an easy one, and her voice danced the notes to perfection.

When it was over, she began to strum as she talked about life on the road.

"One of the hard parts of being a celebrity on the road is the love letters, the requests for dates, and even some marriage proposals."

She rolled her eyes to show her incredulity with such men, and the crowd laughed along with her in response.

"The scary part is trying to discern between the truly dangerous ones and the ones that are just lonely. Are they a threat or just crazy enough to believe I'd go on a blind date with them because they sent me a crazy letter and a picture of themselves?"

Darkness kept Sebastian's features hidden, but even from a distance, Adria could have sworn that his faced changed to a reddish hue. It was minor payback for upsetting her evening.

When she had done several more songs, she walked off the stage to find the band waiting in the wings. Quiet apologies made the rounds between the band and Adria. Adria and the band hurried to the lobby where *Ray's* had a spot set up for all the acts to sell their wares.

The band took care of the merchandise while Adria sat and scrawled autographs.

"There he is," Guy whispered.

Adria glanced up and made eye contact with Sebastian, as he moved toward the door. Her chair scraped back loudly, and she began to move.

"Excuse me," she said to his back.

Sebastian continued his walk, neither hurrying his pace nor slowing, though she was sure he had heard her. Adria sped around the table, nearly chasing him across the lobby.

"Excuse me. Mr. Fox," she called, her voice coming out shrill.

Sebastian stopped and turned. Adria smiled, proud to catch him off guard.

"Mr. Fox, I wanted to save you the trouble of coming to LA."

"It's no trouble, Miss Rider. LA is one of my favorite places to spend a weekend. Getting to dine at my favorite restaurant is just a plus."

"Then you'll dine alone," she said as she searched his eyes.

He shrugged, "Perhaps."

"You didn't get my hint during the show?"

"Oh, I got it. It had all the subtlety of a sledgehammer," he said smiling. "I just decided it didn't change anything."

As she studied him, he extended his hand.

"We haven't been introduced officially. Sebastian Fox, biographer and dreamer."

She took it because she admired his chutzpah.

60

"Adria Rider. Actress and musician."

"I enjoyed your show, Miss Rider, although your drummer could use a bit of work. I'd stay and talk, but your adoring fans are growing restless."

A quick glance over her shoulder showed the attention their encounter had attracted.

"Mr. Fox, I don't need a stalker. I'm quite content without one."

"I didn't stalk you, Miss Rider. I simply asked you out to dinner."

"But you showed up here. I don't need a stalker, Mr. Fox," she repeated.

He regarded her for a moment, and then started to leave.

"What were you going to say?" she asked.

"Does it matter what I was going to say? After all, you just think I'm a stalker, even though you're the one who keeps restarting our conversation."

"I wanted you to know that I wouldn't be coming to dinner," she said weakly.

"Which you could have communicated simply by not showing up," he said with a smile.

He turned and left before Adria could get in the last word.

As the doors swung shut, Adria turned to Guy and said, "I think I'll give him a surprise."

Chapter 10

The next several days were extremely busy. Petey
wanted to hear all about Sebastian's encounter with Adria.
Sebastian made a quick trip to see Duke and squeezed in a
doctor's appointment. Before he knew it, it was time for him to
go to California for the first of the three dates that he was sure
that Adria would skip.

Tuesday he flew to LA, his nerves frayed as he
contemplated a possible meeting with Adria. Wednesday he
took in Huntington Beach, which seemed more crowded than
he remembered it. Hundreds of people, stretching the four day
Fourth of July weekend into a full week, filled the restaurants
and roadways.

Angelino's Pizzeria was a twenty minute drive from his
hotel, and Sebastian left an extra twenty minutes early to
counter the Southern California road demons that seemed to
show up whenever there was something important to attend.
His stomach flip-flopped a couple of times, wondering what he
would say to her if she was there. The small entrance of
Angelinos was covered with pictures of major and minor movie
stars that had visited the restaurant.

Feelings of amazement washed over Sebastian as he
contemplated Angelino's history. It was built on and around the
old stage of a traditional theater that had been converted in the
seventies to a movie theater. Dining on what used to be the
stage made him wonder what drama had played out where his
feet now rested. Old props, mixed with art work from Italy,

were dimly visible in the candle light as they hung from the rafters and walls.

The maître d' met him as he walked in.

"How many in your party, sir?" said the young man in his twenties.

Angelino's had great food and atmosphere, and kept their costs down by hiring good looking, tanned college students from the local schools.

"I have reservations for two under the name of Sebastian Fox."

"Let me check."

He looked quickly at a large book in front of him.

"Sir, we don't have any reservations for tonight. Wednesday nights are usually walk-in."

The reservation log pages were flipped a few at a time, and Sebastian glanced at them as they flipped by. Fridays and Saturdays were evidently packed, if the crowded margins on those pages were any indication.

"Ah. Now, I remember. Your reservation was cancelled last night by a beautiful woman. She had the cannelloni. After dinner, she cancelled your reservations for tonight. I believe she said that you had changed your mind about coming in."

The look on Sebastian's face must have reflected the humiliation that he was feeling.

"I'm sorry, sir," said the maître d', whose name tag identified him as Kurt, "As you can see, there is plenty of room though if you would like to dine with us."

Curse words whistled through Sebastian's head. Adria had come here without him and had gone to the trouble of canceling his reservations as well.

"Sir?"

The maître d' looked concerned, as if Sebastian had lost his sanity. Sebastian, for his part, wasn't about to let Adria nix a perfectly good meal at his favorite restaurant.

"Yes. I'll be dining."

He looked around, found a small corner table, and pointed it out. "What about there?"

"Certainly, sir," said the maître d' and led him to the table, "Are you expecting anyone?"

"Maybe, but probably not," said Sebastian sheepishly.

The man's eyes told Sebastian that he understood and that he shared the embarrassment of his guest.

Wendy, a leggy blonde, appeared and supplied Sebastian with a beer and a small pepperoni, linguica, and sausage pizza. Gradually, Sebastian gave up on his vigil as the diners trickling in bore no resemblance to the beautiful Miss Rider. He lingered, along with his melancholy, making his way through each slice. As he had promised Adria in Columbus, he took time to enjoy both the food the additional room under his table. There was no sense in making himself a liar.

He hadn't really expected to get Adria's attention. Movie stars seemed so other-worldly, even with the obsessive gossip that chased them around the tabloids and the internet. Adria had never been the subject of scandalous video tapes or revelations of self-destructive behavior, but she had done the usual glossy expose on her various homes and the whispered "tell all" interview which, of course, revealed only the enduring traits of the star.

Sebastian had anticipated being alone so he'd brought a book with him. He read with the book in his right hand and a slice of pizza in his left. When a noisy softball team entered and made its way to the bar, Sebastian decided it was time to go. He tipped Wendy generously since her smile had dulled some of his pain.

As he was leaving, a thought crossed his mind, and he stopped at the maître d'.

"I was wondering about a couple of other reservations I had made. The ones for the twenty-eighth and August fourteenth. Were those cancelled as well?"

Both sets of reservations had indeed been scratched out in the reservation log. Sebastian remade the reservations, and this time a note was added that they were not to be cancelled by anyone who couldn't give out the credit card number that they were reserved under.

At the hotel, Sebastian lay in bed and finished the book he'd been reading. When he was done reading, instead of turning out his light, Sebastian fired up his laptop and connected to the hotel's wireless network. When he checked his email, there was one from herself@arider.com. The subject was "Dinner" and the message was brief:

How was dinner? :-)

It was signed, simply, Adria.

Sebastian was flabbergasted.

As he re-read Adria's email, a wide grin spread across his face. A thought that had been swirling around in the back of his mind since he'd been at dinner burst, front and center, into his consciousness.

He was winning.

She had won the battle tonight. The reservation cancellation was a nice move, but the fact that she had gone to the restaurant the night before their proposed date was a significant win for Sebastian. She may have outsmarted him tonight, but he was ahead in the game simply by the fact that there was one going on. He was no longer insignificant, and he obviously wasn't terrifying her. Whatever the reason, they had entered into some kind of relationship.

He clicked on the reply button, and a window popped up addressed to Adria.

Herself –

You went to a lot of trouble to send me a message at the exact time that I was enjoying some of the finest pizza in the world by myself. You, of course, being the fancy sort of person who refers to herself as, well, "herself," probably had something fancier than pizza, like cannelloni, when you were at Angelinos yesterday.

Tonight, while you sat in your fancy house, or fancy hotel room, by yourself, you could have been having another dose of wonderful food. As an extra bonus, you might have even enjoyed yourself.

Himself

P.S. The offer still stands for the other two nights.

He hit send, calmly aware that his winning streak could come to a screeching halt whenever she wanted it to end.

Sebastian woke early since his body was still on East Coast time. Unbelievably, he had another email from Adria. It was a rundown of her night. It began:

Dear Sebastian,

I spent the evening with my meddling sister who tried to set me up. I told her that you were stalking me and that one stalker was more than enough to keep anyone busy these days. I'm not quite sure where she gets these men, but they are complete bores. Tonight there were two of them – a groupie and a lech.

It went on from there. Sebastian read it over a couple of times before rolling back over and sleeping some more. When he woke again, he readied himself to check out. Midway through shaving, the phone in the room rang, and he cut himself.

He answered it, figuring that it must be a wrong number.

"Hello," he said, glancing at the clock to see that it was about eight-fifteen.

66

"Sebastian?" said a soft feminine voice.

"Yes," he said hesitantly.

Only Petey knew where he was staying, and this was definitely not Petey.

"This is Adria Rider," said the voice and Sebastian's heart leapt into his throat.

"I was going to say that I was surprised, but after last night, I guess I really shouldn't be."

She laughed, still tentative, "That was bad of me, wasn't it?"

"Yeah, kind of. Fortunately, they had plenty of tables so it didn't change anything."

"I told you that I wasn't going to show up."

"And you were true to your word. I am going to have to sue you, however."

"Why? Because I cancelled your reservations? You'd have a hard time proving material loss. Trust me. Actresses know all about lawyers and suing people."

"No, I was referring to the physical damage that my razor did to my face you called me."

"Oh, poor baby. I just wanted to see if you liked being stalked as much as you liked doing the stalking?"

"A bit more, actually. I like those aggressive women. I have a question, though, how did you find me out of all of the hotels in LA? Did you pay a detective to follow me from the restaurant?"

"Nothing as complex as that. Your hotel added a banner to your email."

"Wow. You are a very talented stalker, Miss Rider."

"Thank you."

An awkward silence followed.

"I'm a bit curious about something else, since I have you on the phone," he said.

"And what would that be?"

"You described your two would-be suitors from last night as 'a groupie and a lech.' I'm curious to know how you define them."

"Well, a lech undresses you repeatedly with his eyes and harbors some hope of getting into your pants. A groupie just stares across the table at you with these big droopy eyes, hanging on every word like you were some sort of goddess."

"You're not a goddess?" he said mockingly.

"No, Mr. Fox, I'm afraid you'll be disappointed if you think I'm a goddess. I'm sitting here right now on my porch sans makeup and rather stinky after a morning run on the beach."

"That's not very goddess-like at all. I guess groupies are always in for disappointment."

"Definitely," she replied, thinking of an old relationship that really never got anywhere once the guy saw that she was real.

Sebastian heard her pause and disappear. He wondered what part of her lovely brain that she'd floated off to.

"Which are you I wonder?" Adria asked, "The groupie or the letch?"

"Neither, of course. I just want to take you to dinner and hear you laugh."

"Hmm. I'm not sure what type you are, then. It would depend on what happens after dinner."

"I can't imagine anything happening after dinner."

"Not like that! What I meant is, are you going tell all your friends about it? Are you going to squeeze me for information then publish it? Will you try to kidnap me? Depending on your answer, you would be a bore, a gold digger, or a psychopath."

"What if I just wanted to enjoy a meal with you, knowing that somewhere in your memory, you'd think of me from time to time and remember me as a guy who made you laugh?"

"Well, let's see, that would make you either a hopeless romantic or a bit of a fool."

"I've been called both. I'll let you decide which after we have dinner."

"That's very smooth, but you know that I'm a Hollywood starlet, adept at fending off smooth talkers."

In the background, Sebastian heard a dog barking.

"Oh, I forgot. I've got a date with my favorite male. A long walk on the beach and a little vigorous exercise."

The barking grew so loud that Sebastian had to move the phone away from his ear.

"Winston!" she was saying on the other end.

"Thrown over for a dog," said Sebastian.

"Well, he's the most reliable man that I've found yet, Mr. Fox."

"See you in a couple of weeks, Miss Rider."

"I wouldn't count on it."

Chapter 11

Farmington Ranch, Arizona. April 1942.

Charles and Maggie Farmington noticed a change in Duke soon after his older brother Chance had gone off to war. Duke had a new-found interest in physical fitness that wasn't simply a matter of returning his body to the shape it had been in before the bear attack.

He talked about the war, read about the war, and went to town as often as possible to get news on the war. Duke began setting up targets that were further and further away. Round after round obliterated targets until his father asked him to slow down, due to the cost of the ammunition.

"You've got two years before the army will even take you," Charles told his younger son.

Duke wasn't going to wait two more years. He was a man, no matter what his birth certificate might say and sitting around for two years while the war raged wasn't in his plans.

When Duke walked into the recruiting office, it was the same door that his brother Chance had walked through several months earlier on his way to England. Duke picked up the forms and worked his way through the many lines of information. In 1942, the enlistment age was nineteen years old. Duke was not yet even eighteen, but he was smart enough to do the math in his head and change his birth year from 1925 to 1923.

"So you just turned 19," said the recruiting officer.

"Just the other day," said Duke.

"The Army needs men like you," said the recruiting officer, wearing his false grin.

The truth was the Army needed everyone. If the recruiter remembered processing another boy with the same last name, only a few months earlier, he showed no recollection.

"Down the hall to the second door on the left. If you pass your physical, we'll have you killing Nazis in no time."

The doctor was not as excited to see Duke.

"Take off your shirt," the doctor said, "let's give a listen to your chest."

When Duke complied, the doctor's mouth flapped open and closed like a fish that has tossed itself accidentally onto the shore. He had not been to war or seen the like of Duke's scars. Duke was not surprised at the reaction although he blushed and felt his ears turning red.

"What happened to you?" He asked, unable to tear his eyes away from Duke's chest.

Duke wanted to lie. He was afraid that the doctor would keep him out. In the end, he decided that it would be best to simply tell the truth. If this doctor decided to fail him, there were other branches of the service that might accept him.

He told the story of the bear. When the shock was over, the doctor seemed much more concerned with Duke's broken leg than he did with the scars. The doctor checked Duke's breathing, assuring himself that there was no damage to his lungs. When it came to the leg, the doctor ran his finger over the area that Duke indicated. There was a slight bump, enough to give the doctor pause.

"Please, sir. I've spent the last couple of months exercising and getting in shape. I want to serve my country."

The doctor sighed, fighting whatever demons are left to fight for a man who had sent so many innocent boys off to war. Duke held his breath until the doctor had scribbled his illegible

71

signature, giving permission for Duke to go and die with the others.

Charles Farmington wasn't surprised at the news.

"Let's go and tell your mother," was his father's only response.

Maggie Farmington cried. Even though Duke was more than six feet tall, she still thought of him as her baby. In the end, Duke told her that if God had wanted him dead, He would have let the bear kill him. It was not Duke's words, but the look of pride on Charles's face, that helped Maggie let go.

When the day finally came for Duke to leave, Duke insisted on riding with a friend's family to the train station.

"You'll never be able to keep yourself from making a scene," Duke told his mother.

She clung to him before he left, not wanting to let him go. His father drove him to the Gauss's house, where he joined his friend John for the ride.

Charles Farmington clapped Duke on the shoulder. There were no tears or hugs just a manly good-bye and a bit of advice.

"Remember to do the right thing, son. If you do, you'll live without regrets."

At the station, Duke stood off to the side by himself, while John said good-bye to his family. There were a few other boys who seemed to be alone, but mostly the station was crowded with families tugging at their overgrown children.

"So now we're off on our adventure," said John when they had boarded.

Duke grunted. He did not think of it as an adventure, but as simply something that had to be done to preserve the country. He didn't think of himself as beyond the reach of death despite what he had told his mother, but the bear had cured him of his fear of death.

While the train station was a mix of tears and excitement, Camp Maxey was a shock. Duke had never been outside of Arizona so the train ride itself was a big thrill. When he got to the camp though, there were recruits everywhere, and everyone of them was worn to the bone by what the army called its "basic training."

Duke and John were assigned to the same platoon, but they were in different squads of ten. Master Sergeant David Timmons was another shock to Duke. It seemed that there was no limit to his demands or his cruelty.

On more than one occasion, the master sergeant promised to make a recruit look "worse than Farmington's chest," if the recruit didn't increase his performance in some appointed task. The first time the sergeant made such a comment, Duke had actually fallen out of line so great was his shock. He quickly caught up with his squad, but not before Timmons had noticed. Timmons halted the platoon and called Duke out in front.

"Private Farmington, are you having some trouble today?"

"No, Sergeant," said Duke, barely veiling his anger.

"Is the private offended by something I said?"

"No, Sergeant," Duke's tone was a bit more even.

"That's good, private. Now could you please take off your shirt and stand to the side so that the platoon can know what I meant just a minute ago."

Duke decided that he hated Timmons, but removed his shirt and puffed out his chest. Several of the recruits blanched at the sight.

"Privates Sorenson and Herbert."

"Sergeant?" replied the recruits.

"Do you dislike the sight of Private Farmington's chest?"

"No, Sergeant," said Sorenson and Herbert.

"In battle you will see things that are much worse. You will see arms torn off, you will see your friends die, and you will see parts of your own body fall to the ground. And when you do, you will keep going. You will keep fighting. You will not stop. Am I clear?"

"Yes, Sergeant," said the platoon with force.

When the show was over, Duke moved back into line. There was a palatable anger in the ranks toward the Sergeant, an anger that remained even after the march.

Timmons had asked Duke about the source of his scars, but Duke had refused to tell him. The refusal meant that Duke drew the worst of the assignments – including the back of the line during the long dusty runs.

One particular recruit thought that Timmons's disdain meant that Duke was fair game. Tom Radcliff was from Missouri and had a slow, leathery way of speaking.

"You must have won the stupid award where you come from, Farmington. Otherwise, you'd just fess up to Timmons about those scars and make your life easier."

Duke didn't reply. He simply gave Radcliff a look that would have silenced smarter men and went back to polishing his boots.

"I'm talking to you, Farmington. You shouldn't even be here. You're still a boy."

John Gauss's face colored up, and Duke knew that John had let the secret of his age out.

Radcliff walked up to Duke and poked him hard in the shoulder.

"So are you stupid, farm boy?"

Duke grabbed the arm that was still partially stretched between them and pulled the big man toward him. Duke's right fist shot forward lightning fast, and there was a loud crack like the sound of an axe hitting wood.

Radcliff's head snapped back like it was on a hinge.

74

Pandemonium reigned as multiple fights broke out simultaneously. Someone jumped on Duke's back, and he instinctively ducked, letting the momentum carry his foe over the top and past him. Another recruit bowled into Duke, took him to the ground, and managed to land a punch to his face. The tent was about to erupt out of control when there was a shout from a wise private who was watching out the tent door.

"Timmons is coming!"

Disorder and chaos turned into a rush to make things right. Duke pulled Radcliff to his cot and bodily tossed him onto it.

The men stopped, ramrod stiff, and saluted as Master Sergeant Timmons came through the door. Duke tried to look inconspicuous despite the blood that dripped slowly from his nose.

"I thought I heard the sounds of a fight coming from this tent. Would you happen to know anything about that, Private Farmington?"

"No, Sergeant," said Duke.

Timmons grabbed his hand and inspected his scuffed knuckles.

"How did you hurt your hand, Private? And what is wrong with your nose?" said Timmons. Duke wiped his nose.

"I was cleaning my rifle, master sergeant, and my hand slipped and hit my face."

Timmons was about to question Duke further when he noticed for the first time that Radcliff was missing. The sergeant located Radcliff just as the private came to with a moan.

"Oh, my head," he said.

Looking up he saw Timmons and jumped to attention.

"Private Radcliff. Private Farmington told me that he skinned his knuckles while cleaning his rifle and that he also bloodied his own nose. Is that what happened?"

75

"Yes, Sergeant."

"I see, Private Radcliff. How do you explain your failure to come to attention and the large bruise on the side of your head?"

"I slipped and hit my head, Sergeant."

"So I have two clumsy privates, today."

He turned and looked at the rest of the platoon, but no one said anything.

"Tomorrow after drills are done, Privates Farmington and Radcliff will complete the obstacle course three full times, working together as buddies."

He walked to the door of the tent.

"Let me remind you gentlemen that you do not have to like everyone in this platoon, but you do have to be ready to die for them. Now, get ready for lights out. Some of you have an extremely long day ahead of you."

Chapter 12

"Adria did not!" Petey said.

Sebastian took another bite of cake.

"Yes. She did," he nodded his head to clarify his muddled speech.

It was the first time he'd seen Petey since he'd gone to LA.

"How cold can she get? She could have just ignored you. That would have been nicer than canceling your reservations."

"I think she was teasing. We traded a couple of emails. She even called me at the hotel."

"Who are you two talking about?" said Pops, looking worse than usual with a smattering of frosting hanging off his unshaven chin.

Petey turned to Pops, "Sebastian is trying to get a date with Adria Rider, the actress from *Desert Dancer*."

"Whatever. Can I have another beer?"

"No, you can't," said Petey, "You're not supposed to have anything on Mondays. I only let you have one because it was Sebastian's birthday."

"Happy birthday, Sebastian," said Pops hoisting his nearly empty beer can.

After getting Pops situated back into the guest house, Petey returned to the kitchen to help Sebastian clean up.

Petey's insisted that he repeat both the emails and the phone call word for word. When he'd gone over it twice, she shook her head.

"Here's the latest email," Sebastian said showing it to her on his phone.

After reading through it again, he read the last couple of lines aloud.

"My calendar is still open on the 28th. I'll have to find something interesting to do."

"Is she serious?" Petey asked him.

"Who knows? She's been a bit of a wildcard so far," Sebastian said.

"Karma. A woman that famous going out with you couldn't be anything other than you cashing in all of the good you've done over the years," said Petey.

"They say you can't take it with you so I might as well spend it on something."

"She's not really your type, though. You helped get an alcoholic off the streets and set him up in your mother-in-law suite. Cancer patients fill up your calendar. Meanwhile, she's jetting around the world or out on the road singing. Everything in the magazines says she's a very difficult person."

"So what's the difference, Petey? We're not going to get married. I just want to spend a nice evening with her."

"A night trying to look down her shirt, you mean."

"Petey!"

"Well, Sebastian, you are a man after all, and you're not gay – at least not according to your old girlfriends. Don't look at me like that. I checked you out before I took the job. You didn't think I'd work for a friend of a friend without getting all the dirt. I was a little surprised that you didn't hit on me, to be truthful. Not that I wanted you to."

"Well, you are ten years younger than I am, and you made it very clear in our first interview that you didn't like to mix business and romance."

"True enough. But you and Adria Rider dating?"

"Adria is beautiful, but I'm really just, you know, looking for a good memory."

Petey punched him in the shoulder.

"See. A total romantic, and you're going out with a psycho actress girl."

"Woman."

"Psycho actress WOMAN."

"And she's not psycho. Maybe a little high maintenance," he said.

She tugged at his sleeve. "I just don't want you to get hurt."

"What's the worst that could happen?" he said, and Petey had no answer for his sad eyes.

Three weeks later he flew back to Los Angeles and, at the appointed time, made his way back to Angelinos once again and waited.

"You'll never prove it," Adria said to the camera.

She smiled as she stepped into a Mini Cooper that matched her ruby red lipstick. Off, she drove, leaving the intrepid detective coughing in the dust kicked up off the gravel driveway.

"Cut!" yelled the director.

Adria stopped the car and walked back, waving at the dust cloud.

"How was that?" Adria asked the director.

"It was great," he said to her.

Everyone else gathered around.

"Thanks, everybody, that should give us what we need."

Her director gave Adria a peck on the cheek. "Thanks for coming back, honey. I know I probably messed up your crazy schedule."

"Forget it, Cy, but I do have to go."

Adria hurried into wardrobe, stepped out of her dress, and pulled on some jeans and a blouse.

Once she was in her jeep, she punched 411 into her phone.

"Fullerton. Angelino's." The number came up, and she spent the extra two dollars to dial it directly. She waited while the maître d got Sebastian.

"Hello. This is Sebastian."

"It's Adria. I'm running late."

"Running late, but coming?" A whisper of hope snuck into his voice.

"Yes. Running late, but coming. I'm sorry, but I got a call today to re-shoot a scene from a movie that I thought was already done. They had a problem in the studio and lost the film."

"So what does that mean?"

"With traffic, it means I'm an hour and a half away. I'm really sorry."

"That's okay. I'll be here."

Adria walked in, looking like any other harried young woman, who was late for a date. Her eyes searched the room, adjusting to the mood lighting of Angelino's. She wondered if he'd given up on her. Movement drew her eye to where Sebastian was rising from his chair.

His smile greeted her as she approached the table, a nice smile not a crazy one.

"I'm so sorry," she said.

"You got here a little bit faster than I expected after your phone call."

"Well, I may have violated a few traffic rules," she said, smiling back at him.

Adria ordered the twelve layer lasagna, but Sebastian stuck with the pizza.

"So Mr. Fox, how many people have you told about tonight? Some fans who ask me out are in it for the fame, even if it's just within their own social circle."

"Just my friend, Petey. She works for me."

"Her mother must not have liked her to give her that name."

"Petey is short for Patricia – but it fits her. She's got purple hair and more tattoos than appendages. I only call her Patricia when I'm mad at her."

Adria caught the protective undercurrent in his voice.

"So does Petey ghost write your stories?"

The waiter interrupted their conversation with Adria's water.

"No. She doesn't work for me in my publishing business. She just takes care of a few things around the house."

"A housekeeper?"

"Don't you have a housekeeper?"

"No, I do not have a housekeeper," she said, a bit snarkily. "And I haven't had plastic surgery, and I don't own a Mercedes, and ..."

Sebastian held up his hands in mock surrender and laughed, "All right. All right."

Adria smiled back at him. She liked the way that his eyes stayed focused on hers rather than traveling the length of her body. He didn't seem to be nervous or trying too hard. Instead, she realized she was doing what she always hated in her dates, analyzing instead of enjoying. A sip of water covered her for a second when she realized she had missed his question.

"Sorry. What did you say?"

"I said, 'I've told just Petey, how many people have you told?'"

The question caught her off guard. "Oh, a few people I guess. Mary, that's my sister, and Guy, he's my manager, and the band."

"So you're just using me to impress all of your friends," Sebastian deadpanned.

Adria threw her head back and laughed, and that made Sebastian smile.

"That's why I came out with you tonight, Mr. Fox. Even if you are a stalker, at least you're a stalker who makes me laugh."

"Well, it's nice to have a few redeeming qualities. By the way, are you going to stop calling me Mr. Fox some time?"

"Maybe," she said, "So how'd you get into the personal biography business?"

"I wanted to be a writer. Novels didn't really work out for me, and I had a friend whose husband was turning fifty. She wanted to do something special for him so she asked me to write up a twenty-page story of his life and paid me a thousand dollars. One of her friends who read it asked me to write a tribute for their late father, and it just grew from there. What about you?"

"I was more of a singer growing up. My folks had done some theater work. When the school plays came up, it seemed fun so I joined in. One day I got a bit part in a movie and after that, acting took over my life."

They sat for a minute enjoying the ambiance of the restaurant and appraising each other.

"Your tip about this place was spot on, even if you came the wrong night last time," Adria said. "If you dropped it on a street in Hollywood, it would be packed out with celebrities every night. Down here in Orange County, it's a well-kept secret."

"Speaking of celebs, that couple is checking you out, trying to figure out if you're you."

"Let's ignore them and pretend I'm not me. As long as I don't make eye contact, most people leave me alone."

Without staring, Sebastian's eyes flickered over her shoulder.

"The guy wants to come over here, but his wife just got him to leave."

"Fame pretty much cured me from going into public very much. After one film, I think I went for three months before I could finish a meal uninterrupted. The only other bad part of fame is when I'm being stalked by weird men," she said with a smile dancing at the edges of her lips.

"It would be strange for me to be stalked by men, too, weird or otherwise although, if you wanted to, you could stalk me for a while."

At the suspicious look in her eyes, he added, "You know. Just so I could experience what it's like to be stalked by a weird woman."

"Well, that wouldn't help you because I'm not weird. I'm eccentric. Eccentricity is a requirement for being an actress."

Dinner arrived with no special flourish, but it seemed to cement something between them. Adria shared a bite of her lasagna and Sebastian reciprocated with a slice of pizza.

"The pizza is good, but not as good as this," she said, waving a fork full of lasagna in his general direction. They ate silently, a tribute to the food.

"Do you have to shoot again tomorrow?"

She shook her head.

"No, I thought this film was done a couple of weeks ago. We'd already shot these scenes, but they got lost. It doesn't happen often now that everything is digital, but it used to happen a lot. In *Top Gun,* there's a love scene between Tom Cruise and Kelly McGillis. The re-takes were filmed in a barely lit room because McGillis had already dyed her hair for another movie, when they re-shot it."

"So what color did you have to dye your hair for today?"

"Ha, ha. Nothing like that. Just this bright, too red lipstick that makes people stare."

They talked for a while longer then he walked her to her car.

"I know you probably get a lot of mail from fans so I appreciate you actually reading mine and, of course, going out with me."

"Sometimes the volume is mail is crazy, and I get a lot of mail from weirdoes. At least you're a manageable weirdo."

He laughed, and she smiled.

Adria slid into the safety of her Jeep before he could hug her, started the car, and rolled down the window.

"So what now, Mr. Fox? A long plane ride home tomorrow?"

"Well, I don't know what I'm doing all day, but I'll be standing at the entrance to Disneyland at nine tomorrow morning."

"Disneyland?" she asked.

"Sure. I'm a kid at heart."

Chapter 13

The happiest place on earth was bustling with excitement. People pulsed past a sleepy Mr. Fox. Sebastian hadn't slept well. His mind swam as he thought about his date with Adria. Their conversation the night before had settled quickly into normalcy. Adria's tardiness had done more than delay the start of their night.

It had made it.

Adria was so busy worrying about being late, that she didn't have time to worry about how to talk to Sebastian. He had been so busy making sure that she got her order, that he hadn't had time to think about how crazy the whole thing was.

Moments ago these thoughts had come to Sebastian as he leaned against a stone wall, waiting for a movie star to show up and spend the day walking around Disneyland together.

Stealth was in Adria's nature. Moving hidden in crowds was a skill that every public persona nurtured. Sebastian had been looking expressly for her, and yet, she almost was up to him before he realized it. A light-blue baseball cap with the word "Jamaica" written across the front combined with her sunglasses hid the face that millions knew.

"Good morning, Mr. Fox. Fancy meeting you here."

"And you, Miss Rider," he whispered so as not to attract attention.

They walked toward the ticket booths, and Sebastian veered off to the side, where a sign advertised special passes, special promotions, and VIPs.

Adria protested when she saw the sign.

"What are you doing?"

"Getting us tickets?"

"Do you think that you're going to trade on my name?"

"Adria," he said half-turning and pointing at the sign, "this is the ..."

"This is the window for VIPs and such. I don't want people to know I'm here. If you tell them my name just to get a free ticket, the whole park will know I'm here within the hour."

"Sebastian Fox, what are you doing here?" a girl in a blue Disney shirt exclaimed.

"Hi Justine."

"You're not on the list today, Sebastian. Did I miss something?"

"Just a personal visit. I think I still have to see you to use my pass though."

"Of course. Just come over to the booth, and we'll fix you up."

When she had them at the window, Sebastian fished his pass out of his wallet. Justine waved it away.

"Sebastian. As if I need your ID. What is your friend's name?"

"Sarah Rider," put in Adria.

"Well, Miss Rider, here is your pass. You've got the best tour guide in the business. Sebastian's here ten times a year with *Kids with Cancer*. He's one of their patron saints."

After they had walked on a little way, Sebastian turned to her with a bit of a smirk on his face.

"Now, you were starting to say something back there by the ticket booth."

"I'm sorry. A lot of people have burned me over the years."

He took her hands and looked into her eyes.

"I'm not here to change your life, Sarah Rider, and I'm not here to take advantage of you. Now, if you don't mind, I'd like to get to Space Mountain before lunch."

They melted into the crowd, and, before long, they were holding hands just to stay together. Neither of them seemed to mind the simple touch that drew them both physically and emotionally closer.

"So why do you get to pick the first ride?" she asked. "A more chivalrous man would let the lady pick."

"Well, if I had invited you here, I certainly would have let you choose first. However, I just commented that I was coming here, and you decided to stalk me. Not that I mind."

For thirty minutes, the edged their way along the line before screaming through the two minutes and thirty-eight seconds of the actual ride. The FASTPASS+ system at Disneyland allowed them to reserve a certain time window for three rides. Both wanted to ride Space Mountain again so they got a pass for the one o'clock to one-thirty timeslot.

From there, they wandered across Disneyland, making sure to stop at their favorite rides. As they moved through the park, Sebastian glanced around from time to time. His eyes followed the people, watching to see if he and Adria were drawing the attention of anyone. A couple of guys stared their way, but there was no recognition. They were the simple looks of typical young men enjoying a beautiful woman like Adria.

Education, family history, and other topics of small talk came and went with Sebastian describing life as an only child, and Adria talking about her busy childhood home.

They bounced up the stairs towards their next ride.

"What about you? How come no brothers or sisters? Were you too much trouble?" Adria asked as they came back together.

"Mom always wanted a second kid, but it never worked out," Sebastian said. "After they had me, they tried for a while and then gave up."

Sadness sounded in his voice, and Adria squeezed his hand tightly, leaning her head on his shoulder. The line they were in inched forward, but Adria didn't move. Instead, she looked Sebastian in the eye and tousled his hair. He smiled at her touch, took both her hands, and slow walked her back to where the line was waiting to meet them.

I'm in way over my head, thought Sebastian. *I have no right being here with this woman, even if she's the one getting into the spirit of the date a little too quickly.*

They wove their way back and forth along the intricate pathways that Disney and his minions had laid out over the years. Sebastian showed her some of his favorite spots. Most were places he'd found over the years – back alleys that went ignored by the masses, designs inlaid into mountains, and walls that most people ran past without a second thought.

Later they stood in line for Splash Mountain, listening to the crowds around them, guessing at the accents in a quiet voice and pointing out the outrageous T-shirts.

"So who's the prettiest girl in this line? And don't say me." Adria asked.

"Uh, movie star," he said softly, pointing at her.

"You have to pick someone else so I can see what you really like in a woman."

"I guess that girl over there in the Pepperdine shirt."
Adria punched him.

"How can you do that?"

"What?"

"Point out other women when you're out on a date with me."

"But" he started, then the line moved, and she disappeared around the corner, flashing a wicked grin at him. If

88

they ever made a statue of Adria, he decided, that should be the pose they used. It just seemed to capture her. Still mildly annoyed, he caught up with her and called her true name. People turned and stared, and she gave him a reproving look.

"We're supposed to be inconspicuous, remember."

Splash Mountain spun them around several times before dropping them down a fifty-foot waterfall that left them dripping.

"Lunch?" he asked.

"If you'd like," Adria said. "I wouldn't want to interrupt your plans."

Eight dollar hamburgers and cheese fries sounded good so Sebastian handed over the money. They snuck downstairs into the overflow seating of the restaurant and sat in a dark corner, safely tucked away from the ninety degree heat. Part of the time they talked and part of the time they ate quietly.

"Oh no," said Adria suddenly sounding worried.

"What?" Sebastian turned to look over his shoulder.

Across the way was a man with a professional looking camera draped around his neck. The man was holding a photo in his hand and scanning the crowd. When he made eye contact with Adria, he smiled with satisfaction.

"I saw that guy when we were getting off of Splash Mountain. He was standing near the booth where they post your pictures from the ride," Sebastian said.

"That's Charlie Constantine. Not only is he one of the biggest idiots on the planet, but he's also got a personal vendetta against me."

Constantine was making his way toward them and, in his hurry, he didn't see a young girl and her brother who were clearing their family's table. Ketchup, French fries, and chicken nuggets flew in the air as the photographer hit the deck on top of the boy.

"Who is this guy?" Sebastian asked.

"I'll tell you on the way. Come on," she said.

Adria hesitated as she stepped out into the sunlight, not sure what to do. Sebastian grabbed her by the arm and led off toward the jumble of paths that he knew so well.

"I'm not famous enough for most paparazzi to bother with, but Charlie and I had an altercation one time so he's sort of taken me on as a personal project."

"What kind of altercation?"

"I kicked him in the nuts when he trespassed onto my property."

Sebastian started laughing, even as a hurried glance over his shoulder told him that Constantine had spotted them. The photographer threw his camera up, trying for a shot.

"I'm kind of jealous. I thought I was your only stalker."

"Ha, ha," she said as they stopped to catch their breath, "You only wish you were."

"So what kind of money can he get for pictures?"

"Five thousand? Ten thousand? Who knows? Adria Rider and her mysterious boyfriend. It wouldn't be the first time a relationship of mine ended up in Star."

"I would think they'd only care if you were dating an actor or prince or something."

"Well you'd be wrong then, wouldn't you? The magazines will pay for anything even remotely close to a famous person. Don't you read the tabloids?"

"No. I work for a living."

Adria threw Sebastian a dirty look and rushed past him into Fantasyland, which in the surreal moment seemed fitting to Sebastian. He pulled her inside a gift shop, made a quick purchase, and then they were back out on the street.

Over the crowd, Sebastian could see Constantine speeding toward them.

Sebastian looked at his watch and yelled to Adria, "Space Mountain."

90

Chapter 14

Camp Maxey, Texas. June 1942.

The only time Duke seemed to fit in at Camp Maxey was on the rifle range. That's when all of Charles Farmington's well spent ammunition paid off. Even Duke's shooting, though, wasn't enough to keep Timmons at bay.

"Those scars don't seem to hurt your aim," Timmons said, "Keep that up, and the paratroopers will be after you."

Duke finished his firing sequence.

"Who exactly are they?" Duke asked.

"A new group that they're putting together called Airborne. The Krauts have used them very effectively so the Army has decided to try to put together a few as well. Men jump out of planes like human bombs, dropped anywhere the army wants to surprise the enemy."

Duke was still thinking about how great it would be to be a paratrooper when he had his first miss of the day. He took a breath and squeezed the trigger gently, popping another target.

The day turned grim as they moved to the promised hard march that afternoon. Every day was difficult in camp. With the constant running, hiking, and pack work in the Texas heat, Duke had lost nearly forty pounds from the grind. Jumping out of a plane couldn't be much worse than this no matter where he landed.

At the end of the march, Tom Radcliff and Duke were pulled aside while the rest of the platoon fell out for free time.

Sergeant Timmons perched himself on a boulder at the start of the course and prepared the recruits for their punishment.

Both men removed their packs in preparation.

Timmons looked at them and with his most pleasant tone said, "Who said anything about not carrying your packs?"

"You've got to be kidding," said Radcliff.

"Shut your mouth," said Timmons.

The obstacle course at Camp Maxey was laid out in sections. Crawling through sand for a hundred yards was the first exercise for the recruits with the penalty of sharp wire if one decided to rise up too far. Both men pushed their packs ahead of them, plowing wide births in the sand since the course was not built to be run in full gear.

From there, they ran to a ten-foot wall with ropes suspended on either side. With their legs already aching from the earlier run, Duke and Radcliff struggled with the ropes. Duke dug in and used his long strides to pull himself on top of the wall. He glanced over and saw that Radcliff was stuck. The earlier run had sapped the strength in Radcliff's legs. With Timmons's words from the night before still echoing in his ears, Duke dropped his pack over the wall and scooted across until he was above Radcliff.

"What are you doing, farm boy?" Radcliff snarled.

"Helping you over the wall."

"Like hell you are," said Radcliff.

"Like hell I am," said Duke, and with that, he leaned over and grabbed onto Radcliff's pack and yanked him up until both were on the top of the wall.

As Radcliff came over the wall, he purposely toppled Duke from his perch. Duke fell, just getting his feet under him before he hit the ground. The other private scrambled down his rope and landed next to Duke.

"I told you to you leave me alone," said Radcliff.

Radcliff took off running for the next part of the course, and Duke raced to catch him. By the time Duke reached the set of rope ladders that lead to the elevated walks, Radcliff was part way across.

The elevated walk was simply two roughhewn logs with a rope on one side for balance. Duke hurried as he tried to close the gap, nearly falling to the ground. He dropped from the platform on the far side, felt a shove in the back, and went sprawling into the mud. Clawing the mud from his eyes, he watched Radcliff splash down the creek bed and run full speed around the corner toward the end of the course.

Duke sprinted, chasing Radcliff down the muddy trail while his anger consumed him. The two were close to the finish of the first of their three runs.

He was greeted at the end of the finish line by Corporal Clemons, who yelled that whoever crossed the finish line in first place after the second run wouldn't have to run the third time. By this time, Radcliff had opened up a lead of several hundred yards.

Instead of running, Duke began taking long measured steps eating up ground between him and the starting line. Radcliff for the moment had disappeared from his field of vision, but Duke was no longer concerned with Radcliff. When he reached the starting line, he paused and took a breath, pushing aside the events of the whole day.

This time through, Duke pushed his pack ahead of him in the sand mindful of the glare from Timmons. Radcliff was struggling on the wall again. As Duke came out from his crawl under the wire, he saw that Radcliff had taken off his backpack and was trying to throw it over the wall, even though he was barely halfway up the rope. Predictably Radcliff's pack came crashing down striking him on the shoulder.

For a minute, Duke thought that Radcliff would hold on. He swung sideways and grabbed for the rope with his other hand, but the blow from the falling, forty pound pack made him lose his grip.

Duke stared at the wall ignoring Radcliff for the moment. Instead, Duke took a running start at the wall and timed his leap perfectly. Two long, hard pulls and he was at the top. He glanced down at Radcliff, and saw fear and exhaustion in the other man's eyes. Duke let go of his pack on the far side of the wall and dropped back down to the ground beside Radcliff.

Radcliff didn't even respond. He was bent over, hands on his knees, gasping for breath. Duke took the other man's pack and climbed the wall, dropping it onto the far side next to his own. Sitting on the top of the wall, Duke looked down and did the only thing he could think of.

"Soldier, get up on that rope," he yelled.

Radcliff didn't move or even react.

"Soldier, I told you to get up on that rope," Duke screamed again, loudly enough that a few solders passing by turned to see what the excitement was.

Finally, Radcliff responded and began to struggle with the rope. He made it part way before he got stuck once again. Duke grabbed the top of the other man's rope and began to slide down the far side of the wall, pulling his foe to the top. Radcliff half-jumped, half fell from the top of the wall and landed clumsily. His eyes showed the exhaustion he felt and seemed ready to glaze over. They both picked up their packs and moved toward the rope ladders.

Duke went up the rope ladder and dropped his pack on the platform then went back down. This time Radcliff was unwilling to let go of his pack so Duke grabbed his arm, and they climbed together. Once on the platform they took the same log, Duke following close behind where he could lend a hand to steady Radcliff. Once off the logs, Radcliff collapsed on the ground.

"Go ahead. You've earned it," Tom Radcliff said.

Instead, Duke reached down and dragged his fallen comrade from the ground. Together they stumbled on the slimy rocks in the creek and moved toward the end of the second run.

Word of their ordeal had spread, and several men from the platoon stood watching them near the end of the course. Duke brought them to a halt two feet before the finish line and shoved Radcliff across the line in front of him.

Duke, moved quickly back to the beginning of the obstacle course. When he had finished crawling under the razor wire for a third time, he was confronted by a pair of boots.

"Private Farmington," said Timmons in his usual shouting voice.

"Yes, Sergeant" Duke replied

"Where is Private Radcliff?"

"I left him at the finish line," Duke said. "He finished first."

"I find it hard to believe that Radcliff beat you. Especially since Radcliff couldn't have even made it over the wall the second time without your help."

"Radcliff crossed the finish line before me, Sergeant," Duke said deliberately.

At that moment, Radcliff came in to sight. He was being chair carried to the infirmary.

Timmons's understanding was complete.

"I see. Consider your punishment paid, private, and head back to the barracks."

Four days later, Duke and another private, named Kelly, were summoned by Master Sergeant Timmons.

"Tomorrow morning, the top two shooters from each platoon will face off in a shooting competition. You two are our top men. "

95

Any soldier, not on duty, was at the range to watch the competition. Sparks was the odds on favorite to win, and Duke had heard about the man's shooting abilities. Money and IOUs were swapped between men from different platoons as the side bets spread.

Two men stood to the side talking quietly. A few times before, Duke had seen Colonel Weaver, but the newcomer was a stranger to him. He also sported a patch that Duke had never seen, a winged skull with a parachute above it.

Duke's curiosity was satisfied as he listened to the murmurs of the other shooters.

"Lieutenant Leo Hart is the other one," Sparks was telling Kelly, "He travels around recruiting for Airborne. I heard that he's looking for a couple of fill-ins."

All the marksmen were introduced to Lieutenant Hart before the competition.

Each marksman was given a time limit and only enough ammo to take one shot at each mark. Additionally, the further the target hit, the more points were rewarded.

Sparks was the man to beat, and he nailed all of the targets except the furthest one which he missed by a hair. None of the others came close to Sparks's score.

When Duke's time came, he knelt, took aim at the farthest target, and waited for the corporal's signal to begin. Working his way from the farthest target to the nearest, Duke squeezed off shot after shot. Like Sparks, he ran out of time before he could fire at the last target, but having started further out, he had scored more points than Sparks. When the corporal read Duke's score, his platoon erupted and rushed Duke. Sparks complained bitterly that he had hit as many targets as Duke, but the corporal said that the rules were the rules.

Later that afternoon Duke was lying on his bed, writing a letter home, when Lieutenant Hart appeared in Duke's quarters. Duke jumped to his feet and saluted. The lieutenant had a smile on his face and returned the salute.

"At ease, Private," he said.

Duke relaxed, and Lieutenant Hart dropped onto the bed next to Duke's.

"Pretty clever out there today during the shooting contest. You went for the long distance targets first. Don't ever try that in real war. Just take care of the biggest threat."

"Yes, sir," Duke said, reddening a bit.

"How would you like to join Airborne? We're short one squad. Rather than try to mix new recruits in with the older ones, I want to bring in a whole new group. Sparks is coming, too."

Hart, Sparks, and Duke were on their way the next day to Fort Benning, Georgia. Duke was edging ever closer to Europe and the hell that Hitler had created.

Chapter 15

The good news, Adria thought as she ran, is that it's much easier to run from paparazzi than from homicidal maniacs featured in the movies.

The bad news is that in real life, there isn't a director there to yell "cut" and let you rest every hundred yards. As they rounded one corner, Sebastian seemed to disappear. Looking over her shoulder, she saw him crash like a drunken sailor into a couple.

Adria heard Sebastian throw a "sorry" over his shoulder, but she kept running. Space Mountain came into sight and ahead and Constantine was no longer in view although Adria detected a ripple motion in the crowd behind them.

For a minute, Sebastian disappeared completely, and Adria was left searching the crowd for him. Adria saw him running, holding his side. She waved to him to get his attention.

"Do you see him?" Adria asked.

"No," said a breathless Sebastian.

"Speak of the devil," Adria said suddenly, pointing to Constantine as he pushed through the crowd. They turned and scanned their park tickets which validated their FASTPASS+ time. The attendant waved them through. Constantine was running toward the queue, but got stuck behind a group of teenagers who were making their way slowly up the regular line. Adria could hear Constantine's camera clicking off pictures of their backs.

At the top of the stairs, the two lines diverged. Sebastian and Adria's FASTPASS+ line went two hundred yards into the building that housed the ride. The regular ride line ran the opposite direction and began snaking back and forth, adding a half hour to the wait time. Once past the turn at the top of the stairs, Constantine ducked into the FASTPASS+ line which was virtually deserted.

Adria saw Constantine stop and try to get a shot of her, and Sebastian as their tickets were checked again. Sebastian and Adria said something to the employee manning that point in the line and ducked into the building. As they did, Adria saw Constantine running across the concrete towards the ride. She paused to listen to the confrontation that the photographer had with the Disney employee.

"Can I validate your FASTPASS, sir?" the attendant asked.

"I think there might be a problem with the machine when I signed up," said Constantine.

"Actually, sir, you jumped the line when you got to the top of the stairs. The couple that just went in told me that a strange man was following them. Now, I can call security and have you escorted from the park, or you can turn around and walk back."

Whatever else happened, Adria and Sebastian missed it as they hurried down the ramp to where the shorter FASTPASS line stopped.

"So tell me about you and Constantine," Sebastian said.

Adria shook her head as she gathered her thoughts.

"I was dating John Yetzger. We'd made *Going From Gorshem* together."

"You date your leading men a lot, don't you?"

She felt herself flush.

"Probably a little too much. Does that bother you?"

"Why would it bother me? I'm not your director of dating. Besides most people end up dating people from work or school or church or wherever they spend the most time."

"Well, that makes sense, although I never really thought about it that way. I just thought I was attracted to actors. John was so unpredictable – sometimes funny, then dark and serious or generous to a fault."

"Sounds like an interesting and complex guy."

"He was interesting, and we got a lot of press. In fact, I probably got one of my roles just because of the whole relationship. We were at a party that John was invited to, and I met this producer who asked me to say a line from a movie he was putting together. I got the part. Anyway, John and I were dating seriously and thinking about getting a place together. We were getting a little bit closer to something. I don't know what exactly."

She looked away for a minute, answering herself.

"Love? Engagement? Marriage? And I came home a couple of days early from shooting and found him. You know. I found him ..."

"In bed with another woman,"

Adria felt the anger flood back as they stood in the serpentine line.

"And you know what he had the nerve to tell me? That he was sleeping with her so he could get it out of his system before we settled down together."

Sebastian snorted in disdain.

"That's what I thought too," said Adria. "Like I'm going to trust him now that he's sleeping with this slut named Cindy while I'm out of town."

"I'm sorry. What a jerk."

"It gets worse. First off, they were at my place! Not his place, but this little house I had in Beverly Hills. So we're screaming at each other, and she's trying to get dressed. I

100

pushed them out the door into the courtyard. It turns out that the girl has let Constantine in on the little tryst to make a few bucks. So while the whole fight is going on, Constantine creeps through the fence and onto my property. All of a sudden I heard this click, click, click, and I just snapped."

"That's when you delivered the kick line of the story."

Adria laughed and watched Sebastian's face light up.

"I kicked him hard. He was so shocked and in pain that he dropped his camera. John and Cindy just stood there dumbfounded. I picked the camera up and threw it into the fountain in the courtyard. Cindy was still hanging out of her clothes, and no one was saying anything except for Constantine, who was lying on the ground groaning."

"I'm surprised he didn't press charges or sue you."

"Oh, he did, but I also filed criminal charges against him. We finally settled out of court. I bought him a new camera and dropped the charges. He went for the deal because he had some prior arrests and was on probation, but it certainly didn't put me on his good list."

"Do you worry for your safety?"

"No. He's a jerk, of course, which seems to be a prerequisite for his job, but he's not a violent jerk."

They stood there a minute in the semi-darkness, and she watched his eyes while he processed all she had told him.

His eyes flickered back to hers, and she knew she had his attention.

"Now, what about you, Mr. Fox? How come there's no Mrs. Fox?"

Sebastian thought for a minute.

"It just never worked out."

"That's it. 'It just never worked out'? You're a professional storyteller, and that's the best you've got?"

Sebastian looked embarrassed and said, "Yep, that's it."

"Come on. I'm not settling for that."

"Okay. I had a couple of relationships that got serious. There was one girl who I broke up with named Sarah. She went off the deep end. We'd been dating for a while, and one night she starts acting all crazy. Her friends knew she had been using drugs the whole time and were really surprised that I didn't know. I didn't want any part of that scene so I broke up with her."

"What about the other one, you said a couple?"

"There was this other girl named Kathleen. She was tall and lean in that sort of semi-anorexic way that I was into at the time."

"The no-butt look?"

"No curves at all to her, really. We dated a while, and she wanted to move in, but I'm not really a move-in kind of guy, and that threw her a bit. After couple of arguments, she broke up with me."

"You never asked her why?"

"She threw out a half dozen reasons at the time that were all BS. Besides, reasons are just excuses for the choice you've already made."

"That makes no sense," she said.

"When people break up, most of the time, the reasons aren't really reasons. One person has just decided to move on. There's been some sort of turnoff for the one who wants to break up, and they've decided it's over."

"So you don't think I had a reason to break up with John?"

"Maybe in your case or like the druggie's case, but most of the time that people break up, it's just because they don't want to be together any longer."

"Isn't that a bit cynical?"

"No, it's not cynical. Just a basic understanding of how people work. They look at someone and think that they're great for a while. Slowly, they drift away or someone else catches their eye, and, boom, a reason appears and they break up."

When their turn to ride came, Sebastian asked the attendant if they could ride in the back car.

"The backs the best place to ride you know," said Sebastian as he looped his arms around Adria's waist. "That way, you never slow down waiting for the rest of the cars to make the turns."

"I think the front is faster," asserted Adria.

"Nah. It's the back," he insisted.

"What are we going to do about Constantine on the way out?" she asked.

Before he could answer, the ride was grinding up to the top of the first big hill, and all their attention turned to the hills, drops, and curves of Space Mountain.

Adria watched Sebastian walk out ahead of her wearing the t-shirt and a Goofy mask that he had purchased in the gift shop. She spied the photographer shooting as many people as he could. A group of college kids exited Space Mountain, and she fell in behind them wearing her own mask. For a second, she thought Constantine would follow her, but he wasn't sure and by the time he made up his mind, Adria had caught up with Sebastian, and they had headed for another part of the park.

The rest of the day Sebastian and Adria were lucky. They avoided Constantine thanks to the long lines that filled the vastness of the park. They talked about films, about Duke, about artistic creativity.

Sometimes they just stood silently, enjoying the bubble around them, the natural space that others give each other in a crowded line. At the same time, they invaded each other's personal space with the little touches of elbows, shoulders, arms, and backs that happen in a budding relationship.

By nine-thirty, they were settled onto a sparsely filled patch of green on the far side of Disneyland's castle, in a long forgotten corner of Fantasyland, waiting for the fireworks to fill the sky.

They lay on their backs, and Adria settled her head on Sebastian's shoulder, reveling in the safety and contentment of the moment.

Chapter 16

Saturday, Sebastian drove to northeast Georgia to see Duke. The old man was waiting on the porch for him with fishing rods and a jug of mead. Sebastian was trusted with the alcohol but not allowed to touch the fishing gear.

"Do you know how to fly-fish?"

Sebastian shook his head.

"Well, I'll teach you," said the old man.

Sebastian nodded dumbly, knowing, as with the drinking, that this was not a request, but rather a command. A dozen yards behind the house was an old shed that Sebastian had barely noticed in his previous trips. The rough wood planks were nailed with care. Inside were several small cabinets, which Duke opened in some mysterious sequence, finding the building blocks for the flies that he and Sebastian would use.

Duke gave him an education in tying flies, and Sebastian was fascinated at the complexity of picking a fly based on the time of year, the geographical location, and water type.

From there, they trouped out to the lake where the next hour was an education in how to fly-fish. Sebastian worked at it and by the end of the instruction, Duke waved him down the bank. Bees buzzed in the hot July sun and as Sebastian looked back at the old man, he noticed that Duke seemed to be in another world as the fishing rod metronomed back and forth.

Sebastian struggled at first then discovered his own rhythm. The warmth, the water, and the buzz of the insects combined to relax him, even as he came away without catching anything.

After a bit, Sebastian was forced to return with nothing to show for his efforts. Duke's bucket had three good sized trout in it, enough to cover them for a late afternoon lunch. The old man battered the fish and fried them in an iron skillet. A basket of his signature biscuits joined the fish on the table, as well as the ever-present mead.

For a long time, there was nothing but the sounds of silverware clinking on the plates and the scrape of the Mason jars sliding off the table. Duke asked to see Sebastian's notes, and Sebastian pushed the computer to the old man. When Duke had reviewed what Sebastian had written, Duke lit a cigar and stared out at the lake for fifteen minutes.

"You ever had anyone just make stuff up when they talk to you?" Duke asked.

"It's hard to tell, but the odds are that at least a few of them has lied to me along the way."

"I've got something I need to tell you," Duke said. "That first day you were here, I lied to you. It didn't bother me too much at the time, but reading your notes made me feel guilty. The whole thing with Daniel that I told you was made up. Daniel and I don't ever talk. We don't talk because I didn't have anything to do with him going to Canada. Winnie wasn't going to lose another boy to that war. That's what she told me."

Duke's voice cracked. He stopped for a minute, composing himself.

"The day he left, Winnie tried to sneak him out so I wouldn't know. But I caught 'em at the bottom of the driveway. Saw the guilt in their eyes. I told him that he couldn't desert his country, told him that he couldn't just walk away. Not after what his brother had given up."

Duke looked up at Sebastian to gauge his reaction. Sebastian nodded, feeling just a taste of the pain that it must have caused.

"I told him that--" his voice cracked again, "I told him that he wasn't really a son of mine, if he deserted and brought shame on our family. Daniel just sat there and took it. After that, it was just the three of us – me, Winnie, and Lilith. Most of the time, they were doing girlie stuff. Daniel and I just never were able to figure it all out, you know, how to make it right."

Sebastian nodded. Duke put down the cigar and walked off the porch without another word. A couple of hours later, Duke returned. In his absence, Sebastian had decided to take dinner into his own hands and was cooking bacon-and-cheese sandwiches when Duke returned, his eyes red-rimmed and bloodshot. They ate silently and adjourned to the living room. More questions peppered the air after the meal, but not about the war or about Daniel, just about Winifred.

"How did you meet Winnie?"

"There was a dance."

"You grew up in the same town?"

"Don't interrupt an old man, Fox," Duke reproved him. "We were in Alabama after basic training waiting to ship out. There was a dance, and we met a bunch of girls along the way."

Duke continued with his story. Talking about how he met his first love must have whetted his appetite, because, for the first time, he began to open up about the war.

A week later, Sebastian was back in northeast Georgia. As he drove up Duke's driveway, he saw smoke pouring out of Duke's kitchen. Too much smoke.

"Duke! Duke!"

Sebastian pounded up the stairs. Flames danced on top of the frying pan and across the counter top as dark greasy smoke attacked his eyes. He grabbed at a pot holder and

107

dragged the frying pan into the sink, as his breathing quickly turned to coughing. Through the door that led into the hall, he could see a booted foot.

Cursing through his hacking cough, Sebastian dropped below the smoke and crawled to where his friend lay. A trickle of blood ran down Duke's scalp and matted his hair.

Sebastian got the front door open and managed to drag Duke down the stairs. He pulled the old man over to where the Mustang was parked and then called 911.

Sirens wailed in the distance, and Sebastian took a sweatshirt out of the backseat of his car and put it under Duke's head. Duke's eyes fluttered, and he tried to talk.

Fire engines roared up to the house. Another siren sounded from afar.

Two black- and yellow-clad firemen found Sebastian while others started for the house.

"It started as a grease fire," Sebastian yelled over the hubbub to the men working on Duke. "I found him lying on the floor and dragged him out here."

"Is there anyone else inside?"

"No. He lives alone."

Sebastian sat coughing as the firefighters split into two groups, one working on Duke and the other setting up a draft hose to the pond and starting to drench the house. After a minute there was a loud explosion from the kitchen as the flames found Duke's private reserve. In the meantime, the EMS arrived, quickly assessed Duke, and loaded him into the ambulance.

"We're taking him to Mercy East," was the last thing that the EMS said before they roared off, kicking up dust from the driveway.

Sebastian sat, shell-shocked, listening to the retreating ambulance and watched as parts of Duke's roof fell in. The fire roared on and the firemen, who had blocked in Sebastian's car, seemed in no hurry to leave. He dug through his cell phone and located Lilith's number. He got a cool reception until he told her about Duke.

"Is he all right?"

Pure panic filled her voice.

"He was breathing, but seemed confused. He's on his way to Mercy East Hospital."

"Why aren't you with him?" Lilith asked.

"There wasn't room in the ambulance, and I'm stuck right now behind the fire trucks. When they clear out, I'll go over there."

"We're on our way," she said.

A car pulled up that was marked in bold letters as belonging to the fire chief. Sebastian related what he had seen while the chief made notes on a clipboard.

"You should go over to Mercy East yourself and have the docs check out that burn."

Sebastian's arm had started to hurt. He noticed a line where the hair was gone, and the skin looked red and angry. One of the firemen sprayed a white mist on the burn and wrapped it in gauze and restated the chief's admonition that he should get it looked at.

Finding Mercy East proved to be fairly easy, once Sebastian was pointed in the right direction. Compared to the hustle of Atlanta, rural Georgia was a snap to navigate.

"I'm looking for Duke Farmington. I'm ... uh ... his cousin," Sebastian said to the nurse.

He was directed to a waiting area and was so engrossed thinking about Duke that he didn't notice Lilith until the nurse was speaking to her.

"Your cousin Sebastian is over in the waiting room," the nurse said.

Sebastian turned to see Lilith being guided over by a slick looking fellow, who met Duke's description of Calvin.

"My cousin Sebastian?" She hissed out at him.

"Sorry. I didn't think they'd tell me anything if I wasn't family."

"You had no right to say that."

Calvin interposed, "Honey. We can worry about it later. Let's find out about your daddy."

"So what have you heard?" Lilith demanded.

"I haven't heard anything. I just got here myself."

The batwing doors opened, and a female doctor in blue scrubs stood there as several hopeful faces turned in her direction.

"Is the Farmington family here?"

Lilith glanced once at Sebastian then turned with Calvin toward the doctor.

"I'm his daughter, and this is my husband. How is he?"

"Hi. I'm Doctor Branch," said the blonde with short hair, "Your father is resting. He seems to have had a mild stroke of some sort. We won't know for sure until we run a few more tests. For now, he seems stable, and we're monitoring him. I can tell you more if you come with me."

The doctor opened the doors and held them as Calvin and Lilith hurried through, leaving Sebastian behind.

Chapter 17

Fort Benning, Georgia. June 1942.

Duke, Sparks, and Colonel Hart arrived at Fort Benning a few days later, after a long train ride. A couple of the other recruits had joined them on the ride from different forts where they'd been stationed for basic training.

Herman Miller joined them at Benning, and Duke soon came to appreciate his many talents. Miller was a private like the rest of them, but he had spent time honing odd skills like basic medical training and map reading. Newspapers reported on old battles, and Herman kept a set of maps with all of the movements scrawled including unit numbers.

"It's all old news, of course. I can tell you where we were a month ago, but it's good practice for when we finally start doing missions."

Sparks was disappointed that Miller was not another sharpshooter, but as Colonel Hart pointed out, "You can't build an entire regiment simply with shooters. Besides, Miller's not too bad with a rifle."

At Benning they met the rest of their squad. George Rawlings was from Tennessee, the only one in the squad who was married. Frank Sierkowski always went out of his way to make himself look better. Mike Martin was from Arizona, giving he and Duke a lot to talk about. Sparks was part of the group, as was Herman Miller. The last member Duke met on his first day was Graham Carpenter, who had a love affair with his rifle.

When they arrived at Benning, Duke was in for another surprise. Hart had informed the captain there that Duke would make a good squad leader for the new group. The captain had informed the lieutenant who had informed Sergeant Jackson.

Sergeant Jackson gathered the squad together once Duke arrived and announced that based on Colonel Hart's input, Duke would serve as the squad leader.

Jackson looked them over, and Duke knew what he was wondering. Could this squad make up the time that the rest of the company had already put into the training?

"You men should know that by coming in late you have a lot of catching up to do. Rather than try to add you into the old squads, you've been formed as the fourth squad of 2nd Platoon, Hotel Company. The rest of the company has the day off. They return from leave tomorrow afternoon at fifteen hundred hours. You will get no such luxury. I do not know all of your backgrounds, and I do not care. You will not be given any extra breaks. Either you will make it or you will fail. Being a member of Airborne is not a right. It is a privilege. If Lieutenant Hart thinks that you have what it takes to make it, then you probably do. You have thirty minutes to stow your gear, return here, and form up."

If Duke had thought the physical training in basic was difficult, it was nothing like what he was about to experience in parachute school. The physical push began as soon as the squad reported back to Sergeant Jackson. Each recruit did fifty pushups, followed by another fifty. As they were finishing up, one of the MPs on the base came to find Jackson.

"Sergeant Jackson, there's some hotshot at the front gate who says he supposed to join your company."

"We'll come to get him right now since he's already three hours late."

For the first time but certainly not the last, Duke was to see the sergeant get angry. Jackson's breath came faster and faster, but even more so, Duke noticed that his ears turned bright red, as if they had suddenly realized they were allergic to something.

"Squad, it seems our newest member is finally here. As punishment for his tardiness, the whole squad will double-time it to the front gate with full packs to welcome him."

When they arrived at the front gate, they found Tony Marcelli. He was leaning against a wall, smoking a cigarette.

"Private Marcelli?" Jackson asked with obvious anger.

"Yes, Sergeant," Tony said, dropping his cigarette, squishing it out with his foot, and coming to attention all at the same time.

"This is an army base, not some local malt shop. Privates Harrington and Miller, drop your packs," Sergeant Jackson ordered.

The privates consented.

"Private Marcelli, you have the pleasure of carrying your pack as well as these men's packs back to the barracks."

"Private, take your squad to the barracks. Report to chow in thirty minutes," Jackson ordered Duke.

They got lost.

None of them had been on the base long enough to remember where their barracks were. They finally made it back to where they were bunking after feeling like fools for twenty minutes.

Duke pointed Tony to the open cot.

"Stow your stuff, Tony, then you owe us two sets of fifty pushups."

"A hundred pushups?" Tony asked.

"Two sets of fifty. Just like every other member of the squad. We did that earlier while you were out enjoying a Saturday afternoon drive."

Tony tossed his stuff onto his bed, dropped to the floor, and did the hundred in a single set.

"Is that good enough for you?"

The rest of the company filtered in the next day and ignored Duke's squad.

"Not the friendliest guys in the world, are they?" said Tony.

"We'll have to show them that we belong," said Duke.

At 1600 hours, Lt. Paul Thompson addressed the platoon.

"Second platoon is now complete again, thanks to our eight new members. I'd like the company to take the new squad out into the woods and show them how things are done in Airborne."

Sergeant Jackson barked out orders, and soon the whole group was moving at full speed out of the compound and into the woods. They went into the woods until they reached a series of pits, eight foot square and about ten feet deep. One of the squad leaders dropped a caving ladder down the side of one of the pits.

He looked at Duke.

"Get your squad into this hole, and let's see how long it takes you to get back out."

"Squad, down the ladder quickly," Duke ordered.

The squad members dropped their packs and went down the ladder.

Duke followed them in, but held onto his pack. As soon as his feet hit the bottom of the hole the ladder was yanked up. While the men in the pit cursed, the soldiers above dumped water and threw rotten vegetables at their cornered targets. Duke sought a corner and knelt on one knee while the deluge continued. Tony and Frank retaliated and returned fire with some cabbage that had survived the first assault. In particular, Tony's aim hit one of the squad leaders.

"Very funny," the squad leader yelled. "Now we'll take the ladder with us."

114

There was a clanging then silence.

"Now what?" someone asked.

"Sparks, you're the tallest. Does anyone have a knife besides me?" Duke asked.

Several did. Duke opened his pack and pulled out a rope.

"I had a feeling they might do something," Duke said.

"Me too," said Frank.

Duke moved around the walls and stopped when he found a dry spot.

"Tony and Herman, you come over here. Put your hands together."

Duke pointed at Sparks.

"Grab a couple of knives, Jake. Tony and Herman will hoist you up as far as they can then you'll have to pull yourself up hand over hand the rest of the way."

They looped the rope around Jake's waist and tied a quick knot.

On Duke's signal, Tony and Herman hoisted Jake into the air so far that Duke thought for a minute he would fall back to the bottom of the pit. Jake planted both knives as high as he could reach and held on. Tony and Herman could still reach the bottoms of his feet so they stood on their tiptoes and pushed against him for added leverage. Hand over hand, Sparks pulled himself up over the edge. He disappeared for a couple of minutes then the rope dropped into the pit. Herman was the next one up. The rest of the squad was pulled up one by one until they stood outside the hole.

"You think they'll take their time going back?" asked Tony.

"Maybe. We came southwest all the way. It shouldn't be too hard to find our way back, over another path," said Herman.

The squad moved quickly back the way that they had come with Herman in the lead, scouting. After a short time they had caught sight of the rest of the company. Duke led his squad quietly along another trail which angled roughly back toward the base.

Herman led off with a silent trot. After the squad was in sync, he quickened until they were near a dead run. They arrived ahead of the other squads.

"Fresh clothes, on the double," Duke ordered.

When Sergeant Jackson and the other men arrived at the barracks, they were shocked to see Duke and his men in pristine condition lying in their cots. The platoon veterans fumed when they learned that their prank had failed, but also felt a grudging respect for these new soldiers who had outfoxed them.

Duke's squad worked hard over the next couple of weeks to master the various techniques that the rest of the platoon had already covered. Soon there was little distinction between the groups other than the usual friendly banter and competitiveness that infiltrated any such unit.

In Airborne, the men started out jumping off six-foot high platforms onto dusty mattresses, practicing techniques for rolling on impact. By the time they finished, they could do the maneuvers in their sleep. From there, they graduated to a sixty-foot high platform where they dropped over the edge on pulleys hooked through a jump pack.

To become a full-fledged member of Airborne, you had to complete three airplane jumps. The rest of Hotel Company had already completed their first. Soon it was time for Duke and his squad to go. In the first jump, the troopers jumped with a static cord, meaning that the chute's rip cord was hooked into the plane and pulled automatically as the soldier went out the door.

Duke made sure he stood at the front of the line when it was time to go out of the plane. As the air hit him in the face, he experienced conflicting emotions of sheer terror and exultation. He was flying, in a way that few would ever know. No one on his squad hesitated at the door or backed out, something that would have ended their career in Airborne. The rest of the company greeted them at the drop zone. Cheers rang out, and a rare smile crossed Sergeant Jackson's lips. Now, he could begin to mold them into a single fighting force.

The remaining five weeks were some of the most brutal times that Duke would ever experience during his stint in the Army, in or out of combat. Through every trial, the squads grew closer together. After his third jump, Duke was given the special Airborne patch for his uniform.

He was now an official member of the most elite unit in the United States Army.

Chapter 18

Adria wasn't sure what to expect, and a feeling of uncertainty permeated her every thought as she drove toward her destination.

She hadn't told the band where she was going or why she was renting a separate car. She had left them at Hartsfield-Jackson Airport, reminding them that they had an early flight into New Jersey the next morning. Right now she was busy checking and double checking the address on the street until she was sure that she had found Sebastian's house. It was a curious creation, an old brick ranch that had been modified with a glass sunroom on top.

The sight of it made her chuckle as she parked in the driveway near a green convertible and an older VW Jetta.

Behind the house, and to the right, sat a small mother-in-law suite. Just as Adria was getting out, the door of the mother-in-law suite opened, and a punkish looking woman in her late twenties exited and pulled the door closed behind her.

"Can I help you?" the woman said as she walked across the gravel toward Adria.

The woman finally got a good look at Adria and let out an "oh" of recognition.

"You're Adria," said Petey.

"Yes. And you must be Petey."

The front door of the main house opened, and Sebastian walked across the yard to where they stood, a huge smile on his face.

"Well, Miss Rider, what a pleasant surprise."

He leaned in and hugged her. She clung to him for a moment, before realizing with some embarrassment that Petey was standing there grinning stupidly at them. The couple released each other, but stood closely together.

"You have to stop calling me Miss Rider."

"It's an affectionate term," said Sebastian.

"Adria," said Adria.

"All right. Adria. I see you've met Petey. Hopefully, I came out before she had a chance to tell you any stories."

"You did, but the night is young," said Petey.

"Good," said Sebastian, "Now what are you doing here? I wish I had known you were coming though, I made some plans."

"Well, that's okay, I can just stay for a few minutes then drive back if you're busy."

"You could join me, if you don't mind going out with an old drunk on his once a week binge."

"Who's the old drunk?"

"Pops," said Sebastian and Petey simultaneously.

They laughed and Petey explained.

"Pops lives in the small house. He's an alcoholic that Sebastian helped get off the street. Once a week, Sebastian or I take him out drinking. It's not really therapy, but it seems to keep him happy."

Sebastian chimed in, "Tonight's my night to take him out, but you can join us."

"You have an alcoholic living with you who you take out drinking once a week?"

Petey laughed.

"That's the response we always get. Sebastian, you don't have to take him. I'll take him, even if it is a Hooters night."

"Hooters night?" asked Adria.

"Hooters night. Every other week we let him go to Hooters," Sebastian said, "usually on my nights so that Petey doesn't have to go and watch him stare down all the waitresses."

"Sebastian is always willing to make the huge sacrifice to go hang out at Hooters," said Petey.

It was Adria's turn to laugh then while Sebastian turned red.

"Petey, just tell him that he'll have to go to *Dotson's* instead."

"No way, Sebastian, he'd be heart broken. Besides, the waitresses like him."

"For some reason that I'll never understand," said Sebastian.

"Because he's cute and harmless," said Petey.

Just then Pops opened the door and walked out on the porch wearing only his boxers.

"Hey. Who's the hot babe out in the driveway?" he asked

The three younger adults all cracked up.

"You two go out. I'll get him ready to go," said Petey.

"Thanks, Petey," Sebastian said.

Petey turned toward the mother-in-law suite and hollered at Pops, "That's Sebastian's girl from California. Now get some clothes on, and I'll take you to Hooters."

Sebastian led Adria up the front stairs where French doors greeted her. Instead of a small entry way, the walls had been knocked out so that Adria found herself standing in a large kitchen with a breakfast area. Across from her, another set of French doors led out onto a stone patio.

"I redid the whole inside when I bought it a few years ago."

"I noticed the top floor was a little bit different when I drove in."

120

Sebastian laughed, "I like to sit in the light when I write. It clashes a bit with the traditional brick, but fortunately there isn't a homeowner's association to tell me what I can and can't do."

"This is the living room," he said as they walked into another room with wood floors.

In the far corner a stairwell led upstairs. Just then the phone rang.

"Sorry," he said, and went to answer it.

Adria poked her head into a messy master bedroom, a boring guest room, and into Sebastian's office, half of which was taken up with a huge printer and some other odd looking machines. Nearby, there was a desk, with a calendar blotter in the center, and a worn looking book in one corner that turned out to be an old Bible. Bookshelves covered every available inch of wall space. Even the light switch was tucked away inside a bookcase by the door.

The books were broken down by theme. A bookcase for books on writing, another for self-help books, another with what looked like sets of books by author. In the bookcase directly behind the desk, there were biographies. None of the names were anyone she recognized. She realized these were Sebastian's books. There were rows of biographies and a few novels. She picked one up and leafed through it.

"If you read the whole thing, you'll bring the total readership to about fourteen," said Sebastian from the door behind her.

She whirled, "Don't sneak up on people like that. You almost gave me a heart attack."

"Sorry," he said. "There are six of them."

"This one," he said pulling a particular book off the shelf "is the only one that wasn't self-published. It sold a total of sixty-seven copies, and my publisher sends me a royalty check every five years whether he needs to or not."

Something in his tone caught her.

"I'm sorry," she said, rubbing his arm gently with her free hand.

He flushed then smiled.

"It's okay. I finally found my niche."

He waved at the biographies.

"No one famous, but a lot of satisfied customers."

For a minute, he seemed to disappear as he peered at the books. Adria felt the surge of energy. That bookcase represented a hundred lives that he'd recorded, saving their memories for generations to come.

"Maybe it was for the best that the novels didn't get published. You'd just be another famous writer instead of getting to touch all these lives."

"You're quite an optimist."

"Really," she said.

"Maybe so, but when you get the rejection notices, it still feels like your guts are getting kicked out."

She knew how he felt. Whenever the concert audience was too small or the movie reviews panned her, or the audition didn't go well, those were the times where she had to dig down deep and work off of the dream.

"Anyway, that's it except for the conservatory."

"The conservatory," she said drawing out the last word. "Sounds fancy. Is there a secret passage to a study like in the game?"

"No secret passages. I would have liked that, but there wasn't enough money in the budget for it," Sebastian said. "Still, it's nice."

When she came to the top of the stairs, she realized that she could see out in every direction.

"The view is beautiful."

"Yes, it is," said Sebastian, actively studying Adria's outline against the window.

She caught the tone in his voice and looked up.

"Stop it. I meant the view out of your windows."

"Sorry. My mistake," said Sebastian in mock surprise.

The rest of the room was rather nondescript. A desk sat near one set of windows with a large flat screen computer monitor. Nearby on a stand was a TV with the requisite accessories. Scattered across the room were three card tables covered in books and papers.

"Research," said Sebastian with the wave of a hand. "I've never written anything about World War II before so I thought I should read up if I was going to tell Duke's story. So there you go. The grand tour is complete. Now, I was going to eat at Hooters so I haven't had any dinner. Are you hungry?"

"Hungry enough. My stomach's still on California time, but lunch was a bag of peanuts on the plane."

Sebastian held Adria's door as they got into the convertible. A moment later he put the top down and backed out of the driveway.

"Let me know if it's too windy for you," he said."

They drove down the One-twenty to Roswell and parked a couple of blocks off Main Street. The restaurants were packed so they put their name in at *924 South* and walked around the little downtown area, wandering in and out of the art galleries that dotted the main drag.

In one store Adria lingered, admiring a painting, while Sebastian moved on. She stood watching him as he walked, waiting to see if he'd notice that she'd gone missing. He did almost at once, and the look he gave her was the one she had hoped for. There was nothing panicked or desperate in the look, just the even glance of an equal, wondering where his girl had disappeared to.

She rejoined him and was about to say something to him when his phone rang.

He started to hit the reject button when he saw that it was Petey's number. Sebastian answered, and Adria could hear the frantic tone of Petey's voice and instantly knew something was wrong.

Chapter 19

"Slow down and tell it to me again," Sebastian said trying to calm Petey's panic.

"It's Pops, Sebastian. I came out of the bathroom, and he was gone."

"Okay. So how long were you in there before he went missing?"

He mouthed "Pops" to Adria and she nodded.

"I don't know, maybe five minutes."

Adria grabbed his arm and he jumped, cursing as he did so. Not sure what was going on, she stepped back involuntarily.

"Sorry, Petey, I'm not angry. Adria just grabbed my sore arm. Start with *Sailor's Nest* and then work your way north, toward Church Street. We'll drive over and help you out."

After hanging up, Sebastian recounted the whole episode of the fire at Duke's place. He told her about finding Duke, the fire, and how Lilith had treated him badly, despite the fact that he'd saved her father's life.

"And you didn't call me?"

"I don't have your phone number and movie stars aren't listed in the phone book. What was I supposed to do? Email you and say, 'Hey I'm a big hero now, I saved someone's life'?"

"Well, I don't expect you to call me every day or tell me what you had for dinner, but, I mean, you could have died. Was I supposed to just wait for the obituary?"

"I guess it kind of scared me, and later I felt like a jerk for saying that I was part of the family," Sebastian said.

"Sounds like Duke's daughter is the jerk. How is Duke?"

"He's out of the hospital and called to thank me. Lilith has him staying at her house for two weeks. Duke's determined to move back in as soon as possible."

"So was it a stroke?"

"No. They think it was a reaction to some new blood pressure medication."

"What is that?" Adria asked.

She was pointing at the top of the Kentucky Fried Chicken store. On its roof sat a giant chicken, its eye rotating around in circles. Sebastian laughed.

"That is the infamous, 'Big Chicken.' Every merchant in Marietta uses it to start their directions."

Sebastian fell into a Southern drawl.

"Well, what you do is you go down 'til you get to the Big Chicken then you turn right."

Adria laughed. "You shouldn't go into acting."

"What? You didn't think it was a good accent?"

"No. It was horrible. It should be like this."

Adria repeated the line with a flawless Southern accent.

They cruised into Marietta Square and parked. Sebastian keyed Petey's cell phone.

"Hey. We're here. Have you seen him?" asked Sebastian into the phone. "Okay, we'll check *Sherlock's* and go south."

"No luck?" asked Adria.

"Nope. It's not like him to run, but who knows what he's thinking after he's had a few."

"I still don't understand why you take him out like this."

Sebastian got out of the car before answering.

126

"Well, he's too old to get him off alcohol so we bargained with him. He gets to live in a nice place, be waited on hand and foot, get free medical care, and all the beer he can drink one night a week."

"And you get what?"

"The knowledge that I helped someone. God gives me a lot. Seems like I outta do something with it. I can't save everyone, but I can help Pops."

"There he is!"

It came out as a shout from both of them. Ahead of them on a sidewalk, were four young men. They were taunting Pops, pushing him back and forth.

"Hey! Leave him alone!" Sebastian yelled.

The kids looked up and saw Sebastian and Adria running toward them. One of them turned toward Sebastian and Adria, but soon realized his buddies were all running and followed them instead.

Pops shell-shocked, stood yelling "don't hurt me" over and over at the noise.

Sebastian ran a few steps past Pops, to make sure the punks were well on their way to wherever, and then turned around to find Adria holding Pops tightly in her arms.

"It's okay, Pops. It's okay. Sebastian's here, and he's going to take care of you."

After a few seconds, Sebastian saw Pops's hand crawl down Adria's back. She reached out and grabbed hold of his wrist, and firmly but gently pulled herself from Pops's embrace.

"I guess you're doing better," Adria said.

Sebastian cleared his throat, and took Pops by the arm. Sebastian handed his phone to Adria and asked her to call Petey.

"I'd still like her to hold me some more," said Pops.

"Give it a rest, Pops," said Sebastian, "Half of the men in America would like her to hold them. You're lucky that something bad didn't happen to you tonight."

"I'm sorry. I'm sorry. I'm sorry," Pops began to cry as he repeated this endless stream. "Don't get rid of me, Sebastian, I'll try and be good."

Sebastian turned the old man gently around.

"No one is going to get rid of you, Pops. Not ever. Petey and I will take care of you."

"I had to pee and went through the door. Then when I peed, I didn't know where I was so I tried to find you. Looked all over."

"What door did you go through?"

"I don't know. Went through one door and then I was in an alley."

"Well next time, wait for Petey so she can help you find the right door."

"But I had to pee. Had to or I'd make a mess, and the girls wouldn't like me no more."

From the smell of things, Sebastian wasn't sure that Pops had escaped the incident completely unscathed.

Petey was coming around the corner just as they reached the main street. She started to launch into it with Pops, but Sebastian shook his head.

As Petey drew even with them, Adria could still see fire in her eyes. Pops saw it, too, and shrunk back. Instantly, the look on Petey's face shifted, and she reached out for him.

"It's okay Pops, but you scared me."

They led Pops back to the Hooters where he had made his escape. When they came in, the hostess was visibly relieved to see Pops back.

A busboy had cleared their table, but the hostess, Cheryl, sat them back at Pops's favorite booth. They all ordered, and Sebastian left to find a manager and settle up the previous tab.

While they were waiting for their return, Adria turned to Petey.

"So how did you and Sebastian and Pops get together?"

Petey laughed. "Oh well. That's a long story. I got involved through a friend who knew Sebastian. The boys had already been together a couple of years, but Sebastian needed some reliable help. A friend mentioned it to me because I was tired of working at my last job."

"And you didn't find it the least bit odd that Sebastian had an old--" she cut herself off.

"It's okay, missy," said Pops, "I'm an old drunk."

Adria flushed.

"Sorry. That Sebastian had an alcoholic friend who he took out for drinks once a week."

Petey thought about it.

"I guess it was odd. It's been three years now, and I'm more used to the idea. It keeps the old guy safe and off the streets, and I'm actually making better money than I was before. Sebastian's been generous."

Sebastian returned and thumped into the booth.

"I'm starving," he said.

"Me too," chimed in Petey.

The waitress brought a huge basket of wings and set it on the table.

"Compliments of the manager."

Without another word, everybody dug in. After a bit, Adria and Sebastian left and made their way back to his car.

"I hope it was okay that I came out and saw you."

Sebastian smiled into the darkness and held out his arm. Adria took it as they walked.

"You mean," he said, "Is it okay that a beautiful, wonderful woman wanted to spend time with me? No, that's terrible. You should make sure you never do it again."

"Well, it's the least that I could do, you know. Stalking you back for stalking me."

Minutes later they stood on his driveway, holding hands. He stared at her lips. As if reading his mind, she leaned in and kissed him. He dropped her hand and put his arm around her neck, drawing them closer together. When they parted, her eyes stayed closed for just a fraction of a second and then a smile spread across her face.

"What are we doing?" she said.

He kissed her again. "Would you be upset if I said that I didn't know?"

"No. That's okay for now."

Sebastian felt pressure emanating from this beautiful woman. Pressure, but also a vulnerability that seemed amazing given their distinct classes in life.

"I didn't mean to wreck the moment," she said.

"It's still so crazy," said Sebastian as she laid her head on his shoulder.

"Why? Because I'm supposed to be this big star that eats men for breakfast?"

"Breakfast, lunch, and dinner," he said.

She looked into his eyes and hooked her finger under his chin, drawing his face closer to hers. When their kiss was done, he pulled her close again and felt her warmth. He didn't want to let her go, but he knew he needed to.

"You better get going," Sebastian said.

"Trying to get rid of me?"

"No."

"Good," she said.

She climbed into her car and drove back out of his world.

130

Chapter 20

Fort Rucker, Alabama. August 1942.

Fort Rucker was only a long day's drive from Fort Benning, but the company was given a week of leave to make the transition. Tony and Duke drove Tony's car to the new base, arriving just ahead of the deadline that the Army had set. After a couple of weeks, the lieutenant had the sergeants assemble the men.

"While we are here and until we ship out, all men will be given weekend passes. During the week, you will do PT, and work out as squads as well as platoons. You will spend time on the firing range, and once a week, you will do night recon."

No one in the squad heard anything after Thomason's announcement about regular weekend passes. Morale improved even more when they found out that the nearby town held weekly dances on Saturday nights.

Everyone in the company was going to the dance that night, with the exception of George Rawlings whose wife had driven down from Nashville to spend the weekend with him.

Duke, Tony, Herman, and Frank piled into Tony's car. The boys cranked the windows down and started the ten mile drive into town. A few miles from base, they came around a corner and found a stalled car, sitting off to the side of the road. Four attractive women, dressed for a night on the town, were trying to figure out how to put a tire jack together.

Slowing down, Tony pulled just past the disabled car. The boys must have looked comical as they ejected from the car and fairly ran to where the girls stood.

"Ladies, is there something that the men of Hotel Company could help you with?" said Tony, never a shy one with the women.

The girls giggled in unison, as if it were some crazy choreographed play.

"We have a flat tire, which means we'll miss the dance tonight," said a girl in a flower-print dress.

"Oh, I think we can manage that," said Tony. "I'm Antonio Marcelli, but my friends call me Tony."

"I'm Mary. This is Ginny, Winnie, and Caroline," she said, as she went around her circle of friends. Duke caught Winnie's eye, and she returned a look of interest. However, when Duke and Tony had finished with the tire, and stowed the gear back in the trunk, they discovered that Frank and Herman had cut Winnie and Caroline out of the group.

Caroline suggested that they mix and go to the dance together, a proclamation that was unanimously approved.

"I'd suggest," said Duke after clearing his throat, "that Frank and I ride with Mary and Winnie in the girl's car while Ginny and Caroline can ride with Tony and Herman." He had no desire to share a car with Frank, but it would keep Winnie close by. The motion was seconded, and everyone hopped into the cars.

"So are y'all from around here?" said Winnie as they got back under way.

"Duke is from Arizona, and I'm from California," said Frank.

Frank was from Kansas, but he seemed to think that the girls would like him better if he were from California.

"California," said Winnie, "that sounds interesting. What do you do out there?"

132

"Well, I do a little bit of everything," said Frank, "I was working security for a couple of movie stars out there."

"Really?" Winnie said. "Who?"

The question seemed to catch Frank off guard.

"Ah. Well, it changes from time to time, you know, just depends on who needs security that day."

"What did you do before the army, Duke?" said Mary.

"Mostly, I just help on the family ranch."

"Little Duke's only seventeen," said Frank condescendingly. "He lied to get into the service. He's still only seventeen. Four years my junior. Maybe we should call you 'Junior,' Duke."

Duke's eyes filled with anger in the darkness for an instant until he heard Winnie's soft voice, "You sure look strong for being only seventeen."

"When you wrestle calves and clear brush all your life, you tend to get big and strong."

"He handles himself pretty well, for a country boy," said Frank.

"Thanks Frank," he said sarcastically. "Where I'm from, we just try to be who we are."

Frank changed the subject quickly.

"You girls go to a lot of dances?"

"Every chance we get," said Winnie. "Even Mary and she's got a beau overseas."

Mary's eyes shifted guiltily.

"He knows I go to dances with other boys, Winnie. You're just jealous because you don't have someone."

Mary said this last part lightly and, the way Winnie laughed, Duke could tell that it was an old joke between them.

"Winnie's determined to get through the whole war without a serious attachment."

"It makes for less worry, don't you think?" Winnie said innocently.. "So what do you boys do for your country?"

133

"We jump out of planes," said Duke, "we're part of Airborne. A new idea to drop in behind a line of Krauts and give them a little surprise."

He mimicked the firing of a rifle.

"Is it scary jumping out of an airplane?" asked Winnie.

"Nah," said Duke. "Not compared to getting shot at when we get to the ground."

"Let's not talk about the war," said Mary. Her brow was furrowed with worry, and Duke wondered who the boy was that held her heart.

The dance was already packed when they arrived.

Mary and Duke danced together though Duke was uncomfortable. She was by far the superior dancer, and Duke tried to just stay off her feet. He missed a couple of times and muttered his apologies.

"Don't worry about it," she said. "You're doing fine."

Mary seemed to enjoy being held in the close embrace of the dance, and soon Duke relaxed. He thought of Winnie and Frank, but was polite enough to keep his eyes on Mary.

"So who is he?" Duke finally asked her.

"Who is ... oh. He's a sergeant. Sergeant Joseph Casey. He's in England now. We don't have to talk about him."

"It's okay. Do you write him a lot?"

"Some," Mary said. "Sometimes I do. Sometimes he writes. He always tells me to be careful about the boys that I go out with. Does it bother you that I have a boyfriend?"

"No, it's just a dance, and if he knows, then it's okay."

"You haven't complained a bit about getting stuck with me even though I saw you looking at Winnie by the cars."

"Was it that obvious?"

"It might not have been, except she was looking back at you."

Winnie and Frank whirled by. Winnie was laughing at something that Frank had said. Duke suddenly felt sad. He was no match for Frank Sierkowski with the women.

The group of eight danced mainly with their impromptu dates, but toward the end of the dance, Caroline decided that they should switch up so that each girl got at least one dance with each boy. Duke was last in line to dance with Winnie, but the band stopped playing before they had their chance. They all left together and went to a diner. Others from the dance had the same idea so they ended squished up against one another in a corner booth.

Looking up, Duke saw that luck had placed him across from Winnie. He also saw, for the first time, her beautiful brown eyes as they captured the light of the diner. They were a shade of brown that Duke couldn't place. Duke had never seen anything more elegant and engaging.

"What are you going to have, Duke?" Mary asked softly at his side.

"A corn beef sandwich," Duke answered.

"Corn beef, Duke?" asked Tony incredulously. "It's all he eats."

"We never had it on the ranch," he said calmly.

"Maybe not on the ranch, but in every restaurant and diner between Benning and here."

"When I find something I like," he said looking across the table at Winnie, "I want to get as much of it as I can."

Winnie blushed, and Tony just laughed.

After dancing for so long, the group could hardly wait for their food to arrive, except for Duke. The longer the wait, the longer he could have watching Winnie's every move. He drank in every minute of her, her laugh, her smile, the way she drew circles on the table with her coffee cup, and, of course, her eyes. They peered at him whenever she glanced his way.

They flickered to him even when her head was turned toward Frank.

Duke stretched his leg across the space that separated them and slowly rubbed his leg up and down Winnie's calf. Her eyes flashed at Duke, and her mouth dropped open. He grinned at her, and she hesitatingly smiled. Uncertainty turned to joy as she returned the gesture.

In the full light for the first time, Mary noticed the scar that played at the edge of Duke's neck, peeking above his collar.

"What happened to your neck?"

Duke reddened a bit.

"If you think that little scar is something," said Frank, running off at the mouth as usual, "you should see him with his shirt off. It looks like he got into a fight with a set of knives."

Everyone at the table stared at Duke, and the girls waited for the rest of the story.

"If I told you, you wouldn't believe me anyway. So there's really no point in starting."

"Now, that's not fair. How do you know what we'll believe?" asked Ginny.

"Unbutton your shirt and show your scars off, Duke," urged Herman.

"I'm not going to undress in the middle of a diner," he protested.

Tony grabbed Duke's wrist with an iron grip and peeled Duke's sleeve back despite his protest. There, along his right arm, the bear had left a long scar. The girls oh-ed and ah-ed.

"You can give up asking him how he got them though. He won't tell you," said Tony.

"C'mon, Duke," said Winnie.

Duke looked at her for a moment, but the waitress saved him from compromising his secret by setting a heaping corn beef sandwich in front of him. He immediately dug in, as

136

did the others. As he ate, he felt the press of Winnie's foot against his leg again. When he looked up, she glanced away, but she left her foot right where it had been.

Ginny and Winnie excused themselves and headed for the bathroom making a short stop to say something to the clerk at the counter. When they returned, it was time to call it a night, and the ladies presented hugs all around to the gentlemen.

Winnie's hug lingered a bit on Duke although he wasn't sure if anyone else had noticed. It wasn't until he was getting into his skivvies that he found the napkin stuffed in his pocket. On it, she had scribbled her address and a time: 48 Fern Street, tomorrow, two o'clock, Saturday.

Chapter 21

Adria was smiling when she left the stage. For the first time in a while, the band had made it through every set without having a breakdown.

"Way to go, guys."

As excited as Adria was about their performance, she couldn't help but wonder if they'd be able to keep the momentum going. This was their last night on their Florida swing. The band was leaving tomorrow for California, while Adria left for San Antonio to film several scenes for a new movie. There was no celebratory post-concert drink with the band. After some obligatory interaction with a couple of fans and feeling a little nervous about how small the crowd had been, she made her way back to the hotel, packed her bags, and crawled into bed.

It was at that moment that Guy Davies called her with news that the studio was pulling the plug on the tour.

"They made a commitment," Adria fumed. "They said two years, and it's barely been nine months."

"I know, and that's what I told them today in two different meetings. They claim that the contract says that the band has to be breaking even for the concerts to continue."

"Wait a minute! That's not in there. The contract specifically says that we have two years to tour. Are they saying that the CD sales aren't covering the costs of the concerts?"

"No. They aren't saying that at all. But, the contract is worded in a very odd way. If you read it one way, then it seems to say that the 'break even' part includes the CDs, but if you read it another way, it says something different."

"But the more exposure we get, the more CDs we'll sell. It's as simple as that. A concert means interviews on local radio and promotional advertising."

"I know, but they are checking the store by store sales in the areas where the band performs, and we aren't generating the buzz to push the volume up. I'm sorry, Adria. I tried to get them to change their minds."

"I know," she said, sounding her defeat. "Listen. Do me a favor. Don't tell anyone in the band tonight. I'll tell them in the morning. I want them to enjoy this evening."

Fierce angry tears started the flood. When they were done, the tears of self-pity followed. A shower usually helped revive her, but tonight it simply gave her another sad metaphor – her dreams washing down the drain along with the last few tears. She found Sebastian's phone number and stared at the clock. It was past two.

She pushed the button, and a sleepy Sebastian answered the phone.

"Adria?"

"How did you know?"

"LA number came up on the caller ID."

She was near tears, as she tried desperately to hold them back and think of the right words to let him know that she was a failure.

"It's two-fifteen in the morning. Is everything alright or did just you forget about the time change?" Sebastian asked.

"There is no time change; I'm in Miami," she said. "And no, it's not alright."

She said it softly and was surprised that there were any tears left to dribble down her face.

"What's going on?"

"I just don't know if I can keep it together right now," she managed to choke out, "and I was so flippant about your books not getting published, and now I'm calling you when something goes wrong for me. The tour's cancelled. The label pulled the plug."

Now that it was out, it lifted a great weight from Adria's shoulders. She replayed her earlier conversation with Guy for Sebastian.

"At first I was just mad," she said. "Now, I don't know if I'm scared or hurt."

"Probably a little bit of both. Why don't you come see me? I've got a place up in the mountains where we could go and hide out. Do a little bit of honest work with our hands, that sort of thing."

She smiled despite herself. "It sounds nice actually, but I'm on an airplane in the morning for San Antonio to shoot some stuff in the desert there. Two weeks's worth, which means I won't be able to make our third date."

"Well, more pizza for me."

"Shut up. I want to see you. Can you change your flight dates to a couple of weeks later?"

"No problem. Get yourself to San Antonio and do your acting thing. You're good, and you'll be in your natural element. Knock that out then take time off to figure things out."

She sniffled into the phone, "I guess that's all I can do. How am I going to tell the band? We just had one of our best shows tonight and now this."

"You can't worry about them Adria. They're all adults. They'll handle it."

The band was angry and frustrated when Adria talked to them the next morning. Kim, her newest backup singer broke down and cried.

140

"I quit my other job to do this. I thought this was my break."

Jimmy tried to find the bright side.

"Hey, it's the music industry. If we all wanted stability, we'd be sitting in an eight by eight prison called a cubicle. Are we still on the label's dime for the rest of the day?"

"Sure," said Adria. "Just don't go overboard with it."

They found a nice restaurant for breakfast and proceeded to drink mimosas until there was some question about any of their sanity, not to mention their ability to drive the rental van back to the airport. Adria, having foreseen this possibility, had stopped at two drinks and took the wheel.

The rental car was returned undamaged, and the group split up.

"The label will come around," said Jimmy.

"Let's hope," Adria said.

She passed around hugs like they were going out of style and wandered through the airport until she found her flight. A magazine stand caught her eye, and she bought the latest *Cosmopolitan*. When she turned back, her bag was gone, and she freaked out. It took her only an instant to find the man who had grabbed it. He was standing less than five feet away from her, wearing a prankster's smile and holding both her bag and a dozen roses.

"Sebastian! What are you doing here?"

"Stealing your bag."

"But what are you doing in Miami?"

He led her to her gate, finding a couple of seats together in a corner.

"I flew down on the 7:14 flight, and I'm flying back this afternoon. I had free tickets so I thought I'd come down and cheer you up. Are you any better?"

"A little. We decided we're going to fly back to LA, catch the executives from the label by surprise, and slice and dice them."

"Well at least you're thinking about doing something productive."

Adria felt herself smiling her big, dorky smile. The look embarrassed her, but she couldn't help it. It was good just being with Sebastian Fox. She felt her heart pound a little faster, and the pain from the tour cancellation ease just a bit.

They chitchatted for several minutes until the flight attendants began announcing the boarding. Adria put her arms around his neck and let him hold her, a pocket of silence in the chaos of the airport.

"Cheesecake Factory," she said suddenly.

"Excuse me?"

"For dinner, let's go to the Cheesecake Factory at Marina Del Ray. It's really beautiful. Three weeks from today at six o'clock."

"Three weeks from today. I can do that."

She stopped and threw him a wave and a kiss before turning for the plane.

Chapter 22

Sebastian was back at Disneyland, running from Constantine. Only this time, Constantine didn't have a camera. He had a long spear and every time he threw it, a new spear would appear in his hand. Pain filled in his lungs and couldn't catch his breath. Suddenly there was a white-hot pain. He looked down and saw a spear sticking out of his chest.

The leap from his bed into the middle of a dark room swept the dream away, but the pain remained. His lungs ached and he shuffled to the bathroom, he found his pain prescription and took a dose.

It was five-thirty in the morning, scarcely worth going back to sleep when dawn was just around the corner. Instead, Sebastian climbed to the observatory and began to work. His phone rang, and he found a strained woman's voice on the other end.

"I'm sorry to call you so early, but I've been up for hours, and I couldn't think of anyone else to talk to."

"That's okay. Who is this?" Sebastian asked.

"It's Betty Hudson. You made my son Charlie a dragon on his birthday. I didn't know who else to call."

"Is Charlie all right?"

It was a most ridiculous question to ask about a child with leukemia.

"He's fine," a sniffle, "but Dick left us."

"I'm sorry, Betty."

"Why would he leave us?" she asked, the pain clear in her voice.

There were several responses that flew through Sebastian's head. Because major illnesses often break up marriages. Because he's overwhelmed. Because he's a loser.

"I can't tell you, Betty. It's probably because he just didn't know how to deal with it all."

"Well, I don't know either," she wailed.

"I know, and I wasn't saying it was right for him to leave, I was just trying to answer your question. People run away from the things they can't fix."

"Why now? I mean it's actually going a little bit better. Not great, but you know, better. And to leave his own boy," she said, crying.

"I know," said Sebastian again, "and he's a great kid."

"Charlie's blaming himself, and he's only seven."

"Betty. I'm sorry. Charlie's got you, and you're obviously very dedicated. The only thing I can suggest is that you talk to Charlie about adults making mistakes."

There was nothing but tears, on the other end of the phone. Sebastian listened for a minute, an idea forming in his head.

"Would you like me to do something with Charlie?"

"I don't know. I'm just so confused right now."

"Why don't you talk to Charlie and see what he thinks about it? Maybe even a few hours would be a good break from the house for him and a good rest for you as well."

"Where would you take him? I don't want to expose him to any germs or anything."

"It won't be any place dangerous to him. Maybe we could go to a drive in movie or something?"

"Are there still drive-ins?"

"One in Atlanta at least. I was just thinking it would be a way for him to see a movie and stay out of the crowds. Just think about it and tell me what you want to do."

"Okay. I'll call you."

144

A week later, Sebastian picked up Charlie. With the summer hours, the earliest they could run the shows was nine-thirty at night and even that was pushing it a little bit. Sebastian figured they could spend some time at his place first.

Sebastian arrived with the top down on the Mustang. Charlie was wide awake and almost bouncing off the walls.

"Mom gave me Mountain Dew so I'd be awake for tonight."

"I can see that," said Sebastian with a laugh.

Betty was all smiles, seeing Charlie getting a chance to do something normal. Only her eyes betrayed the loneliness that she was feeling. She triple-checked Charlie's clothes and decided to add a light jacket despite the eighty-degree temperature.

"Isn't it early for you to be going?" she asked. "It's only six o'clock."

"Well, we're going to do dinner at my place, where Charlie won't get any more Mountain Dew," he said with a smile, "otherwise he might launch himself into orbit."

Back at Sebastian's house, Charlie ran up the staircase to see the view from the windows. When he came back downstairs, he looked at Sebastian.

"I like the cool glass bubble on top of your house."

"Thanks. I like it too. Are you going to help me make tacos for dinner?"

"Like Taco Bell?"

"Much better than Taco Bell."

Sebastian fried the corn tortillas on the griddle and showed Charlie how to use the cheese grater. While Charlie worked on that, Sebastian cooked meat and beans and pulled out some vegetables from the fridge that he'd cut up earlier.

Charlie finished the cheese, and Sebastian handed him bowls to put on the table.

145

After they had eaten, Sebastian duplicated Duke's technique for making popcorn. He filled a large Tupperware container to take to the movies.

"Mom just microwaves it," said Charlie.

"I do that sometimes, but it tastes better if you make it this way."

Popcorn and people were packed into the car, and they were on their way.

"I like your car. It makes me feel like I'm flying," yelled Charlie as the convertible raced down the interstate.

"It makes me feel free," said Sebastian.

"What's your car's name?"

"I've never named it," said Sebastian, looking curiously at Charlie and smiling at the mind of a little boy.

"But it still has a name. It knows what its name is even if you don't," the boy insisted.

"Can you talk to it and find out its name?" Sebastian asked.

"I don't know," said Charlie, "normally when I look at stuff its name just jumps out at me. Oh! I know. Riding in your car is like flying, and dragons can fly, so I think its name is The Green Dragon."

The Green Dragon carried them to the drive-in movie, into a spot with a good view of *Planes*. They had some time to spare, but Sebastian had brought Uno with him and proceeded to teach the card game to Charlie.

"Uno!" Charlie yelled as he played the red three. He tipped his other card forward, the way that kids do, and Sebastian saw that Charlie's last card was a green six. Fishing through his hand, Sebastian found a green three to play.

Charlie slammed his card down and yelled "I won! I won! I won!"

"Good job, buddy," said Sebastian reaching out his hand to Charlie.

Charlie slapped down "five" and held his hand out for the return from Sebastian.

The movie started and Charlie snuggled over next to him, his light wind breaker discarded into the back seat. Disney had re-used the classic underdog script, this time with airplanes. Charlie bounced in his seat for the first part until he began to tire. He made it through the whole film, but fell asleep as they waited in the parking lot for the traffic to clear.

Sebastian put the top up and drove to Charlie's house in silence. When he pulled into the driveway and parked, he scooped the still sleeping Charlie up easily. Betty led the way to Charlie's room, pulling back the covers so Sebastian could lay the boy down. She tucked Charlie in.

Sebastian noticed that Betty had changed into a pair of shorts and a tight fitting shirt. Betty wasn't in Adria's league, but she was definitely attractive.

"Well, I should go," said Sebastian.

"Thank you," said Betty, she reached for Sebastian, pulling him close. He smelled her perfume, felt her body close against his, and then she was kissing him.

He slid out of her grasp till they were standing there, almost, but not quite touching.

"I'm sorry, but I'm seeing someone right now," Sebastian said.

She nodded slowly, sadly, and then began to weep.

"I'm sorry, too. It would feel really good to spend a few hours in someone's arms," she said. "Please don't let this get between you and Charlie."

"Betty, I'm flattered. If I wasn't seeing anyone, things might have gone differently."

"Well, if you ever need anyone to hold you, think of me."

"Okay," Sebastian said, still edging away. "Tell Charlie I'll call him sometime."

147

Chapter 23

Alabama, August 1942

Duke had slept little after the dance, spending his time instead thinking of Winnie.

Sweating in a cot in the August heat, Duke thought of her lingering hug, her foot pressed against his leg, and her mahogany eyes.

Mahogany was the color that Duke had settled on as he wrestled with the memory of those eyes and tried to describe them to himself. He had seen the dark wood in the hotel lobby in town where he used to sit and read his brother's letters from the war. Even in the dark, he could see her eyes that had shone so spectacularly.

He was still thinking of those eyes when he picked two large handfuls of goldenrod from an open field around the corner from the address that Winnie had given him.

Tony had driven Duke part way and said he would pick him up later. The door of the two-story blue house with the white shutters opened as Duke was closing the gate of the white picket gate behind him. Mary and Ginny saw him, screamed, and ran back inside.

"Winnie, he's here. He's here," they shouted into the house.

"Girls, stop it," said an older female voice.

Miss Walker came to the door and frowned at Duke. Mary had mentioned her name the night before as the woman who ran their boarding house.

"Young man, may I ask your business?" said the plump Miss Walker, as she looked him and his flowers over with suspicion.

"I'm here to call on Miss Winnie," he said.

"Let me see if she's here. Are those goldenrod for me?"

"Actually, ma'am, they're for Miss Winnie."

"Hmm. The manners of boys these days, not bringing anything for the hostess."

The door shut in Duke's face, and he sat down on a nearby bench and waited, listening to the loud tones as Miss Walker laid down the rules for Winnie. Winnie's muted responses were barely audible beyond the door and when she reappeared, her head was bowed.

Duke thought for a minute that he had done something wrong, but as the door swung shut, Winnie's eyes lit up with fire, and she stuck her tongue out at the closed door.

He rose from the bench to greet her and received a hug in exchange for the flowers.

"Thank you. They're beautiful."

Duke fought the tug of her eyes. Whenever he saw them, he felt himself pulled in further. There was silence then as neither of them knew how to start the conversation.

She smiled suddenly, "Do you usually attack the ankles of your friend's dates?"

Duke grinned. "No, ma'am, but I didn't want you to waste your time on Frank."

"Is he secretly married?"

"No, he's not secretly married. He's not from California either."

"I know," she said, "Tony told me while we were dancing. He told me that I'd do a lot better with you than with Frank."

"And what did you say?"

"I told him that it was just a dance, I didn't need to get tangled up with anyone."

She gestured vaguely toward the cold eastern sky and shuddered.

"Do you know many boys who are over there?" Duke asked.

Winnie nodded.

"Everybody does, I guess. My cousin is in the Pacific. Another boy, whom I met at a dance here, was killed in an accident on a ship in transit to Europe."

The door opened and Miss Walker came out on the porch with a pitcher of water and two glasses. She set them on the small table in front of Duke and Winnie. They thanked her, and she disappeared back inside. Winnie poured them each a glass. They sat for a minute, trying to remember where they had been in the conversation.

"You mentioned a boy," Duke prompted.

"Charles. Charles Fischer. He was funny, like your friend Tony."

She didn't say anything else and Duke suggested that they go for a walk.

"Miss Walker feels that we should remain on the porch while you are calling on me."

Duke nodded, but he said, "I'm going to war where I may die; I think I should be able to go for a walk with a girl."

She looked at him, a deep sadness playing on her features.

"Hey, I didn't mean it," he said. "I'm not going to die over there. I can't. I have to come back and see you."

He pulled her to her feet. As they paraded down the stairs, the door opened and Miss Walker started to say something, but Duke just smiled and kept walking.

"She will be mad when I get home," Winnie said when they had gone a block.

"We can go back," Duke said.

"No. You're right. We're old enough to make our own decisions."

As she said this, she caught hold of his hand and led him down to where a stream ran through some woods on the edge of town. Duke stopped, worried that Winnie would be in trouble if they didn't go back. Winnie thought he had stopped for another reason and swung around like they were on a dance floor. She arched her arms up over his broad shoulders and found his surprised lips. His eyes popped open, but hers were closed so he joined her in the darkness, letting the feel of her in his arms sink in.

She broke the kiss off and led him down by a stream. A well-worn rock served as their bench.

"So do you like the South?" she asked.

"I like that you are here," he said.

"Now you sound like, Frank," she said, with a smiling rebuke.

"Ouch," he said, covering his heart, "that hurt. I like the corned beef and the girls. I could do without the humidity."

"I thought you lived in Arizona. Isn't it hot there?"

"Hot, yes, but it's a dry heat. It'll burn the life out of you in the summer, but out here it seems like all you do is sweat."

"I don't sweat at all. I'm a lady."

"I didn't mean `you`, I meant everybody."

She leaned on his shoulder, and he leaned over to kiss her. She let him, not really joining in, but not minding. The stream babbled past them. Noise from the town died when it hit the edge of the trees, leaving them alone in a peaceful world.

"I hate the war," she said. "The newspaper says we're losing in the Pacific, and Hitler seems unstoppable. I meet these boys then they disappear."

"Like Charles?"

151

"Yes. He wanted to kiss me, but I wouldn't let him. I felt so guilty when he died."

"Is that why you kissed me? So you wouldn't feel guilty when I died?"

She looked at him, her beautiful eyes boring deep into him. He couldn't tell if she was angry or sad. Her sobs tore through the air as she buried her head into his chest. He held her, waiting for the tears to stop. She said something into his shirt, but he couldn't understand it.

After several minutes, she stopped and wiped her face.

"I'm sorry. I didn't mean to lose control like that," she said.

"I didn't mean to upset you."

"You didn't. I've just held it in all this time, but I can't do anything about Charles anymore, can I?"

She reached up and slowly traced the edge of one of Duke's scars.

"Now that I've bared my soul, tell me how you got these scars?"

Duke shuddered at the thought of the bear as he sat in the shelter of the thin woods. He didn't say anything, and Winnie drew him close.

"Never mind. You don't have to tell me," she said.

He looked into her eyes and saw that she had opened her heart wide to him.

He unbuttoned the top two buttons of his own shirt. The scars were deep and thick.

Intrigued rather than repulsed, Winnie leaned over and kissed them.

"Last November I was out hunting, and my shot disturbed a bear," he said.

Winnie's eyes grew wide at the mention of the bear.

"He was..." Duke hesitated. "He was huge and mad and wanted to kill me. I shot him, but it only made him madder. I

152

lost my gun, and we fought. I crawled to get away, and he came after me. Somehow I got into the river and got away."

"How awful."

"My dad and my brother Chance found me. Chance is over in England now."

"You didn't go with him?"

"The bear broke my leg. I was laid up for a few months before I could really run again."

The sun was sinking behind them as they finished talking and hurried back to find a disapproving Miss Walker waiting for them on the porch.

The following weekend, Duke told Winnie of a plan that he had. Instead of going out walking, Duke set about working around the house. A pile of wood in the back had been neglected for some time. It needed to be split and stacked in the basement to dry for the winter.

Winnie had told Duke that Miss Walker would usually hire one of the boys in town to split the wood, but most of those had gone off to the war. Duke split wood for an hour. When the axe first began to fall, Miss Walker had appeared on the back of the porch. Duke didn't make eye contact with her, but a quick glance revealed her usual sour expression.

"Don't think that this makes up for walking off with my charge last week," she said.

"Of course not, ma'am," Duke had replied before going on about his work.

In the days that followed, Miss Walker was much more amiable toward Duke and her lectures to Winnie ceased. They fell into a comfortable pattern. Duke and Winnie would go out on Friday night, usually with Tony and whichever girl caught Tony's fancy that weekend.

On Saturday mornings, Duke would arrive and work around the house. Winnie would make them a small lunch, and they'd go down to the river where Duke would clean up. They would sit and talk about Arizona, about Chance, about Winnie's two younger sisters, about anything but the war. When the afternoon sun had waned, they would start their climb back up the hill to where the boarding house stood.

After the fourth weekend, Miss Walker asked Duke to join them for supper.

"How much longer will you be here?" Miss Walker asked as they ate.

"Another month they think, ma'am."

"Well, I appreciate the help that you've been around the house, and I'm sure that Winifred is glad that she'll have your company for a while."

Outside a horn honked, and there was a sudden pounding of feet on the stairs. An urgent knocking sounded on the door and everyone pushed back their chairs.

Tony stood there.

"We're shipping out at midnight," he blurted out.

Winnie started to cry, and Duke took her and held her in his arms in front of all of them.

"Come back, Duke Farmington," Winnie said as she let go of him.

"I will," he said and took a long last look at those eyes that had so captured his soul.

Chapter 24

Marina Del Rey sparkled like a jewel. The deep, blue water was punctuated by the white dots of the houseboats docked in the Marina, resting placidly, as they rolled to the slow rhythm of the ocean.

Adria saw that Sebastian was early. She came up behind him and rubbed his back. He turned and his arm naturally slid around her shoulders.

"It's a beautiful day to be staring out at the ocean," she said.

"I could stand here all day with you, or maybe we could shanghai one of the boats in the harbor and sail out to sea."

"That won't work," she said. "I'm starving. If we stand here much longer, I'm going to get cranky."

She felt her stomach rumble and wondered if Sebastian could hear it over the hubbub of The Cheesecake Factory. Adria always got a kick out of The Cheesecake Factory's decor. The booths were the red leather of a 1960's diner.

When they were seated, they debated the wisdom of an appetizer for all of about thirty seconds before settling on the chili cheese crisps. They talked about flights, the view, and the menu before Sebastian asked her about her current shooting in San Antonio.

"It was fun. I have to go back next week, and I'll be there for a couple more weeks."

"Isn't that a short time for a movie to shoot?"

"That depends," she said with a wry smile, "on how far into the movie you get killed."

He laughed. "I could see where that would make a difference."

The waitress brought their appetizer and took their orders. It was a shrimp theme – his, the Jamaican Black Pepper Shrimp, and hers, the Big Bang Chicken and Shrimp.

"I'm due back on Tuesday. You were the only reason that I came out. You've actually been one of the few pleasant surprises in an otherwise unpleasant year."

Adria almost laughed at the quizzical look on his face.

"An old boyfriend showed up back in January, the tour cancellation, and one of my dogs died."

"I'm sorry."

"Thanks. Brutus was a crabby old thing and he wasn't really mine anymore, but he was when I was in high school."

"So what's the latest with the tour?"

"The latest with the tour is that it's cancelled, and there doesn't seem to be any resurrecting it any time soon. I've scheduled some film time and some vacation time. A trip back to Colorado to see my folks. A little bit of free time in case something comes up."

"So what's that mean for you and singing?"

Her face fell a bit.

"Well, it's never good. I guess I have to decide how much I want to sing. I wasn't trying to leverage my acting and jump to the big time, but I was hoping for at least the medium time."

Adria searched her tone to make sure she wasn't whining.

"What's it like being up in front of everyone?" Sebastian asked.

"Well, the first time, it's really odd. You either feed off it or are scared of it. In the movies, you film without an audience so the toughest part is learning to focus and ignore everything around the camera that isn't a part of the scene."

156

She thought back on the first time that she'd seen herself projected to the size of a giant and the surrealism of the whole event.

"On stage, whether it's acting or music, I always feel like I want to puke, and then I get this adrenaline rush. It's the realization that the audience, on a subconscious level, is willing you to succeed. They want you to do well."

Pandemonium ensued as a group of college girls were seated a couple of tables over from them. Adria and Sebastian's mildly peaceful dinner turned into a yelling match.

"What's the biggest audience you ever performed in front of?" he hollered.

"I don't know. A few thousand I guess, for some of the plays. Why all of the questions? You never seemed interested in this kind of stuff before."

"Just making conversation," he said with a smile. "Wondering what's going on inside that head of yours."

Adria laughed at that. She barely knew what was going on inside her own head. She couldn't imagine a man who could follow it all. Except, when she looked at Sebastian, she thought that maybe he could.

They mixed their two shrimp dishes together and settled into a steady rhythm of eating until they were suddenly confronted by the college girls at the next table.

"Are you, like, Adria Rider?" asked a co-ed in a lime green tank that matched her gum.

"I'm not only 'like' her; I am her," she said, putting on her showbiz smile.

Giggles all around.

"Can you sign this? It just came in the mail."

She handed a tabloid to Adria, who took one look and turned it to back to Sebastian. "Look. You're famous."

On the cover of *The Star*, scrunched into the upper right corner was a picture of Adria and Sebastian on Splash

Mountain going over the edge of the big waterfall at Disneyland. The header read "Adria Rider takes the plunge with new boyfriend."

Adria autographed the cover and passed it back.

Lime Green handed the magazine and pen to Sebastian. "You, too."

"Oh, no. I don't think so," he said, refusing to take the magazine.

"Oh, come on. It won't hurt," said Lime Green.

"I'm not famous so I don't see the point," said Sebastian.

"Well," said Adria, helpfully, "you are on the cover of a national magazine."

"Yeah," said Lime Green, as all her friends bobbed their heads along with her.

"You're a lot of help," he said sarcastically to Adria, but he took the pen and carefully scrawled his name.

The girls giggled before retreating to their table.

"You know you like it," Adria said.

"I do not."

"Well, I do. I mean, me being on the cover, not you. It's free publicity. If it gets enough buzz, it might get the tour back on schedule."

She was soon lost in those thoughts as they raced from magazine cover to tour to stardom. After a few minutes, she looked up to see Sebastian staring at her with a slight smile on his face.

"Sorry," she said. "Just thinking."

The waitress offered dessert, and they just looked at each other.

"Give us a minute," said Adria prompting the waitress's departure. "I have an idea. How about we decide on what we want for dessert and wrap it up? You can follow me back to my place, and we can eat cheesecake and listen to the ocean."

Sebastian smiled.

"I think that may be the best offer I've ever had."

The drive south was short. It was the first time that he had ever seen a gated community made up entirely of trailers, but, as Adria had explained, the trailers and the beach had been there long before the security gate. Her trailer was down at the end where the beach took a turn and a narrow cliff ran down to the water's edge cutting off all entrance to the area. She had paid extra for the privacy and solitude.

Adria pulled up to her trailer and checked her rear view mirror to make sure that Sebastian had pulled in behind her. She pranced back to him, pounding on his door and startling him while he was fiddling with the keys to the rental car. Adria laughed at him as he climbed out with a bemused look on his face.

"Well, what do you think?" she asked.

She made like a game show hostess showing off the Pacific Ocean, or what could still be seen of it with the sun barely above the horizon.

"I think it's great," then a pause as he looked her in the eye. "Really, you found something special."

She poked him in the belly, ignoring his suddenly serious mood and ran past him.

"Wait till you see the inside."

Outside the mobile home ran a simple deck with two chaise lounges. Four stairs lead down to Adria's parking spot. Adria opened the front door, and Winston shot out, racing between the two of them as he tried to decide between giving a welcome home to his master and checking out the new guy. Finally, Winston bounded over to Sebastian, jumped up and almost knocked him down the stairs.

"Winston! Winston! That's no way to behave," Adria chided.

Winston ignored her as Sebastian knelt and gave the dog a big hug. Winston's back feet bounced from side to side while he tried his best to plant a wet doggy kiss on Sebastian.

"I think he needs a W-A-L-K," said Sebastian.

She made no attempt to leash the golden retriever, letting him run free as they headed down the beach. Winston charged toward a flock of seagulls.

"Does he ever get one?"

"What, a bird? Absolutely not."

Winston led them on a merry chase up the beach as he covered twice as much ground as either human. Eventually, the trio reached some invisible end of the walk that Adria had chosen, and they turned back towards home, retrieved the cheesecake from the car, and sat down in the sand. When the cheesecake was gone, they played fetch until the dog tired of the game and lay down panting nearby.

"So how often do you get to sit here at night?"

"Depends on how business is. If it's good, then I'm gone a lot. With the tour and the films all interspersed, it hasn't been that often. Half the time, he can't find the ball, and I can't see the green in the water."

"That ball's green? Looks more like a mushy brownish, swamp marsh color."

"Well, it was green. Once upon a time."

Adria snuggled up close to Sebastian as the cool breeze began to blow in, whispering in their ears that it was time for the little people of the world to sleep. Her long hair fell against the side of his face

He smelled clean and wonderful. Adria slipped her hand up the back of his shirt, and he turned his head toward her.

They kissed for a while and eventually, Sebastian lay back while Adria wiggled her head against his shoulder until she found a comfortable spot.

"You could stay."

It was a question.

"I'd like that, but I don't know," he said.

She put a hand on his lips.

"I'll just take that as a 'Yes.'"

Chapter 25

Sebastian made the long walk to her trailer, fighting the battle of conscience and desire. The most beautiful woman he had ever met was walking beside him up the beach and into her house. Regardless of where he thought the relationship was going, he was sure he could have her tonight if he wanted to.

Adria made small talk as she lead him slowly to her bedroom. She left the room dark and led him in. He felt her arms as they wrapped around his neck, felt her kick her shoes off and draw herself against him. His hungry lips met hers. She pulled him toward the bed, but he resisted. Instead he held her, oblivious to the confused look on her face.

The kissing started again – intense and passionate. He nibbled her ear, and she yelped, but in the darkness he could see her smiling too. Adria stepped back toward the bed again, and the kissing stopped for a moment as he steadied them in place near the door.

He listened to her breathing, heard her heartbeat, and felt his sync up to hers. She let him go and stepped back.

"What did I do wrong?"

"Nothing. I just like to move slower than this."

"Well, that's a change," she said, obviously disappointed. "Most guys try to get me in bed at the first opportunity."

He smiled into the half-darkness.

"I haven't been most guys for a long time."

A dry chuckle escaped her lips. "I guess not."

Sebastian drew Adria close to him and brushed her long dark hair away from her face. He started at her ear and kissed along her neck until he found her lips. Reading this as a change of mind, she tried tugging him toward the bed, but he stood his ground.

The kissing stopped, and he whispered into her ear. "Why don't you show me where you want me to sleep?"

"I already did," she said.

He smiled at her, but didn't move.

With a sigh, Adria led him to a spare room where she dislodged Winston from the bed. Sebastian tried to pull her toward him again, but the mood had evaporated.

"I'm going to take a shower," she said, still pouting as she turned for the door.

Sebastian turned the lights off in the room and opened the blinds to let in the moonlight. He dropped his jeans on the floor and crawled into bed. As he lay there, he heard the shower turn on in the other room and fell asleep to its rhythmic pounding.

The squeak of the floor woke him.

"Winston?" he said into the darkness.

There was no answer, but clearly that it wasn't Winston who was moving across the room wearing shorts and a T-shirt. The smell of soap from her freshly washed skin went before her like a red carpet.

"Will you at least hold me?" she asked, fear impregnating the question.

"Yes," he whispered, barely loud enough to be heard.

She pulled the sheet back, crawled in, and moved against him. They lay quietly soaking up the moonlight, and each other's presence until they both slept.

In the morning, Sebastian slipped from the bed, pulled on his jeans, and found the bathroom down the hall. He glanced back into the guest room, and saw that Adria was still asleep, a dark-haired angel in the half-made bed. She hadn't stirred despite the light peeking under the shade.

As Sebastian turned, Winston followed him down the hall. He left her a quick note, and slipped out into the crisp salt air. It was all so different from his mountain cabin getaway, but similar in a way that he couldn't quite put into words. Freedom filled each step as he and Winston stalked the beach. Sebastian's arm tested Winston's resolve to retrieve the ball and the dog rewarded Sebastian with persistence.

Sebastian didn't know how far he had walked. Far enough to get caught in the surf a couple of times, and to have the bottom of his jeans completely crusted with sand. Finally, Winston gave up on chasing the ball and walked alongside Sebastian, panting heavily. Together they headed back toward Adria's place.

Instead of peeking, the sun was above the horizon, as he and Winston caught sight of Adria walking toward them. White Capri pants, a yellow tank top, and a slim white cover-up set the scene as a sudden wind whipped her hair back, giving the illusion that she was riding in a convertible. Winston sprinted toward her with a happy bark.

She looked like a sun goddess, and at that moment, Sebastian would have gladly fallen down and worshiped her.

Adria bent over and gave Winston a quick hug before peeling away from his dampness. Her laughter carried to where Sebastian made his deliberate way to meet her.

"I thought you'd run away," she said, giving him a quick kiss on the cheek.

"And I stole your dog."

"You thief," she said, an expression of faux distrust in her eyes. "When do you go home?"

"This afternoon. Oh! I forgot about checking out of the hotel. I need to drive back down there by eleven. Any idea what time it is?"

"Probably about eight. Time for a quick breakfast before you make your mad dash?"

"Sure. What is the cook serving up today?"

"What are you serving up today, Mr. Fox?"

"I thought you were cooking for me."

"Who said I was cooking the quick breakfast?" she said with a grin.

They turned toward home, her hand sliding easily into his.

"I'm sorry about last night," her voice was fragile like the wind.

"That's okay," he said.

He looked at her, but her face was turned down at the sand, steadfastly avoiding his probing gaze.

Air swirled around them and silence stood between them. Sebastian listened to the water as he walked, waiting for the sounds to smooth out everything between them, the way it smoothed the sand at their feet.

"So how much longer will you be in San Antonio?"

"Not sure," she mumbled under her breath. She broke free from his grasp and took the ball from Winston and threw it far, driven by anger.

"I just don't understand. You seemed pretty interested when we were kissing on the beach," she said after a few more paces.

"We had this discussion last night. I like to move a little bit slower."

"Yes, but you wanted to last night. I could tell."

"There are a great many things that I want to do, Adria, but that doesn't mean that I'm going to just jump in bed with someone after three dates."

"You don't like to jump into bed with anybody, but you think I do?" Adria demanded.

"That's not what I said."

"It's what you meant. Face it. You don't approve of me, do you?"

He could sense her anger rising as she talked.

"Why are you acting like this?"

"Why can't you just answer me?" Adria said.

"Because you're acting insane. Have I ever said anything that implied that I didn't approve of you? Anything?" Sebastian voice was tinged with emotion.

"Which still isn't an answer."

"Adria, you're picking a fight for no reason. Do you do this all the time? Pick fights with everyone?"

"No, I don't. Do you avoid every difficult question that someone throws at you? Did you skip having sex with me last night because you are afraid of commitment?"

"No."

"You're not going to explain it to me?"

He looked at her, biting his tongue.

"Maybe a lack of communication is the reason you're a forty year-old bachelor," Adria said, poking at his chest in agitation.

Sebastian's mind raced, but he let the comeback die on his lips. He looked her in the eye, cursing his future.

"You're right. It is."

Leaving her there, he put his head down, and began walking at an angle across the beach toward her condo and his car. She stood watching him go, rooted until the tide washed up to her knees. The surge snapped Adria out of her funk, and she chased him down.

"Wait. I'm sorry," she caught him and turned him around, pulling his head up gently. "I'm sorry. I didn't mean it."

The sadness she had caused him was written on his face.

"No," she gathered him against her chest.

The tightness in his body relaxed, and she cried into his hair while he clung to her, emotions moving through his veins that he couldn't process.

"I was just being cranky," she said.

After a time, she lifted his chin and kissed him gently. Adria tried again to explain.

"I'm sorry. Really, I was just hurt and scared."

She trailed off as he checked his emotions visibly.

"No. Please don't be upset, Sebastian."

They walked the rest of the way to his car, silently, and Sebastian felt her cling to his hand like a drowning man grabs the hand of a man in a boat.

Sebastian stopped at his car rather than follow her in.

"I think I need a rain check on breakfast. I don't want to be late checking out."

"Okay," she said in a defeated voice.

He felt her eyes probing, trying to read all the emotions that he was feeling, but he had buried most of them now as best as he could.

Sebastian's hug was stiff and kiss good-bye unconvincing.

"Call me," she said, as he climbed into the car.

It was his turn to say okay.

"Sebastian, really, please call me," Adria pleaded.

"I will."

Chapter 26

England, November, 1942

The Army took Hotel Company and reassigned them to the 2nd Battalion of the 509th Division. Another target had come up for Operation Torch, an assault designed by the US and British war planners to get the French more involved in the war, and the 509th was the weapon of that attack. With France occupied by the Germans, the plan was to take control of the lightly secured North African colonies of France. This would allow the free French government a base to launch attacks against the Germans and would expose Italy coast as a weakness in the Axis defenses.

The assault was slated for November of 1942, and the planning had been going on for months. After the army had hurried Duke and his comrades to England, they had put them on hold. Time was spent mostly playing cards and hiding their gambling from the officers.

"Come on, Duke," Tony was saying. "Just play for a few hands. I'll spot you the money."

"That's what you said last week, Tony," Duke replied, "And now I owe you most of my next pay check."

"It won't matter at all in a few weeks," said Jake, morosely.

They were all feeling the coming combat in different ways. Jake was sure they would die. He had gotten word that his brother in the Pacific had died, and he was sure that he was next.

"Stow it, Jake," Duke barked.

Duke stormed out of their temporary quarters and ran straight into Sergeant Jackson. The look on his face spoke volumes to Duke.

"Sergeant?"

"Is your squad all here?"

"Most of them, Sergeant. Private Sierkowski ran into town about two hours ago."

"Get them together. We leave in a week. Everyone is confined to base until then."

"Where to?"

"Some place where there are bad guys waiting to shoot you."

Their chutes were packed and re-packed. Gear was sifted. Packs were loaded with rations for ten days. Hastily written letters were prepared in case they didn't make it back.

The 509th was loaded into C-139s. On board the planes at last, Hotel Company was given their orders from Lieutenant Thomason.

"The operation that we are a part of is called Operation Torch. Hotel Company's destination is Maison Blanche. There are roughly two hundred German and Italian troops in town. Because of its location, Maison Blanche serves as a communications hub for the area. The four platoons will shoot for different drop zones. First and Third Platoons will exit the plane first and come down the north road into town as loudly and with as many fireworks as you can muster to draw the majority of the troops toward your position. First platoon will take up a position on the highest hill to the northwest of town. From there you can command the road."

He went on with the details of the drops for Second and Fourth Platoons.

"After Second Platoon lands, you will make your way into the town to their headquarters. Once there, you will secure the building at the direction of Mr. Smith."

At this point, Lieutenant Thomason introduced the one man in the back of the C-139 whom no one knew. He was wearing the uniform of a reporter.

Tony leaned close to Duke.

"If he's a reporter then I'm the king of Italy."

Duke nodded, but said nothing. He was still getting over the fact that 2nd was going to be commanded by someone from outside the unit.

"For those of you who are wondering who I am," said Mr. Smith, "you can simply call me Mr. Smith, as the lieutenant mentioned. The building we are targeting contains important information. On the way to the building, kill anyone you encounter. Once we get to the building, do not kill any officers."

Lieutenant Thomason spoke again.

"Corporal Gleason's squad and Private Farmington's squad will jump with Captain Smith and accompany him to the objective."

He ran over their plan of retreat and asked for questions.

Corporal Gleason raised his hand.

"Does Mr. Smith know how to jump out of airplanes, or are we going to strap him to something?"

Derisive laughter filled the space.

Mr. Smith stood up again, "I've made twelve jumps, six behind enemy lines. I think I'll be able to keep up with you."

The time to jump finally came. First and Third Platoons bailed out of the plane. A couple of minutes later it was Duke's turn to line up. He found himself behind Mr. Smith.

"Remember, Private, the Germans hate you. It'll be easier if you hate them, too."

"I don't hate them, Mr. Smith."

"You will."

Smith disappeared, and then it was Duke's turn to step through the door. He shot through the air watching Smith trail off behind him. When he finished his count, he pulled the rip cord. As he neared the ground, he could see flashes off to the north. First and Third were already in action. Staccato gunfire welcomed Duke to Africa.

Momentary panic struck Duke as he hit the ground. Freeing himself from his chute, he scrambled for cover. Gunfire was coming from what looked like an old barn about a quarter of a mile from their position.

Duke looked and found Mr. Smith safely tucked behind a large boulder, trying to focus his rifle on the enemy. From where he lay, Duke could also Tony, Frank, and Herman plus a few guys he recognized from 4th Platoon.

"Where's our mortar team?"

No one knew. The platoons had always trained with a full complement of men, but the first live night jump had shown them all that the wind could change your plans in a heartbeat. Every NCO had been carried far to the South, and it left Duke as the man on the spot. As he sat trying to make a decision under all the fire, Frank Sierkowski suddenly spun around, fell to the ground, and cried out. Duke crawled to him and yelled for a medic.

There were no medics nearby so Herman, the jack of all trades, crawled to Duke. Tony and Jake began to put down a constant fire with their M-1s on the barn. Duke sat holding Frank as he cried. There was a hole in the right side of his chest. Each time he tried to speak, a puff of pink seemed to come out of his mouth.

"It hurts," he told Duke.

"I know, Frank, just hang in there."

171

Duke looked at Herman, but Herman just shook his head.

Frank's eyes fluttered, and he looked at Duke and said, "Duke?"

"Yes?" Duke said.

Whatever Frank had intended to say floated off with his soul into the African sky.

Duke swore bitterly, looking up to find Mr. Smith squatting behind him.

"Your men are waiting for you to do something. You're a squad leader, so lead."

Duke looked up, really looking at the situation for the first time. At about the same time, Corporal Gleason appeared with most of his squad.

"Gleason," he ordered, despite the fact that Gleason outranked him, "take your squad west. My squad will open fire to get you over to those trees. You take out that barn."

Gleason didn't hesitate.

Duke glanced at Frank's sightless eyes. He wanted to reach over and close them, but there was no time.

"Squad, fire."

Duke's men began to fire. As Duke watched, Gleason's men were able to get within twenty-five feet of the barn.

Grenades flew, and the barn went silent.

The Americans moved from street to street encountering very little opposition. As they closed in on the building marked on Smith's map, they saw movement inside and flames leaping from several fires; the Germans were burning Smith's precious documents. Gleason positioned his men to cover the windows. Smith, Duke, Herman, and a dozen others filtered through a side street and made a rush for a side door. Jake stood back in the shadows for a short minute. They heard his gun fire once then again. A body dropped to the street from above them.

172

Tony nodded to Duke, kicked in the door, and tossed in a grenade. Herman tossed another and pulled the door closed. After the detonations they swarmed the downstairs room. A few Germans who had survived the blast were quickly cut down. Moving upstairs was trickier. Duke and Tony alternated cutting the angles. Once they were close to the top, they threw grenades into the room, waited for the concussion, and moved in. Duke saw no one as he entered the wide room, but then on the far side of it, shrouded by smoke, he could make out two Germans feeding documents into a fire barrel.

Making eye contact with Duke, one German reached for a pistol on the desk, and Duke shot him through the shoulder. Tony was also firing.

Smith and Duke disarmed the live German officer, and frantically stopped the blaze of documents. Several other Germans surrendered in light of the superior number. Prisoners and papers were herded south of town toward the rendezvous point.

Duke and his squad went back to get Frank's body on the way. They stopped at the barn to face Frank's killers. Inside Duke found two young German soldiers who were mauled from grenades and had their hearts pierced by a bayonet thrust.

"Oh my God. They're just kids. They can't be more than sixteen," Herman cried out.

Duke looked at Herman for a second then stepped forward and spat on both the bodies.. Without another word, he left the barn and walked to where Frank lay.

Duke closed Frank's eyes and helped Tony wrap Frank in a rain poncho.

"Goodbye, California," said Tony in a simple eulogy.

They loaded Frank, the only American dead, and the wounded from both sides into two trucks and started their fifty-mile march toward an airfield. Thankfully, the Americans tasked for the job had captured the airbase. Even still, it was

173

the next day before they arrived. Duke and his squad found an empty building. Exhausted, they quickly fell asleep on the hard floor.

Duke woke to find Lieutenant Thomason and Sergeant Jackson standing over him.

"Good morning, Private," said Lieutenant Thomason.

"Sir," said Duke, jumping to attention.

"Private Farmington, in recognition of the job that you did yesterday, you have been given a battlefield promotion to the rank of corporal. That way when you order Corporal Gleason around the next time, you will at least be the same rank as him."

Duke reddened, but his men cheered. There were smiles all around, but no real joy. Each was thinking that they could have been the one who died instead of Frank.

Chapter 27

Adria thought Sebastian's call would never come and, in fact, it didn't – it was an email instead.

Dear Adria,

I'm sorry about the argument we had. Hopefully, we can see past it and remember the good time that we had at dinner, on the beach, and afterwards. Those were moments that I'll never forget. You asked if I approve of you the other day, and the answer is yes. I hope that you still approve of me as well, even with my go-slow approach.

I wanted to call you, but couldn't decide on the best time to do it. Petey has been all over me because of the picture in Star. I'll never, ever hear the end of it.

I want to see you again.

Sebastian.

She wanted to call him, but he had emailed her so she emailed him back, and said he could call her any evening.

When the call came, the cast was out having margaritas, and she barely heard her phone over the blaring music in the Mexican restaurant. Outside, the din of the party was more muted.

"I'm getting drunk with my fellow actors sort of like you and Pops," Adria said. "The way we're putting away the alcohol, we'll be dancing on the tables soon."

"I'll look for the pictures in *Star*," he said.

She felt like they were back to wherever they had been. His voice was full and rich.

"What would you say about coming out and staying a few days?" he asked.

"I'd like that a lot."

"Okay. I thought you'd like to come up and meet Duke and maybe go drinking with Pops? I also need to do some work out at my cabin and thought I could enlist your help."

"Well, I don't know about the work part, but the rest sounds good. If nothing else, I'd get to drink some of that moonshine that you're always talking about. When did you have in mind?"

"Whenever you can make it would be good for me. A flexible schedule is one of the perks of being a writer."

"I'll let you know. I've probably got a few more days here."

A few days later, she was in Atlanta. Sebastian met her at baggage claim with a bouquet of mixed flowers. They kissed in public, and Adria didn't even wonder about cameras. After a minute, she ran her hand along the length of his face to ensure he wasn't a fantasy after all. At first, he didn't seem as though he was completely there. The vision faded quickly, and he smiled again. As they went through the terminal, he pulled Adria's bag along with one hand and wrapped his other around her shoulder.

In the car, he had a shoe box-sized package waiting for her. Adria opened it, not really sure what to expect. She looked inside and started giggling.

"And I was worried you'd gone and gotten me a serious gift," Adria said, waving the can of bright orange tennis balls in his face.

Sebastian smiled back. "Well, it's really more for Winston so he'll be able to find them more easily."

"He's a dog. He's color blind," she said.

"Well then, maybe it really is for you."

They stayed at Sebastian's that night, and the next morning they drove to Duke's, idling away two and a half hours by taking turns asking questions about each other. He'd wanted to be a lawyer, but started writing instead. Later, it had been too late to go back, or maybe just too inconvenient. She'd told him about her family, her friends, and her favorite vacation spots.

Adria's first thought when they started up Duke's long winding drive was that it was something out of the movies, a long country lane leading up to the big house on the hill. Only the burned corner of the house detracted from the picture.

"That's odd," Sebastian said. "Lilith's car is here. I didn't expect her to show up for a work day."

Adria's first impression of Calvin, for it was Calvin not Lilith, was that he looked so uncomfortable in jeans it was as if he'd never worn a pair before. Along with them, he was wearing a weight belt that you'd normally associate with the Olympics and a pair of boots that didn't have a scuff on them.

"Hi, I'm Calvin," he said, extending his hand to Adria.

Duke stood quietly behind him, rolling his eyes at Calvin's fawning.

"I'm Adria," Adria said. "You're Lilith's husband."

At the mention of Lilith, Calvin dropped her hand like it was white hot.

Sebastian stepped in, "And this is Duke, who's been relegated to foreman duties."

"Thanks to my darling Lilith."

He gave Adria's hand a solid but gentle squeeze, and held her eye contact.

"So you're the Hollywood tart who's been keeping poor Sebastian awake at night."

"And you're the old fart who almost burnt his own house down around his ears," she shot back in a startled clip.

From one corner of her eye, she saw Sebastian's jaw drop and Calvin's face contort as if he were trying to ease through the floor. For a moment, she wondered if she had gone too far.

Instead the old man threw back his head and laughed until it turned into a cough.

"Don't die on me now, old man," said Sebastian, coming forward to help Duke.

Duke waved him off.

"The tart and the fart. Well, Adria, I'm glad to see that you're not one of those hot house flowers who doesn't know how to talk to an old man. I can definitely see why Sebastian would be enamored with a fabulous looking woman like you. Did you eat on the way up?"

"No. Sebastian promised me some of your biscuits and mead," she replied.

"Well, all I've got to cook right now is the camping stove, but we should still be able to rustle up some biscuits."

Inside, the kitchen was a hodgepodge of the old and the new. The old stove had been pulled out as well as the gas line that had fed it. Lilith had insisted that Duke switch to electric since she said it was safer.

Half the cabinets were in, but the ones over the stove were still in their extra-crispy state. The one in the corner, Adria noticed, was different from the others as if it had been added at a later time. Both the handles and the carving were similar, but it didn't quite match.

The biscuits were cooked and eaten with the requisite amount of butter and jam. Just a taste of mead was given so that the workers would be able to see straight.

The cabinets were worried and pried at until they began to come down. Calvin and Sebastian pulled each one down, and Adria dragged them out into the back yard and threw them onto a roaring bonfire that Duke had started.

178

After one trip to the fire, Adria walked with Duke back into the house and found that Calvin and Sebastian had made it to the final cabinet in the corner. Duke sprang forward.

"Hey guys, let's take a break. Calvin, why don't you go pick up some fast food?"

Calvin stopped at what he was doing.

"Sure. Just let us finish up with this cabinet then I'll go."

"No. It's just one. The three of us can handle it."

Sebastian interposed. "Duke, it will take two minutes."

"Listen, I'm a hungry, tired old man, and I want some food. If Lilith were here, she'd get it for me."

That was enough to get Calvin's attention. At the mention of Lilith's name, he hopped off the counter and put down his crowbar.

"I'll go. What does everybody want?"

Arby's was the only place close to Duke's so everyone gave an order. The minute Calvin's car headed down the driveway, Duke moved forward.

"Okay, you two, now that Lilith's eyes and ears are gone, let's get this last cabinet down."

Sebastian and Adria stared at him, unmoving.

"Oh come on, Fox, don't tell me that you of all people fell for my little act. Have you ever heard me once talk about fast food? Adria, you're going to have to help."

Adria climbed up onto the counter top eyeing Sebastian who just shrugged as if to say, "Who knows?"

Adria worked the crowbar while Sebastian steadied the cabinet. When it was almost off the wall, there was a flutter of white from behind the cabinet, and Duke scrambled to pick up the letters and envelopes. A couple were stuck to the wood as they brought the cabinet down, and Duke grabbed those as well and disappeared with a hoarse cry into the back of the house.

179

Adria clamored down off the counter. Sebastian started to follow Duke, but Adria stopped him.

"Let me go," she said.

Down the darkened hall, she heard the stifled sobs of a grown man. She moved silently, gliding into Duke's bedroom like an angel. The letters had been tossed haphazardly onto the bed. The old man sat at the end, looking like a worn out shell.

He was clutching a picture of a young man who looked a lot like Duke. A wife and two small boys completed the photo.

Duke didn't move when Adria joined him on the bed, but he let her pull his face down to her shoulder. Adria had never heard such an awful sound in all of her life.

The tears went on for ten minutes. Through it all, this proud man, wailed out the anguish of a family lost over the years.

Sebastian's voice came from the hall.

"Calvin's coming up the drive."

Duke sprang off the bed.

"What do I do?" he said.

Adria took control.

"Go and wash up. If he asks why your eyes are all red, tell him you had another coughing fit."

"But the letters."

"I'll do it. Just go."

She shuffled them together making no real attempt at organization and found a drawer in the bureau on the far side of the room to put them in. Sebastian poked his head in, holding a final letter that had escaped Duke's notice. Adria put it in the drawer and hurried back, arriving on the kitchen stage just in time for Calvin's return from Arby's.

Chapter 28

Sebastian stared for the hundredth time at her jaw line, watching it flow down from her ear and back around the other side. Doing so, led his eyes to the top of a very kissable neck.

Adria was asleep now, probably due to some combination of celebratory mead, and the long twisty road that was taking them to Sebastian's cabin in the North Georgia mountains. The lights on the dash illuminated her porcelain skin. In that moment, she snorted in her sleep, and Sebastian almost laughed aloud. Despite her beauty, she was human after all. They had almost stayed the night at Duke's instead of going to the cabin, but Duke had waved them off.

"What am I going to do with you under my roof for a whole night? Sebastian can't hold his liquor so he'd probably wake the lot of us up puking his guts out," Duke had said.

If the liquor had any effect on Duke, it wasn't to loosen his tongue. He wouldn't talk about the letters despite repeated questions by Adria and Sebastian.

Sebastian had almost spilled what he knew of the secret in an attempt to force Duke to talk. The extra letter that Sebastian had found told him that there were still a few things about which Duke wasn't being totally honest. It was a letter from Daniel, Duke's younger son, the one who had run away to Canada rather than go to Vietnam. The letter was dated only a few months before Winnie's death and was postmarked in Montana even though Duke had said he thought Daniel was still in Canada.

181

Adria and Sebastian had pleaded and cajoled, citing friendship, cabinetry, and shared sweat, but Duke had not relented.

"Can't an old man have a little bit of privacy without everyone wanting to know what he's up to," had been his final word on the issue.

After that, they had given up. Just before they had left, Adria had whispered in his ear. Whatever she said brought tears to Duke's eyes.

Preoccupied with Duke, Sebastian almost missed his turn, slamming on the brakes at the last minute. The suddenness roused Adria from her slumber.

Still yawning, she said, "What time is it?"

"Ten o'clock. That's only seven for your West Coast body. Why can't you stay awake?"

"Oh, that honey mead."

Sebastian laughed.

Adria glared. "I should vomit on you. Then we'll see how funny you think it is."

"There are some keys in the glove compartment. Can you get them?"

"Eww," she said, holding up two long, black keys with skulls at the end of them.

"That's them. They're skeleton keys for all the locks at the cabin."

"Ugh. What a terrible pun."

"I had those made up about a year ago."

Sebastian pulled off the road onto a paved piece of driveway that was barred by a locked gate. He put the car in neutral, unlocked the gates and swung them back from the road.

The driveway disappeared as it angled up to the left away from the main road. A wall of red-tip bushes soon engulfed the view on that side. Two more switchbacks put

182

them high above the main road pulling up before a modern looking cabin.

Sebastian unlocked the screen porch door and hauled everything inside. He quickly found the light switch in the small kitchen. The refrigerator was humming away, and the clock on the microwave constantly blinked twelve o'clock.

"It's nice," she said.

He started unloading the cooler he'd brought, and Adria spotted a bottle of champagne.

"Champagne?" she said in a slightly mocking voice. "What's the big occasion?"

"Having you here, of course."

Another bag held the linens. They made the beds together, turned on the window air conditioners in both bedrooms and the living room, and generally made the cabin livable.

"You take the master bedroom, Miss Rider."

"No. It's your place. I can sleep in the guest room."

"The guest room, as you saw, is a dismal place, barely big enough for the full size bed. I wouldn't want to upset your prima donna actress sensibilities by forcing you to stay there."

He took her arm and pulled her close.

"Not to mention the fact that the air conditioner in the guest room doesn't work very well."

He kissed her solidly then held her while she laid her head on his shoulder.

"Thanks for being here today. I don't know what I would have done with Duke if it hadn't been for you."

"It's so sad," she said. "He's so lonely and doesn't seem to get along with his family. He'll die all alone in that big, beautiful house. "

"Probably but sometimes the pain of death is too great to share with anyone."

"You've seen it?"

"A couple of the kids with cancer. Their parents asked if I would come, and I did. They were so scared, and had that look in their eyes. Wondering why."

Adria looked up to see the hot streaks of tears flowing down his face, and she tried in vain to wipe them away.

"I've got to stop doing that. There are a lot of good things in the world. Far more than the bad ones. Not the least of which is you," he said and kissed her forehead.

"And Duke," she added. "He's your friend, Sebastian. He likes and trusts you, too. He's coming to the end of his life all alone and there you appear on his doorstep. It's not just him, though. You've been working on his book for months. Much longer than usual. You're afraid to lose him."

"Maybe," Sebastian said.

"You know I'm right."

Silently, he deposited her bag in the master bedroom despite her continued protests.

"Are you going to tuck me into bed, too?" she asked hopefully.

"Not tonight," he said, "although I'm tempted."

One last time, he kissed her and then closed the bedroom door, separating them for the night. In the guest room, Sebastian stripped to his underwear and crawled into the sheets. Different noises caught his attention in this room, one he had never slept in. Adria pushed into his thoughts. He wondered if she was asleep or if she was in the other room thinking of him. He felt a twinge of guilt, but pushed it aside. The buzz of the air conditioner was the last sound he heard before sleep overtook him.

After a quick breakfast the next morning, Sebastian and Adria were outside. Sebastian had suggested a hike in the morning, then he had some work to do. He led her along the pathways that he had created, showing her rows of trees. In one place, there was a series of oak trees only a few feet tall.

"That's my greatest gift right there," he said proudly. "It'll be another fifty years before people will get to enjoy them in all their glory."

They hiked for another fifteen minutes before Sebastian came to an abrupt stop. Adria closed her eyes at his request. Once he was sure that her eyes were closed, he led her around the corner.

"Okay. You can open them."

A dazzling twenty-foot high waterfall greeted Adria as she opened her eyes. Its flow was low because of the season, but it was still beautiful. Sebastian had planted several varieties of flowers along the small basin that formed beneath the foamy waters. Standing nearby was a small shack, the walls screened in against the dime-sized mosquitoes that lived in the grotto.

"It's beautiful," she said turning to him.

They walked to the shack. Along the one full wall was a row of shelves which was empty except for a box of trash bags. A few folding lawn chairs were stacked neatly in a corner. Sebastian knocked the dust and spider webs from two and set them up.

"Sometimes when I come up to the cabin, I'll bring a sleeping bag and sleep out here, listening to the waterfall while I drift off. It's not the best shelter in the world. There's no clean water and no way to cook, but it's not bad for an overnight trip. I'll bring an extra battery for my laptop and stock the shelves with food and put some bottled water in the edge of the pond."

"It would be perfect for writing," she said.

"I don't think I would have bought the place if it wasn't for the waterfall."

"I like my ocean better," she said.

"You have to share your ocean. This is all mine."

"What about me?"

"Okay, it's ours. Someday when my time comes, I'm going to come up here and fall asleep for the last time to the sound of that waterfall."

"That's kind of morbid when you put it that way."

"It's not a pleasant part of life but it is part all the same. I used to tell my friends that I'd go over Niagara Falls when it was my time to go, but I like this better."

She leaned on his shoulder, and he slipped his arm around her slim waist.

"We should sleep up here tonight."

"I didn't bring sleeping bags."

"I'm sure you'll figure something out," she said.

Sebastian looked into her eyes, knowing that he wanted to share his whole life with her, but he didn't know to tell her. He should tell her. He would tell her now.

"Adria," he started.

Before he could say anything else, she began kissing him. Telling her was forgotten, along with the work he had planned to do around the cabin.

The waterfall whispered quietly in the background as the two enjoyed the afternoon.

Chapter 29

North Africa and Italy. September 1943

Duke's company was pulled out of the airbase after a few days and put into a reserve position in Africa, waiting for the next time the Army brass decided to put their lives on the line.

The first weeks after the jump, the company was nervous and stayed ready. It became clear, however, that the Army was still working on plans to put them into action. With summer coming on, they spent the heat of the day indoors, keeping as cool as possible. Only in the late evening did they venture forth.

Duke wrote Winnie, not knowing when she would get his letters. He got one from her, written just after he had left. Miss Walker passed along her greetings. Winnie hoped Duke wouldn't mind if she still went to the dances, although she promised not to kiss anyone until Duke came home. They hadn't had time to talk about it before his hasty departure.

In early July, the army informed the men that they would be doing a jump in the next week. Each man packed their bags, said their prayers, and wrote letters to be delivered in the case of their deaths. A few days later, Duke and his men were told they were not going after all. The 504th would make the jump, which turned out to be into Sicily. Several other companies, including Duke's, were being held in reserve for a larger attack.

Rather than the initial jump, the army decided to gamble Duke's life on an attack on the Italian mainland in early September of 1943. Duke and the rest of the 509th were moved to Sicily to use it as a jumping-off point. Salerno was the obvious choice for an allied beachhead, and a constant stream of reports told of the German effort to reinforce the area.

On the thirteenth of September, the 509th was informed that they would be dropping into the area around Avellino, with the goal of cutting off the supplies for the Germans headed toward Salerno. Radio equipment would guide the planes over Avellino. If the city could not be held, then the squads were to filter their way back through to the lines the best that they could, hitting the German supplies and communications along the way.

Duke's squad was the first into the plane. Because of the rough weather, a static jump was ordered despite the protest of the veteran jumpers, who liked the flexibility that a regular jump gave a parachutist.

Jake sat furthest from the jump door. He liked being the last one out of a plane.

"If I'm the last one out, I don't have to worry about any of you landing on top of me," he had replied when they asked him why. The truth was that he had been the last one out on every jump he had made, and now, he was afraid to change anything.

"Cut the German supplies off for us, and we'll be able to hold the beach head, and get a foothold on Italy. Cut off Italy, and we'll have the Germans running for cover."

Now, the adrenaline rush that had been ignited during their briefings spilled over into the belly of the plane. Toward the back, two other members of Hotel Company were pounding on each other's shoulders. Several were praying. Duke was weighed down so heavily with extra ammo that he all he could think about was how hard he would hit the ground.

The plane's flight became erratic and the jumpers began to get nervous.

"What's taking so long?" Duke heard one of the sergeants yelling to the jump master.

"I don't know. I'll go up and find out."

He was gone for several minutes and when he returned, he wore a frown.

"The navigation equipment isn't working because of the weather so we don't know exactly where we are," said the jump master to the sergeant.

"Can we turn around and go back?"

"No. They radioed headquarters, but headquarters told them to make the drop as best we could. Nothing we can do about it."

The sergeant nodded and went to report to the lieutenant. Duke and Tony sitting nearby heard the whole discussion.

"This is bad," Tony yelled to Duke over the roar of the engines.

"We got a job to do. If you land on top of a German armored division, just think of all the medals you'll get when you kill them."

"That's not a job, that's a suicide mission."

"Jumpers, up!" yelled the sergeant by the rear door.

"I hate static jumps," said Tony, yelling into Duke's ear.

They hooked their lines in, ready to go. As Duke neared the door, the plane gave a shudder as the wind suddenly caught it, and the turbulence popped everyone off their feet. It took almost a minute before Duke could regain his footing. He stepped toward the door again, and the jump master caught his arm.

"It's too late," the jump master shouted as Duke and his men got to the door, "You won't be near anyone else."

"We'll find them," Duke said.

He saluted and went through the door. Instantly, he was jerked upward by his chute. Below him, he saw other chutes opening. One, two, three. Tony, Herman, and Jake. All of them had made the jump. Behind him, he had hoped to see the rest of the company, but as he looked now, he could spot only a couple of parachutes that were miles away.

One minute he was looking up, as he heard the plane turn back toward the sea, then he was busy looking for a place to land that wasn't covered with trees. Fifteen minutes later four friends were together.

Three of them were busy digging with their latrine shovels into the side of the dried up creek bank, carving out a natural hollow so that they could hide their chutes.

Tony started to complain again, but Duke cut him off.

"Shut up, Tony. What's done is done. It will all work out one way or another."

"What will work out? We don't know where we are. We don't know where the rest of the company is. We don't know where the army is."

Tony rambled on. Duke looked to where Jake stood unmoving against a tree. Jake was their lookout, and only the eyes of the sharpshooter roved the landscape.

"Look, Tony, we know we need to get to the other side of these hills. The rest of the company is operating around Avellino so we need to find it. If we see some Germans on the way, then we send them on their way to hell."

Duke stood suddenly, surveying their work.

"That's good enough. Kick some dirt down from the top, and it'll have to do."

Jake swung himself into the creek and knelt beside the others.

"So now what?" he asked, looking at Duke.

"Now, we do what we came here to do," said Duke. "We kill the Jerrys, we cut their communication lines, and we work our way back to the front."

Jake nodded and said, "Let's do it."

Tony stared hard at them, his jaw clenching and unclenching. Finally, a sarcastic grin spread across his face.

"I love you, Duke," Tony said. "We're fifteen or twenty miles from the closest ally forces, and you're still thinking about getting the job done."

All of them were aware of how precarious their situation was. The pilots might be able to relay where Duke and his men had jumped, but even in the best of the planning scenarios, the Americans were going to be outmanned. Hope lay in being a small group and knowing that they had no one else to rely on but each other.

For a few days, they saw very few signs of life. Twice they skirted small villages, taking great care to climb higher into the hills and away from chance meetings. On their third night, they saw headlights of several vehicles on a road in the distance. The road brought renewed hope of a way over the mountain, but it also reminded all of them that they facing real enemies.

In the coldest part of the night, Duke was awakened by a tap on his shoulder and a hand across his mouth. Duke felt Tony's breath on his neck before he heard the whispered words.

"Patrol coming."

Duke got carefully to his knees. He pulled Tony close to him and whispered back, his mouth almost touching Tony's ear.

"How many and where?"

Tony held up eight fingers and pointed southeast. Duke could see them now, maybe a quarter of a mile away. There was no way to tell if they were Germans, Italian regular army, or partisans. The enemy was bunched together, ripe for the taking. Here was his chance to avenge Frank.

However, this patrol was not a threat to Duke and his men, not yet at least. If they had been out looking for a particular group of soldiers, they would be scattered out to kill.

"We stay here, but keep them under our guns. If they go on by, let them pass. If they get within a hundred yards, we take them out."

Tony let out a deep sigh of frustration, but Duke stuck to his plan. After the Germans were gone, Tony demanded to know why they hadn't killed the patrol.

"We could have taken them out with two shots each."

"What if you didn't get them all?" asked Duke. "What if you got seven of the eight? There could be a hundred men nearby for all we know. They dropped us in here to wipe out logistics and help with the frontal attack, not take out a backwater patrol."

They moved in the morning, and by late afternoon, the busy road they had seen the night before was no longer a distant mirage, but a wide, grey snake that led over the foothills to where there was real fighting.

"They're stopping in town, before they head over the hills."

"Gassing up, I bet," Jake said.

"Is a gas depot a big enough target for you, Mr. Squad Leader?" Tony asked.

"Yeah, Tony. That's big enough. Now here's what we're going to do."

When night fell, they were in position. Duke's plan had sounded crazy the first time, but it had grown on them. Splitting up when they were already down to a handful made no sense. Still, darkness was a great equalizer, and one man can be missed in darkness.

Tony and Jake went east near the section of road that led weary soldiers into town for fuel. Tony edged nervously close to the road, while Jake set up to provide covering fire. The first part of the plan was simple. Make as much noise as possible by lobbing hand grenades into the line of trucks. If the plan worked well, every gun toting German in the place would head right for them.

Tony worried that it might work too well.

He threw the first two grenades as far as he could over the trucks. Counting off fifteen seconds, he waited and then threw another six as fast as he could in succession. The first two carried over the trucks and onto the far side of the road. When the first one went off, several of the trucks swerved to a stop. The second one blew near a truck, and there were screams from inside.

A couple of the other grenades missed, but one landed on top of the canvas and tore it apart. The last truck he had targeted actually blew up like in the movies as one of Tony's grenades ripped open the fuel tank, and a second aimed at that truck ignited the fuel.

Jake for his part was shooting at officers and non-coms as Tony crawled up the mountain. The sharpshooter put down three, moved further up the hill toward the rendezvous point then fired again as a group of soldiers decided to move toward Tony's position. From where he was sitting, he could see about twenty dead and at least two trucks burning. He crawled further into the trees where he could view Tony's progress.

While Tony was throwing grenades, Duke and Herman waited near the fuel dump a half mile away. They were hoping that the Germans would rush out of town to aid the trucks that were under attack. In the meantime, Herman and Duke would blow up the main fuel dump. Herman realized that they had made a mistake. Rather than rush to help the trucks, the attack had simply caused the Germans to send patrols in all directions.

193

Now that the soldiers were out in force, Herman realized his position would quickly be overrun.

Herman's first grenade came up short and exploded harmlessly in a field. It did draw considerable attention, and soon the enemy started shooting randomly up the mountainside.

Duke swore as Herman stood suddenly, exposing himself to fire. The grenades that Herman threw in rapid succession reached out to the fuel dump, setting off a huge explosion. Duke closed his eyes against the flames.

He reopened them just in time to see Herman spun around by a slug and knocked to the ground.

Chapter 30

Adria stood at the stove, cooking a wonderful, nameless mixture of chicken and mushrooms, sautéed in butter and garlic. While she cooked, she kept one ear open for the sound of Sebastian's return from the shack, where he'd gone to take their gear before it got dark. It had taken a small amount of feminine whining, but she had finally talked Sebastian into sleeping there overnight.

She put the plates on the table, feeling like she was playing the role of a homemaker in some new film. Only, it didn't feel like acting. It just felt right, waiting for her man to come back from what he was doing. Adria fiddled with the dimmer switch in the small breakfast area until the lighting matched her expectations.

The door swung open on its hinges, and seconds later, Sebastian stood in the doorway. He smiled across the room.

She smiled back.

"You pour the champagne while I get the rest of it on the table," she said.

As they ate, they talked about her music career.

"The big places aren't going to fit me, and a lot of the little places book far in advance so they can guarantee that they've got some sort of talent. Maybe I should just give up."

"Nonsense," Sebastian said. "I love your music. In fact, I wished I could have spent more time in California so you could serenade me."

"But you're my boyfriend, you have to like it."

She watched him, hopeful that he'd come up with a stronger argument for her doubts.

"Well, I think you should just keep at it. Write music, practice music, and play music whenever you can. The crowds won't be huge, but if you're singing full time and making enough to pay the bills, then that's not half bad."

"Is that why you kept writing?"

"You mean, is that why I kept writing despite being a miserable failure?"

"Nobody said you were a failure. You just didn't get as far as you wanted."

He sat as if digesting this take on his writing career.

"That's pretty accurate, but music isn't your only option. You can decide that you want to stick to acting. There's nothing wrong with that either if that's what you want to do."

Dinner cleanup went by quickly as both were thinking of their hike out to the shack by the falls. By the time they were settled, the crickets were out in full force.

"There's your serenade," she said as she lay in his arms, letting him hold her.

She took it all in for a few minutes.

"I'm falling in love," she said, after a while.

"Me too," he said.

They rested against each other, sometimes with his head on her shoulder and sometimes, the other way around. Water fell steadily down the cliff creating a shroud of intimacy around the shack, intimacy that declared the night their own.

Sunrise found Adria still in the arms of Sebastian. Whatever he wanted from her seemed to be human-sized. Not money, not fame, not anything related to what she did for a living. For once, she had found a man who wanted her for herself.

He woke slowly to find her staring at him. Immediately, he began to play with her hair, which seemed to be his favorite pastime when she was in his arms.

"Wow," he said after a few minutes.

"Wow?" she asked with a smile.

"This is the best morning I've ever had, waking up with you here, in my favorite place."

Adria smiled and snuggled closer.

"Me too. We should just come up here and ignore the rest of the world. No movie executives, no band, no producers."

"No money. No Mary. No Winston."

"Oh, we could bring Winston. It wouldn't be as quiet as it is now, but we could still bring him. This shack might be still, but I'm sure he could find a corner to call his own. We could visit those other people once a year, then come back and disappear."

The rest of the morning was a pleasant helping of cleaning up and being okay with seeing each other looking less than sparkling after a night in the shack. They packed the Mustang and locked the place up and headed down from the mountains with a plan to stop by Sebastian's house before taking Adria to the airport. Sebastian's cell phone chirped as they made it back into cell phone range.

Sebastian spoke for a few minutes with someone named Betty as Adria listened to one side of the conversation. Betty Hudson was throwing a party for Charlie because he was doing so much better, and she had called to invite Sebastian. He had declined because of their plans.

"How do you know him?" Adria asked.

Sebastian explained about the party and about taking Charlie to the drive-in. He also mentioned Dick Hudson leaving the family.

"How can he be so cruel?"

197

"It happens all the time, and it usually makes situation worse, as you can imagine. It's not just leukemia. Sometimes it's a miscarriage, a stroke, or a heart attack. One study said that men are three times more likely to leave as women."

"So much for 'in sickness or in health.' Do you know Charlie's dad?'"

"The only time I ever saw him was at Charlie's party. He seemed overwhelmed, like he'd given up hope."

"He'd rather leave the boy to die without him?"

"It sounds cruel. I don't know what I'd do if I were in his position."

"You know full well that you'd stick to it. It's in your blood. You wouldn't go back to see these kids if you didn't have what it takes."

"I guess. It's too bad about the party. It would have been nice to make it."

"What if," she started, "we skipped hanging out at your house and went straight to the party? Could we go for a while and still make my flight?"

Sebastian picked up his phone.

"Betty. This is Sebastian. It looks like I'll be able to come for a little while. I'm with my girlfriend so would it be okay if I brought her along? Okay, great. She has a flight to catch later, but we can come for a while."

At the park, there was a maze of people, and it took a few minutes for Sebastian to figure out which group belonged to Charlie. When Charlie saw him, he threw his arms around Sebastian's legs and squeezed as tightly as he could.

"Isn't this cool? Mom hasn't let me go to the park in months."

"Hey Charlie!" another kid called, "I bet you can't beat me to the top of that hill."

Charlie was off and running before Sebastian could say a word.

Betty disengaged from the group she was talking to and walked over.

"Sebastian, thanks so much for coming," she said, as she gave him a chaste hug.

She turned to Adria and held out her hand.

"I'm Betty Hudson. It's nice to meet you. Sebastian told me he was seeing someone, but was a little mysterious on the details."

"Adria Rider," said Adria, wondering what Sebastian had said exactly. At the same time, she was struck by how much the woman reminded her of her sister Mary. She had the slightly wider hips and extra weight that women add at childbirth while still retaining a physical attractiveness that was accentuated by the care that she took with her makeup and clothes.

"Thanks so much for coming to the party," Betty said. "When Sebastian said that he had plans today that he couldn't change, I should have realized it involved an attractive woman."

A woman in jeans and a white top joined them.

"Did you say your name was Adria Rider?"

"Yes," said Adria, dreading where the conversation was headed.

"You're the actress. The one who dated the guy from *Hunting Honey.*"

"John Yetzger."

"Right, John Yetzger. He was great in that and in the one you did together."

"*Going From Groshem.*"

Betty joined in, "That was you. Wow. No wonder you look so familiar. I was thinking the whole time when you were walking up that you kind of had that look to you."

Sebastian threw her a "what are you going to do" shrug and wandered off, leaving her stranded in a sea of fans. Adria watched him find Charlie, alone on a swing.

"So what was that like?" someone was saying to her.

"I'm sorry, What was what like?"

"Kissing John Yetzger in the movie. I've always thought that he looked so yummy."

"Well, not to spoil it for you, but it's a bit like licking an ashtray. When he's not on screen, he's pretty much always smoking."

"Oh, that's too bad," said one of the women.

The mingling that had encompassed Adria ended when a kid in a wrestling melee came out of the pile with a bloody lip, and the flock separated, each one making sure their kid hadn't caused the problem. Betty was back immediately, seeing Charlie safely with Sebastian.

"Sebastian's quite a guy, isn't he?" said Betty.

Adria detected a faint hint of wistfulness.

"Yes. He is." Adria said, watching him with Charlie.

They talked for a few minutes then Betty made her excuses to Adria and moved off in the direction of the other guests. Adria turned toward Charlie and Sebastian who seemed lost in their own world. Their words drifted across the grass as she came up behind them.

"I was scared before, Sebastian," Charlie was saying. "Have you ever been scared?"

"Of course. Everybody gets scared. Courage is going on even when you're scared."

"How can you go on when you're dead?"

"Well, you can't, but you aren't dead. You were just sick, but sometimes when people get sick, it's hard for them to go on because they are so scared that they give up."

"Everybody dies or leaves you," Charlie opined. "My dad left. You won't leave, will you Sebastian?"

200

"I'd never leave if I had a choice, but we don't always get to choose."

"I guess not. I don't understand life sometimes, Sebastian."

"Cake, everybody," came the cry from one of the moms.

Charlie was off the swing just as Adria reached them, but he stopped when he saw her.

"You're not as pretty as in the movies though," said the young boy.

"Thanks a lot. Just for that I'm gonna go eat all your cake."

She made the beginning of a dash for the table while Charlie sprinted away.

Sebastian grabbed her arm and yelled, "I'll save your cake, Charlie."

"Traitor," Adria screamed in faux surprise.

Sebastian pulled her toward him and wrapped her up. She fought him for a minute then started laughing.

Chapter 31

Sebastian smiled and fiddled with Adria's hand as they drove from the party to the airport. Relationally, a bridge had been crossed. It was their first event together as an official couple, and it had felt perfect, and, yet, he was troubled. There was just too much there to let go of, but he couldn't see his way through to the end of it.

Sebastian stared off into the Atlanta sky as they drove. He didn't realize he had zoned out until Adria broke their silence.

"When I get back, I'm going to do what you said. Start calling around to places where I can do little shows. There are a million of those places in the LA area. Bars, coffee houses, or wherever. "

"Some of them here have regular shows on Friday nights," offered Sebastian.

"Yeah, but others have different people. If I have to play for tip money then I'll play for tip money."

"Maybe I should come watch you play."

"I'd like that."

"Just watch out for weird stalker guys."

"Right," Adria said with a smile, "They're trouble."

At the airport, Sebastian handed over her bags to a curb side attendant. Adria kissed him once, a long full kiss. Sebastian followed her progress all the way to the door of the terminal where she disappeared into a sea of travelers.

The next day, Sebastian wrestled with his story. Specifically, he wondered about the veracity of Duke's account of his family history.

Duke said he hadn't heard from Daniel since Winifred's funeral. Since the letters had been to her, it's quite possible that had really been the last time that he'd seen him. So, why lie about Daniel being in Canada? Of course, Daniel's disappearance correlated with the family falling apart. Rather, it had been when the oldest son, Antonio, had been killed in Vietnam. How many families fell apart during crises, moving from functional to dysfunctional?

Montana. Sebastian iconified his word processor and got on the Internet. Yahoo, Google, all of them had brought the world that much closer. He searched on Daniel Farmington, but got no results. Next he tried 'D Farmington.' No free listings showed on the screen although Yahoo offered him information on all the "D Farmingtons" for a mere $19.95. He glanced at the preview of the information and saw there was one in Bozeman, Montana. That was the town where the letters had come from.

He found what he was looking for and grunted. There was an D Farmington, listed with a birthday in 1950 which matched what he knew and from the looks of things, there was a Mrs. Farmington as well plus a couple of boys, a Carter and, he saw, an Antonio. Six digits into the phone number, he hung up.

What was he going to say? Hi. You don't know me, but I thought I'd interject myself into your dysfunctional family, and see if I can make it all better? Duke hadn't moved in forty or fifty years. Daniel could certainly have found Duke by now, sometime in the last twenty years since Winifred had died.

Sebastian sighed and called again. He would use his book for an excuse.

"Hello," said the woman who answered.

"Yes. I'm calling for Daniel Farmington. I'm writing a book about his family and wanted to talk to him about it."

"A book about the Farmingtons?" she asked.

"It's sort of a commissioned book."

"Commissioned by who?"

"Well, Lilith was the first one to have the idea, but Duke decided that he wanted to pay for it instead. Duke is Daniel's father."

"I know who Duke Farmington is. It took years to undo the damage he did to D.H. I'm quite sure that I don't want to talk about Duke Farmington."

"Would it be possible to speak to D.H.?" Sebastian asked, picking up on the new name.

"He's at work, and I doubt he'd be interested."

"Please, ma'am. I won't take up much of his time."

She hesitated, and he could hear the wheels cranking.

"I'll make no promises, but you can leave your number."

Sebastian did and told her that he was in Atlanta.

Late at night, as he sat over his manuscript, he heard the chirp of his cell phone. He found it among stacks of papers on the desk.

"This is Sebastian Fox."

"This is D.H. Farmington. Daniel."

"Hi, Daniel. I'm a writer, and I've been doing some work on a book about your father."

"I don't have a father."

"Oh. Well, I thought I might talk to you about Duke and maybe add in some memories that you have of him."

"Duke Farmington cares more about himself than any person I ever met. The last time we talked was at my mother's funeral, and that's good enough for me. He cut me off almost forty years ago. Do you know about that?"

204

"I know there was a disagreement over Vietnam," said Sebastian.

"Disagreement," D.H. snorted into the phone. "That's a fairly mild word for telling your son that you never want to see him again."

"Well, he's getting old, and his heart is giving out. I think he'd want to see you."

"I was hoping he was dead. When my wife said someone had called about Duke, I was thinking he had died and maybe left me something in the will."

Sebastian tried to keep himself calm, but he was angry. Death was not something to be wished on anyone.

"Well, you almost got your wish. He's got heart problems that will probably kill him soon enough, and there was a fire at the house that almost cost him his life. Luckily, he got by with only a concussion and a large repair bill."

"Why should I care? Antonio was his favorite growing up, the good son. The son who was willing to die."

The bitterness was clear in his voice.

"I'm sorry, D.H., I just thought that maybe you two could work things out."

"Well, it's very little that you know about Duke Farmington and me. He left me in my hour of need, and I don't care if he dies a slow, painful death."

"What about your sons?"

"What do you know about my family?" D.H. demanded.

Sebastian felt the rage coming through the phone.

"Not much, I just saw their names when I found your phone number. Maybe they'd like to meet their grandfather, see the old house, and maybe even let the old man show them how to tie a fly."

Herman grunted on the other end.

"They know how to tie a fly. I may not have any feelings left for my father, but I would never let him come between me and fishing."

"Well, at least you've got your priorities straight," said Sebastian, a harsh edge to his voice.

"Are you sure you're a writer? You sound like some kind of shrink."

"I'm just someone who believes that we can make choices in life, no matter what's gone on before."

"Great. How's this for a choice?"

Silence in Sebastian's ear let him know that D.H. had hung up on him. He set down his cell phone, realizing that he was flushed with embarrassment. What was he doing? Trying to save Duke from himself, trying to save the world, trying to put a family back together because his was gone?

His mind spiraled away, thinking about Duke and D.H., wondering what Duke thought of when he saw the old pictures. Did he regret what he had done?

Before he knew what he was doing, he had dialed Adria's number.

"You okay?" she asked.

"Oh. I've just been thinking about Duke. He's all alone, and he's got family. They should be together."

"It is sad," she said.

"I called his son today just to see if there was anything left of that relationship."

"Sebastian!"

"Was that bad?"

"Not bad, but definitely not any of your business."

She paused for a heartbeat and then continued.

"And it is sad, like I said. When I got home last night, I called my Mom, Dad and Mary just to tell them how much I loved them. I don't want any of us reliving what I saw Duke go through."

Sebastian stared at the frame across the room, thinking of his own dead parents.

"Are you still there?"

"Yeah, I was just thinking about my folks."

He didn't say anymore. She had heard all the details as they lay in the shack near the waterfall in the mountains.

"I didn't mean to upset you," she said. "Sometimes people make bad decisions. They fight or turn little problems into big problems. Or they simply stop talking altogether, even after the anger passes. One day, they wake up, and they've gotten old, and backed themselves into a corner."

"Duke seems so different from the person the D.H. describes. He's kind, not the dad who screws up everybody's life."

"Or did," said Adria. "Who knows what he'd be like if he could start over now? I doubt that he and Lilith have given one another an even chance in a very long time."

"I know," he said, "but it seems like there's something that could be done."

"Oh Sebastian, you've got such a good heart, but sometimes you just need to write your book and move on," Adria said.

He thought for a moment about his situation, and a cough came involuntarily out of his chest.

Move on.

If only there was a way.

Chapter 32

The hills above Avellino, Italy. September 1943.

Duke slid down the hill and was almost out from under cover when he saw Herman dragging himself.

"Caught one in my shoulder, and it hurts like hell," Herman shouted.

Behind him, the fuel dump continued to explode in an unbelievable domino effect. Herman and Duke edged along, Duke providing balance for Herman as they hurried, bent over in half run. Duke kept his gun loosely pointed with one arm while he used the other to help Herman. Finally, they managed to make it up to the general rendezvous area. The wounded man let go of Duke's arm and moved ahead into some trees. German voices swirled up the hill behind them. Duke swung his head, and saw three Germans come running out of a clump of trees. Their eyes found Duke, but they had to stop to bring their guns up, and Duke's was already level. Before he knew what he was doing, he had already dropped the first one, and he kept his fire up as he tried to get to Herman. A gunshot came from above them and then another.

Jake and Tony hurried down the hill. It was they who had fired from above.

"Herman's hit."

They found Herman lying on the ground, moaning and holding his shoulder.

Duke and Tony hoisted Herman between them, and headed straight up the hill. There was a wild animal trail that

208

Duke had seen earlier. They took it now, following its rough angle up the hill. After a quarter of a mile, they crested a ridge and dipped into a different valley.

Jake grabbed Duke and pointed.

A smile broke out on Duke's face when he saw that the line of trucks was no longer moving up the mountain. Flames lit up the sky and enough of the road to demonstrate that they had halted the German reinforcements. Both men enjoyed the moment before moving on again.

Halting in a bowl in the hills that appeared to be secluded from the rim and the road, the small group huddled and outlined their next move. Tony and Duke made a fire for Herman's sake, despite the obvious risk. Jake worked on Herman's wound, cleaning it, but unable to remove the bullet.

Duke walked away unable to watch any longer and sat alone on the edge of the hollow, questioning his judgment. He looked up as Jake appeared.

"How is he?" Duke asked.

"Not good, I'm afraid."

Duke shook his head.

"What I wanted to tell you," said Jake, "was that it was a good plan. Even if we'd had a whole company, it couldn't have gone any better."

Jake squeezed Duke's shoulder. "He'll get better."

"What if he doesn't?" Duke said, lashing out. "What if I've gotten him killed with my carelessness?"

Jake spread his hands, but had no real answer for the rage. They joined Tony, and Duke drew a map on a piece of bark.

"Best I can tell, we're about here," Duke said. "My guess is that our troops are here. If we're lucky, we can move down this direction and find them. I figure we can march north toward the foot of the hills and rest there for a day or two."

Duke tossed the map into the fire.

They debated for a while over the best way to move Herman, and finally rigged a crude stretcher out of two stout sticks and pieces of Herman's pack that they shredded for the purpose. Duke and Tony each took an end, and Jake led off into the trees.

Twice they saw patrols from a distance and melted into the scenery. Just after noon, they stopped and ate half of their rations for the day. Herman's wound looked bad, despite being bathed whenever they stopped. An hour later, as they crossed difficult terrain, Herman started screaming from the pain and came fully awake. They eased him to the ground and tried to calm him.

Jake moved further out to see if the screams had drawn any attention. Seeing nothing, he returned to camp. Herman had calmed down, but was begging them to get the bullet out of his arm, despite the pain.

Duke put a stick between Herman's teeth and rolled him over onto his stomach. Tony pulled his knife out and made the cut that Herman had recommended near his shoulder blade. Herman cried out painfully, and Tony had tears in his eye. Reaching around to the front of Herman's shoulder, Tony located the slug under the skin and pushed it out the incision that he had made. Herman grunted and passed out as Tony finished.

"Duke, we need to move it," Jake said. "We'll be sitting ducks if we stay where we are."

Looking around, Duke realized for the first time that they were exposed to view from down the slope. They had simply stopped when Herman had begun screaming.

"Strap him face down," Tony said. "It will keep the weight off of the cut."

Duke privately dreaded starting again. He was thoroughly exhausted from carrying Herman all morning. It was a great relief when Jake offered to switch places. They had gone a half mile when Duke held up his hand for a halt. He knelt slowly. Jake and Tony lowered Herman to the ground and swung their rifles into position.

Tony crawled up to where Duke was and took a look.

He pointed toward some movement below them in the valley. From where they rested, they could see two figures moving through the trees.

"Those are women," Tony finally said.

Duke nodded.

"They've got company," Tony said, "Looks like seven or eight Krauts. They're arguing with the women and motioning toward the hills. We've got to rescue them."

"No way," Duke said. "We can't risk it."

Duke took one more look back through his glass and as he did, one of the girls turned toward him. He focused on her eyes. The scared eyes were a color he'd only seen once before, looking back at him from a shapely Alabama girl named Winnie. His heart melted inside of him. One of the Germans grabbed the girl and began to drag her away to privacy. Something inside Duke snapped.

"Jake, work your way a bit down the hill but stay under cover. Don't shoot until I give you the signal, but then shoot as fast as you can. You'll have the best field of vision. Tony, you and I will circle around to where the girls are and get them away quietly if possible."

Duke could hear screams and the sound of an open-handed slap as he got closer. He caught a glimpse of German grey wrestling with the beige of the girl's dress that he had seen earlier. As he came up behind the German, the Italian girl's eyes flared open, and the soldier wheeled toward Duke. Duke's bayonet slid into the soldier's throat. Duke turned the bayonet and pulled it out before the flesh could trap it. The girl tried to run, but Duke grabbed her and tried to quiet her. She flailed at him and escaped his grasp.

211

Duke heard thrashing from where Tony was, but ignored it and moved forward. He caught Jake's eye as he brought his rifle up and began to fire into the crowd of Germans. Jake started on the right and Duke on the left. The Germans dove for cover.

A shot came from Tony's location, and suddenly, a German bolted out into the open directly under Duke's gun. Duke fired, and the German spun around and dropped.

There was no more firing, but Duke was taking no chances. He waited and looked around to get Jake's signal that everything was clear. He turned, and instead of finding Jake safely up the hill, Duke saw him ambling down the hill at a leisurely pace.

"Now what, Duke?" said Jake.

A shot rang out, and Jake toppled forward.

One of the "dead" Germans had fired, and Duke quickly fired into his body. Tony, still in hiding, put a bullet into the head of every German he could see, and Duke did the same.

Tony ran to Jake and turned him over.

There was a bullet hole in his forehead. Jake was dead.

Noise sounded behind him, and Duke swiveled. It was the girl with the mahogany eyes. The beauty of her eyes was filled with the flames of hatred, and she was holding a pistol in her hand.

Tony covered her with his rifle and told her, in Italian, to put her gun down. She shook her head, and Tony told her to put it down or he'd kill her. The girl dropped the gun and retreated into the brush, but her friend stood there shocked by the violence of it all.

Tony walked over to girl who had not fled.

"Ask them where they are going," Duke said. "Tell them we need a place for Herman."

Tony had forgotten about Herman. As he walked toward them, the girls backed up, pointing at the blood on his shirt. Tony said something and the one girl smiled. Even the girl with Winifred's eyes had a hint of a grin on her face.

"Whatever you're telling them, keep at it."

"I told them that I'm actually Italian and, that after this is over, we're going to get rid of the American. They were down in the town because they had to bring money to one of their cousins. None of the men could come because the Germans would try to press them into service. So they came. About five hours from here is a village we can stay at."

One of the women pointed toward Jake and shook her head. Tony shook his head and pointed back up the hill, and the women answered him with rapid Italian.

"She says that she might be able to help Herman."

"Go ahead. I'll be up in a minute."

Duke, tears running down his face, went to each German and made sure they were dead. Kneeling down, he went through each of their pockets taking their money, stripping their rifles, and gathering their ammunition.

He looked up to find the girl with the beautiful eyes standing next to him. She reached for one of the rifles, and Duke pulled it back. She rattled off something in Italian.

"What she's saying," said Tony, coming down the hill behind them, "is that only a stupid American thinks he can carry five rifles and his injured friend."

Duke set his jaw stubbornly, but eventually gave in and handed the rifles over.

"Grazie," Tony said. "The one you keep staring at is Maria. The other one is Rosa."

Maria rattled off something and began slinging the rifles over her shoulder.

They carried Jake up the hill and walked until they found a natural shallow in the ground. Duke took Jake's tags and whispered a prayer of his mother's over Jake. Rosa pulled wild flowers and left them on Jake's chest.

213

"I don't like leaving him here," Tony said.

"Me either," said Duke. "But we have to get Herman and these girls out of here."

Duke and Tony took the stretcher and began to follow the girls across the hillside. They marched for hours past burnt out houses and barns.

"A lot of the partisans are from this area, and so the Germans have swept through and cleared it out," explained Tony as he talked with the girls.

Italian partisans hated the regular Italian Army, made up of fascists who were sympathetic to Mussolini. They hated the German Army even more. Duke said as much.

"I would guess they hate us, too," Tony said.

"When people stomp on your country, hate is easy."

For a while, no one spoke and they simply hiked, the men with their load and the girls laboring under the strain of the rifles and ammunition. Herman remained oblivious to it all. Darkness was falling as they wound their way into a deserted village. Rosa and Maria hurried along paths that were obviously familiar to them. At last, they came to a farm house, built long and low against the base of a hill. Inside there was a hearth which soon had a roaring fire going.

"Ask them about the Germans, whether or not they ever come this way."

The girls said the Germans hadn't been in this part of the country for months. It was too far off of the beaten path to be strategic, now that the partisans had been chased away.

Duke got Herman settled into a bed. He couldn't even think about Jake. Rosa disappeared into a back room and reappeared with a bottle in her hand.

Rosa took the bottle of brandy into the room where they had stretched out Herman. She ordered Duke and Tony to take his boots off and roll him onto his stomach. After they did, she took the stinking bandage off his shoulder. The wound looked terrible.

Herman came abruptly awake, screaming at the fire that he felt as she poured the brandy on the wound. Wild eyes looked at Rosa as if he was seeing a ghost.

"Relax, buddy. Rosa's trying to fix you up. It's been rough," Duke said.

Herman was given a long drought of brandy to drink. They rolled him back onto his stomach so that Rosa could bathe the wound again. Since Herman was awake, they took the opportunity to move the bed into the main room so they could be closer together. The girls huddled together in a far corner, while Tony slept near the door and Duke near the window. The last thing that Duke saw, as the fire died down, was Maria looking at him.

Maria -- the girl whose eyes alternately mocked and reached out to Duke.

Chapter 33

Adria squinted her eyes against the darkness of *The Olde Harbor*. She'd located the bar and its minder more by following the smell of beer than by any sort of organized layout in the little club. Even GPS had been no match for the odd little corner of the town where she now stood. Instead, the GPS had "re-calculated" multiple times as Adria wandered in circles. Finally, she had seen her name on a couple of tacky, cardboard signs secured with grey duct tape onto lampposts that stood like sentinels in front of the establishment.

Her guitar case and movie star face undoubtedly would have lead the bartender to her identity, but she introduced herself anyways. The bartender said his name was Brad.

"Is there a table I can use to put some CDs on or something?"

"Not likely," Brad said, smiling through yellow teeth. "We're expecting a big crowd just like every Friday night, and I don't have a table to spare. You can set them on the ground up front, if you'd like. The mike should be plugged in, but don't change the volume. You play from eight to eleven with a ten minute break every hour."

"Okay," she said hesitantly.

The volume wasn't quite to her liking, but when she glanced toward the bar, she saw that the surly bartender was watching her like a hawk gliding over a meadow on the first day of spring.

"Okay," she thought to herself. "Relax. I won't touch your precious volume switches."

Adria had wavered on the drive down from L.A. Was it worth it? She had a million dollars in the bank from years of acting and living frugally, at least by Hollywood standards. Why was she out here? Was she trying to prove to her high school music teacher that he was wrong when he told her that she sounded like a frog when she sang?

She started with a ballad, focusing on the couple that sat closest to her. In her mind, she pretended she was a minstrel, commissioned by a royal prince to perform. In the past few weeks, she'd already set up a pattern -- Work through her repertoire, make eye contact with the groups of men, and avoid the men who were there with a girl so she wouldn't cause any jealousy.

At the end of the night, Brad handed her a hundred dollars and seemed pleased, noting that some of his regulars had stayed longer than they usually would to watch her. He made sure to emphasis the word "watch," with a hint of leering in his voice. Adria felt the implied grime wash over her, guessing where Brad's mind was wandering. It ruined her whole evening.

She hurried to gather her stuff up and spilled some CDs onto the floor. One of the waitresses stopped to help, as Adria fought to keep the tears from spilling out.

"You okay?"

"Yeah," she nodded, then, "No. Just Brad."

"Say no more. I admire you though," said the waitress. "We don't get many stars at the Olde Harbor. And you are a star, even if you're working your way up from the bottom in music."

Adria heard a snort from behind her and turned to find Brad.

"What it was Ms. Rider, was a lot of BS songs about love that no man would ever believe. But you've got a nice body which will bring the guys in, and the sappy music brings in the ladies so it just might work for you. 'Working your way up,' like you have someplace to go with this."

He shook his head, pushed on by, and headed for the back room.

Adria's tears found form, flowing down her face as she packed the last few CDs away and closed up her guitar case.

"Don't mind him," said the waitress, "Brad hasn't gotten laid in twenty years."

Adria enjoyed a brief laugh at Brad's expense, packed up her car, and drove back to the hotel where she was staying overnight. She thought about Sebastian, but didn't call him since it was four in the morning on the east coast.

Instead she cried and doubted every decision that she'd made in the past the year. She remembered when she had gone back and bought a guitar again. Fooling around with it, picking out chord sequences that she liked and building up calluses. No pressure, just fun.

Her first song was about a boyfriend who had dumped her in college. Her second about a guy she'd met while out surfing. A cut surfer who had drunk her in with one look, then spent the rest of the afternoon using his eyes to flirt with her. Each song had its own history, and that didn't even include the ones that she'd dumped in the trash to die, muffled and unsung.

She couldn't remember now if she was the first one to consider recording them or if there was someone else she could blame for all of this. Her last thought as she fell asleep was that she'd have to play at *The Olde Harbor* again tomorrow night, under Brad's watchful eye.

In the morning, she dialed the number she'd been thinking about since last night then listened to Sebastian's phone ringing a thousand miles away. When Sebastian came on, Adria forgot to ask him what he was doing because he asked her first.

"I think I'm going to go to the beach."

"Ah," said Sebastian, "the rough life of a Hollywood starlet."

Her voice caught in her throat and it all came pouring out. She sat down on the edge of the bed, one shoe on and the other falling, unnoticed, to turn sideways against the dresser. All the emotions of the concert tour collapse, the songs, the expectations, and the night before turning into a mocking at the hands of Brad.

"There will always be Brads in the world, Adria. They tend to be short-sighted people who wouldn't know a dream if it came up and sprinkled pixie dust on them. Brad's view of life tapped out when he was twenty-two."

"What if he's right? What if my music's just a bunch of romantic nonsense?"

"In that case, you could be in for a great career, since most music in the world is about relationships. Even if he's right, you still use it. Make some changes and write the next song."

She sniffled and leaned back on the bed. "I wish you were here."

"Me too. Instead of spending time watching you sing last night, I got to go watch Pops drink beer."

"At Hooters!"

"Okay, at Hooters, but that doesn't change the fact that I would have rather sat in hell with you last night than sat in Hooters with Pops."

"*The Olde Harbor* wasn't quite hell, even if Brad is the devil."

"Brad will be a distant memory after tonight. Besides, this little tour of yours is supposed to be for you and the music, remember?"

"Sort of. I mean I remember us talking about it, but it's hard for me to feel it."

"Adria, just think about the best time you ever had sitting on your porch, playing your music, and staring at the sunset then take it with you to the club tonight."

"Sebastian Fox, I love you."

"I love you, too, Adria."

Adria made her way back to *The Olde Harbor,* reluctantly, after a day of half-hearted shopping at the multicolored, multistoried, multi-block Horton Plaza in the heart of San Diego's revitalized shopping district. She'd found a new outfit to help her through the grueling evening that she was expecting then settled down to read a book in a corner café that seemed to have gone unnoticed by the general public.

Now, striding through the front door of *The Olde Harbor*, she wasn't sure if an outfit was going to be enough. Maybe a couple of stiff drinks would help, but the last thing she needed was to get drunk in public.

She waved at Brad, but didn't bother stopping by the bar. Set up was automatic tonight, and she didn't care about the volume. Julie, the waitress from the previous night, stopped by and whispered a word of encouragement.

Friday had been busy, but the place was completely packed for Saturday night.

Before Adria opened up, she thought about Sebastian's advice. It seemed silly in some ways, like a bad comedy about finding your happy place. In her mind, though, she saw it – the sunlight flashing across the Pacific, a light breeze blowing her hair in swirls around her head, and the music coming together for the first time. Just before she took the stand, she captured the feeling right down to the smell of the ocean.

Her first session sold her a dozen CDs, and a glance around the bar told her that the tip jars were way ahead of the night before, but the biggest difference was the buzz of the crowd. She smiled as she walked into her break, and not even Brad could think of a negative comment.

Partway through the next set, she saw a camera flash from her right. It happened again then a third time. Constantine was walking toward her as she sang. She turned away from him, finished up the song.

"Ladies and gentleman, the photographer who is interrupting your meals is an uninvited, unwanted, sort of personal stalker of mine. Let's ignore him and hope that he will find his way home to his mommy."

Several people laughed, and one guy stood up, barring Constantine's way. Brad waded into the fray, getting a solid grip on Constantine's belt and collar. Constantine struggled a bit, but a waiter joined Brad in escorting him to the door. Julie did her part, grabbing Constantine's camera and clearing out the memory.

"I'm sorry about that, folks, give me a sec, and we'll get back to the set," Adria said.

She took a break and drank her water. When she came back on, there was a mild round of applause.

The crowd was solidly behind her for the rest of the evening. When she finished her final set of the evening, there was a thunderous applause from one back corner. As she cleaned up, she turned to find her sister Mary and her husband Jimmy, along with Guy and Karlie Davies.

She hugged them all at once.

"What are you guys doing here?" she finally said after the hugs and faux kisses.

"Well," said Mary with a devious look on her face, "we got a call from someone who said that you were having a bit of a hard time so we thought we'd come on down to cheer you on."

"Sounds like Sebastian's been meddling again."

Guy pulled out his I-phone, pushed a button, and handed it to Adria. Sebastian appeared on the screen, his conservatory framed behind him.

"Adria, I'm sorry I couldn't make it out to see you and encourage you to keep chasing your dreams tonight, but if you're seeing this then Guy and his wife made it. I'm planning on sitting and listening to your CD all night while I do a bit of writing. Now, I've got to run so I can get this to Guy before he drives down for the concert. I'm thinking about you, and I'll talk to you tomorrow."

Adria stood looking at the people around her with a completely different type of tears filling her eyes than the night before.

Chapter 34

Sebastian and Duke finished bolting down the new linoleum counter tops. Duke's job was to sit on top of each one and hold it flush with the support, while Sebastian lay on his back, working the drill with the screwdriver bit to tighten things up. Sweat dripped down the side of Sebastian's face from the hot work lamp that shared the cabinet space with him.

His hands were sore from all they had accomplished – installing the dishwasher, putting in the sink, hooking up the garbage disposal, and doing the counter tops. Finally, this last part, putting the top on the kitchen island, was almost finished.

It had been two weeks since he and Adria had torn out the cabinets, and the kitchen finally looked ready to use. Duke waved Sebastian off to the shower saying that he could handle the unpacking from there.

Sebastian scrubbed to get the grime off, and when he returned to the kitchen Duke was standing there, staring at a pile of boxes.

"Fox, do something with those while I see if this stove is worth the money."

Sebastian carried the boxes out to the fire pit, weighed them down with heavy stones, and lit them, hoping the ashes wouldn't start the whole place on fire again.

When he returned, Duke was making the dough for some afternoon biscuits and bacon began to sizzle filling the room with its enticing aroma. Duke decided he wanted to watch a football game so they sat in the den eating, watching, and talking very little to each other, the way that men often do.

"Hey Fox, maybe we should put off tomorrow's session. I'm pretty tired out from all this kitchen work."

Sebastian murmured without committing to anything.

"We could make it a fishing day instead. Not here, but down on the river."

Sebastian crossed the river whenever he came out to Duke's, but Duke hadn't ever mentioned any interest in going there to fish.

"Duke, if you don't want to talk, we don't have to talk. You've come a long way in the story, and it seems like we're getting pretty close to the end. I'd say we finish it up."

"Not tonight. Tonight I'm going to get good and drunk. In fact, it's about time to get a pitcher and start working my way into oblivion."

"Tomorrow, then."

"Tomorrow."

It was more a question, the conscious Duke asking the subconscious one if he was ready to relive it.

"You don't have to worry about what you have to say," said Sebastian. "I'm your personal biographer and nothing more."

"I wish it wasn't you, Fox," said Duke.

Sebastian flushed red and started to say something, but Duke held up his hand.

"It's not what you think. When I started all of this, I was expecting a nameless stranger who could be my anonymous

224

confessor, without having to worry about how it would affect our friendship."

"That's what I am," Sebastian argued.

"No you're not, Fox," said the old man, his hand clutched tight to the arm of the chair. "You're the first friend I've had in two years. My old friends have all died, and I burned the bridges with my kids a long time ago."

Sebastian thought about D.H. and their conversation. That was a burned bridge without a doubt. It would take a colossal apology on the part of Duke to even begin to pry the doors open. Lilith was present but disliked, and D.H. was distant and ignored, ostracized for the choices he made as an eighteen year old. Old hurts rarely healed on their own.

"I won't judge you, Duke, no matter how your story ends."

"Won't you? You don't know how you will feel, and you aren't a very good liar. I'll see it in your eyes."

"I might be shocked or upset, Duke, but it doesn't mean that I'll judge you. I just don't see the point in it."

"God will judge me for it," said Duke, "or maybe he already has judged me in this life."

"Because of Lilith and D.H.?"

"D.H.? Who told you he went by D.H. now?"

"I saw one of the letters. The one I brought down to the room when you and Adria were talking. It was signed D.H. and it was sent from Montana, not Canada."

The accusation hung for a moment, taking on a life of its own.

"And that's not all. Here's his address and his phone number," said Sebastian. "He and I talked last night, and you're right, he's not very keen on making up."

Duke erupted in anger.

225

"Daniel made his decision twenty years ago. He walked away from his country, he walked away from his brother, and he walked away from his family."

"And he walked away from you?" Sebastian asked hotly.

"You bet he did. He walked away from everything that was ever a part of who he was."

"And you closed the door on him, forever."

"What I did is none of your business."

"Duke, I'm trying to be your friend. Don't you care that you've got a couple of more grandkids, a daughter-in-law, and hardly any time at all?"

"You already told me that he doesn't want to make up, so why even bring it up?"

"Maybe if you apologized," started Sebastian.

"Apologize? Apologize for what? For trying to make a man out of him? For insisting he stand up for his country?"

There was silence for a minute.

"He never wrote me a letter. Not a single letter."

The pain was evident in Duke's voice.

Sebastian watched Duke, the fire and pain fighting for control.

"He wrote his mother."

Duke shook his finger at Sebastian.

"You leave Winnie out of this."

"He wrote his mother, but not you because he didn't think he had a chance at your love."

"Fox, I told you to leave her out of this."

Sebastian saw Duke's fist start toward him, but astonishment froze Sebastian in place. The punch connected and sent him reeling backward. Sebastian touched his lips and found blood.

"I'm sorry Fox. I didn't mean to do that." Duke said.

Sebastian wanted desperately to return the blow. Instead, he just glared at Duke and stormed out of the house and headed toward the pond. Duke came out on the porch and called after him. As Sebastian walked, he silently cursed the old man and himself.

What had he been thinking? Duke was right. It was none of Sebastian's business. Only, it seemed like such a waste of a family. Sebastian knew it from Duke's manner and from his physical appearance that time was running out. The old man had aged in the months they had known each other. If Sebastian had returned Duke's blow, it might have put the old man in the hospital. Whenever Sebastian watched Duke, he seemed to shift from the fiery fighter to the aged man, moving between the two like a shadow.

Sebastian found his fishing rock and sat down, staring across the water at the house. He felt the old pain well up inside him, breaking down the walls that he had used to shield his loneliness. What did Sebastian know about family? Perhaps it was best that they had died a long time ago. At least he remembered them fondly because of the distance in time and space.

If Sebastian's dad had lived, would he have chastised Sebastian's choices and driven him away like Duke had done? Would he have walled Sebastian out like Duke had done with Lilith? It seemed unlikely. Duke wasn't his dad though. Duke was Duke, an ornery bull of a man who had been through hell. He had watched his friends die in front of his eyes and had learned to harden himself. Loyalty had helped him live through a war that killed so many, and Daniel had turned his back on that loyalty.

Sebastian heard movement and turned his head. Duke was coming through the tree line toward him, two jars of mead clutched in unsteady hands. He stopped as Sebastian's eyes came to rest on him.

"I'm sorry." The words came out quietly. "I didn't mean to hit you."

Sebastian nodded, his eyes flickering from Duke to the sweet brew.

"It's all right," said Sebastian after a while, "I guess it's a personal problem. My family's all gone, and I was hoping I could help your family. Should've known better than to turn my back on a vet."

Duke smiled a little and crossed to the rock, sitting down on it and handing Sebastian a jar. They sat sipping and watching a group of fish break the surface.

"You can take a free shot at me if you want," said Duke, setting down his drink and jutting out his chin.

"Don't tempt me," said Sebastian.

"Go ahead. It'll make you feel better."

"If I was going to hit you, I would have already done it," said Sebastian.

"Fox," Duke was serious. "I'm really sorry. You've been my best friend these past few months, and I never should have hit you. I don't know what came over me."

"I was pushing too hard, trying to find some way for you and Daniel to put things back together. You deserve it after all these years."

"Sometimes I think I'd like that," said Duke wistfully, "Not that I deserve it. I'm quite sure that I'm getting exactly what I deserve. It's just such a screwed up mess that there's no way it could ever work out."

In the morning, they drove to the cemetery, and Duke talked about Winnie's funeral. She was buried there with Antonio, and there were two open slots in the family plot. Duke would fill one of them soon, he said.

"It's kind of odd staring down at that patch of dirt when I come out here to visit their graves, knowing that I'm going to be under it in a few months."

228

They stopped at Sebastian's parents graves as well. It had been a cold dark day when he'd buried them. Georgia had drawn him back down to where they were and fifteen years later, he realized that you couldn't run from your past. The scenery might change, but sooner or later, you were going to have to deal with your baggage.

Duke and Sebastian got so busy telling stories that night that they never got back to talking about Italy, the war, and the secret that Duke had so successfully buried for all of these years. It would have to wait for another time.

Chapter 35

The hills above Avellino, Italy. September 1943.

In the morning, the girls wanted water for cooking and
to bathe Herman's shoulder.

When the Germans had raided the town, they had
dropped rocks and caved in the closest wells, but above the tree
line, was a spring with a good flow of water. Tony and Rosa
stayed at the house while Duke and Maria went for water.

The climb up the hill went fairly easy although Duke
made sure to watch for German troops. He kept his eyes away
from Maria's as much as possible. The drop down to the actual
spring was steep, and Duke had just reached the bottom when
he heard a startled cry.

He turned just in time to catch Maria as her momentum
knocked him off his feet. The large wooden bucket slid out of
his hand and skittered across to the edge of the spring.

Maria's face ended up a few inches from his. She
looked up at him, and her eyes pulled him in. He leaned toward
her face, and she held still, neither moving to meet him nor
moving away. Thinking Winnie, he knew he should stop. This
was a girl who'd been attacked by soldiers yesterday. A girl he
would never see again.

He kissed her.

For an instance, she remained as she was. In another
instance, she pushed her lips against his. After they broke the
kiss, she reached up and slapped him across the face. Long
strings of Italian stung the air as she pushed her way out of his

arms. Her steady chatter increased as she climbed to the bank while Duke filled the bucket. None of it made sense to him, but he was quite sure that several of the words were not fitting for a lady to use.

While she stood, watching and chiding, Duke stripped to his waist and washed in the cold mountain water. When he revealed his scars, Maria went mute. He didn't look around at her until he realized that she had slipped off the bank and walked up behind him.

"Leone?" she asked, tracing the marks on his strong chest.

"Lion? No, it was a bear." Duke said. The word obviously meant nothing to Maria.

"Maria," she said pointing to herself.

"Duke," he responded.

"Dooke," she drew out the syllable.

"Close enough," he said and started putting his shirt and field jacket back on while she watched. He flubbed the buttons like a five-year old trying for the first time, starting one hole too high and ending up with a button at the top and nowhere to button it.

She laughed at him and stepped closer. Brushing his hands away from the button, she undid them and then slowly, with a serious look on her face, buttoned them back to the top. When she was done, she brushed his cheek with her lips.

"Dooke," Maria said as she picked up the bucket and started back toward the house. Duke just stood there, trying to work it all out, even more confused when she threw a penetrating look over her shoulder that cut to his heart. He followed her up the path caught up with her, and took the bucket. Halfway to the cabin, Duke realized that he'd been watching Maria and not the rest of the terrain. He was suddenly alert, frightened of the danger he felt.

Herman was looking better and talking to Tony when Duke and Maria got back.

"Herman, you're awake."

"I was just asking about Jake."

Duke felt a pang. All he had been thinking about was Maria. He had traded Jake for Maria and Rosa, he realized. The thought made him sick to his stomach.

"Jake's dead, Herman," Duke said. "We were in a fight. It was when we stopped a German patrol that was bothering the girls. We all thought it was over until Jake got shot."

"Not Jake," Herman said. "Everyone was sure he'd make it through. Did you bury him?"

Tony started to say something, but Duke interrupted.

"The best we could. We had to get you and get out of there."

Herman nodded, but his voice was choked when he spoke again.

"Where are we?"

"Thirty miles from the front. Three or four days march once we get you on your feet."

Herman lay his head back down.

"I don't know when I'll be able to go, Duke. It feels good to be here."

Duke stared out the windows. Warm and safe. He remembered something Timmons had said back in Texas.

"It's never going to be safe. We'll be in different countries where people have lost loved ones and hate everyone's guts; it's a war that will kill you as easily as you might squash a bug."

Duke looked around and understood Herman's reluctance though. Maria and Rosa's soft voices carried from the kitchen where they were mixing some sort of grain into boiling water.

"Looks like it's hot mush for breakfast, Duke," Herman said.

"Hot mush beats what we've been eating, Herman, but we got to get you on your feet in the next couple of days."

"I need longer."

"Two days, Herman. We move in two days."

Herman got a hurt look in his eye, and Duke clapped him on his good shoulder.

"You're still a soldier, aren't you, Herman?"

"Yes, Corporal," he said, faking a smile.

"Tony, there's a barn out back. Go out there and keep watch till I relieve you."

"Why should I go sit in a barn?" Tony demanded.

"Because," Duke said, finally letting the rage loose, "This just the way Jake acted when he got himself killed. We're not on vacation. It's war."

Duke took the bowl that Maria offered and his face softened a bit, but he still strode out the front door to sit on the porch. Tony stomped past Duke a few minutes later with his rifle and his helmet. He had slurped down breakfast inside.

When Duke was done, he brought the bowl inside and handed it to Maria. She started to refill it, but he shook her off. He went to Herman who was awake. Looking around, Duke took a flat piece of firewood and drew a map for Herman like he had for Jake and Tony a day earlier.

"How do we get through the lines to our side?" asked Herman.

"I don't know. Hopefully, we'll figure that out when we get there."

Duke and Herman sat there for a couple of minutes, and Duke looked at him.

"You did a great job on that gasoline dump."

"I don't even remember it."

233

"You tossed a half-dozen grenades and blew the hell out of it. It's probably still burning."

Duke forced Herman to walk with him to the spring despite Rosa's incomprehensible protest. Herman had to start moving, had to get used to the idea that they couldn't stay here forever. When they returned, Tony was there to interpret Rosa's complaints.

"She says that he is sick and shouldn't be moved. It is mean to make him walk when he is so sick."

Before Duke could respond, Maria came forward.

"Bear?" she said to Tony, only when she said it, it sounded more like "beer."

She walked to Duke and traced the scar on his neck.

"She wants to know the Italian word for bear, Tony," Duke said.

"Orso," Tony said, looking at Duke.

"Orso?" she repeated, disbelieving.

Maria crossed herself and Duke, embarrassed by the attention, slipped out to the barn.

When he came back in, Tony and the girls were talking with Herman. Herman was asking all about where they were, adding to the map that Duke had made earlier.

"I think we're closer to Avellino than you think, Duke," Herman said. "More than likely, it's less than ten miles."

Duke fell asleep with Tony on guard. When he woke up, Tony was gone. He had left a message with Rosa who repeated it in broken English.

"Say go to bury Jake."

Duke kept watch toward the East where they had come from, but saw no sign of Tony. Herman took a turn watching out the window during the night. It wasn't the most effective watch, but it let Duke sleep easier knowing that someone was watching.

Herman woke him in the darkness.

234

"I think it's about 3:00 A.M."

Duke nodded, and Herman was asleep before Duke had pulled his boots on and slipped outside. The perimeter was quiet, and Duke listened for the night sounds then settled himself into a corner of the barn loft where he could watch without being visible himself. A time or two, he drifted off to sleep only to jerk awake. Dawn was beautiful, as the sun painted the hills with golden light.

The front door of the house opened, and Maria stood on the porch with two buckets. Duke dropped down to the ground and walked to where she stood. He poked his head inside to find Herman sitting up and getting his shoulder bandaged by Rosa.

"I'm going to take the buckets to the spring. Will you be okay here?" asked Duke.

"Sure. I'll stand guard once Rosa's done with the bandage."

Duke closed the door and Maria stood waiting for him. She had brushed her hair somehow and was looking fresh in the new light of a beautiful day. As they walked, she chattered on in Italian knowing that he didn't understand a word. Maybe she was talking about the sunrise or maybe she was telling him that she'd never met a boy like him. The sound of her voice made Duke smile. When he smiled, she smiled back and kept on talking.

While they waited for the buckets to fill at the spring, she suddenly turned serious.

"Dooke go?"

"Yes. It's about time for me to go."

"Maria go," she paused as if reaching for a word. "Home?"

"Maria go home. Dooke go home?"

"Home? Not for a while. Duke goes to kill Germans."

235

Maria nodded solemnly and kissed him. Guilt about Winnie fought with the loneliness and fear that washed over him every day. Winnie lost out, and he felt another pain in his heart.

Duke started to lift both buckets and walk back down to the house. Instead, Maria motioned for him to put the buckets down, took his hand and led him away from the spring.

Tearing through the veil of the darkened forest ahead of them was a blaze of sunlight that cut through an opening in the trees and warmed a giant boulder. Maria led him to the top and sat down. She pulled his head down until he was lying on his back with his head in her lap.

The song started softly. Duke had heard her hum the song before, and as she sang, he made up words to go with the melody. He had never heard anything so beautiful. She smiled at him then leaned her head down toward Duke as their song came to a close.

The crack of the gunshot was a strange accent to her voice.

She made one last chirp then a drop of crimson rolled out of her mouth and splashed onto Duke's chin.

Chapter 36

Adria was getting used to the grind of playing two or three nights a week. Some places hired a permanent band and others took whoever they could find for a given weekend.

Johnny's Beach House was one of the former. When the phone initially rang, Adria hadn't been thinking about *Johnny's* or any other venue. Instead, she was thinking about Winston who had escaped her notice while she was reading a book and sunning herself on the porch in front of her trailer.

The dog had come clomping up the steps of the porch and proceeded to drench Adria and her paperback before she could move it out of harm's way. Adria yelled the dog's name, and he barked happily, unaware that she wasn't glad to see him. Still wet, Winston jumped up on her before she quite had her balance, so that she toppled backwards on the chaise lounge.

It was at this moment that her phone rang. She stretched for it, where it had been lying on the deck, dropped it, swore and picked it back up.

"Adria, it's Guy, and ..."

"Guy, what a time to call. Winston just tried to break me in half right here on the deck. If I didn't love the beast so much, I'd kill him right here and dump his body in the water."

"Adria, I've got someone on the line with me."

"Oh," she said carefully, but with humor, "not someone from the humane society I hope."

There was a laugh on the line, but not one that Adria recognized.

"No, I'm not from the humane society."

The laughing voice had turned out to be Cranston Newberry, the owner of *Johnny's Beach House*. *Johnny's Beach House* had a regular crew that played week in and week out. Adria had made inquiries when she had first started her self-proclaimed Tour of the Dives. *JBH* wasn't a dive. In fact, it was a nice bar and grill that sat just north of the pier at Newport Beach.

"Shouldn't your name be Johnny?" she inquired.

Newberry laughed again. "I doubt people would be interested in going to *Cranston's Beach House* so I decided to go with Johnny's instead."

"That was a good call," said Adria, warming to the voice on the other end.

"Well, here's the thing, Adria," said Guy, "Mr. Newberry's regular band needs a break for a month or so. He was thinking of doing something a little different while they were out."

"Guy, you've got to stop calling me Mr. Newberry," Cranston said, "The band is going to go into the studio to do a CD so they asked for a month off. Listen, Adria, I'm going to do a series of shows with an all-acoustic theme. Johnny's Unplugged. Different groups on different weekends, sort of a change of pace. I've heard good things, and I want you to play one weekend."

Adria smiled at the compliment.

"That would be great, Mr. Newberry. Let me double check the dates, but I'm sure that is going to work out for me."

Having a venue come looking for her was a step in the right direction.

"I know you've been playing some smaller places lately, coffee shops and little bars, but we do things a bit differently. We don't have tip jars, and we don't allow artists to sell their CDs. It has a cheesy feel to it that I don't want people to associate with Johnny's. To make up for that, we offer a five-hundred dollar a night payout on the weekends."

"That's very generous," she said.

"My band thinks so, that's why I've kept them so long even though they're good enough to be playing somewhere else. I know you make a lot more when you're acting, but that's our standard amount. I'd need you here at five o'clock on Friday night and an hour earlier on Saturday, will that be a problem?"

"No, that will be fine, both the money and the hours. I don't expect acting money when I'm playing."

"Great," said Cranston, "I'll see you next month."

The month flew by. Now as she faced the front door of Johnny's, she was feeling good. She marched up and was met by Cranston Newberry himself, decked out in loafers, khaki shorts, and a light blue shirt. His blond hair was parted down the middle, and he greeted her with a mild handshake.

"Let me show you where you can set up," Cranston said.

He draped his arm generically over her shoulder and walked her through the restaurant.

"The Friday night crowd comes out in three phases. An after work drinking crowd, some couples out for dinner and music, and finally, the partiers who don't have anything better to do than to drink up as much of my booze as my bartenders will serve them."

Adria nodded as if this knowledge was essential to the planning of her show.

"I might not have asked you to play, but my brother saw you in San Diego," said Cranston.

"Well that was nice of him to say something."

"Brad doesn't have much of a sense of humor, but he does know talent. He said he was hard on you the first night at his place, but you held up and got it together the second night."

"Brad?" she said with a mild amount of surprise.

"You might remember him as the guy who threw a photographer out who interrupted you." Cranston laughed. "Throwing people out is Brad's favorite part of owning a bar."

Adria remembered Brad clearly, but was surprised that she had gotten any kind of positive endorsement from him.

"Most people are in for an hour so play for forty-five minutes then take a fifteen minute break and then do it all over again."

With that, Cranston wandered off, and Adria went through her now familiar routine of setting up. The wind shifted, and a cool ocean breeze began to blow her way. She thought to herself how much this really would be like sitting on her deck at home. All that was missing was Winston and a slobbery tennis ball.

Everything went well the first night. As she was leaving, Cranston stopped her.

"Tomorrow's a little different. The crowd is a bit more casual at first. A lot of people will wander off the beach for a cold one. I've got one large group coming in around eight for a birthday party so maybe you could sing happy birthday for them."

"Sure," said Adria, "that's one thing I haven't done from the stage yet."

"Great, people like that."

Saturday, she got up early and went surfing. It was the first time in months that she'd indulged herself. A few hard spills convinced her that the night before an acoustic concert probably wasn't the best time to risk a sprained wrist. As she showered off, she felt a growing frustration that she had to worry about such things. Suddenly, the ease of acting full time pressed in on her, and the old doubts began to creep in. She called Sebastian's cell phone and got immediately tossed into voice mail. On a whim, she decided to try his home line. Petey answered.

"Hey, it's Adria. Is Sebastian around?"

"No. He's up with Duke. They are wrapping up tonight, do you want me to leave him a message?"

"Oh, just tell him I called."

"Is something wrong?" asked Petey.

"No. Well, it's just one of those days, you know. I've got a big show tonight, and I was feeling a little bit down about the whole thing."

"You'll do fine. Sebastian told me that your concerts were going really well."

"They are, but you know how it is sometimes."

"No. Not really," said Petey, who would rather have her skin scraped off than make an appearance on a stage, "but I'm sure you'll do fine. By the way, Adria, when Sebastian first started dating you, I thought he was making a mistake."

"And now?"

"I think you're great, and I hope that you guys stay together."

"Me too. He's been a surprise."

She stretched out on her couch for a long nap and fell asleep thinking about an obscure writer on the East Coast, who was probably drinking moonshine with a crotchety, old man. When she woke up, it was after noon, and she began to make preparations for the concert at *Johnny's*.

The crowd really was different the second night. Cranston knew his clientele, and the different waves of people shifted through the crowd like the tides. Midway through the evening, Cranston sat down at a table with a number of people, and Adria recognized Guy among them. Adria played her set, mixing in a new song. The song, not that anyone cared, was about Sebastian. The title, *Surprise My Heart*, had been in her mind when she had told Petey that Sebastian was a surprise.

241

During her break, Adria went looking for Guy. He was in the middle of a hushed discussion with Cranston and a tall, serene stranger with grey hair.

Everyone turned as she approached the table.

"Adria, have a seat, we were just talking about you," said Guy. "This is Les Foley, from Paragon Music. Les is now our contact over there."

"It's good to meet you, Adria. Paragon just decided to assign you to me last week. The next day I ran into Cranston, and he mentioned that you would be playing at his club tonight. I took the two events as a sign."

"What kind of a sign?" Adria asked.

Foley leaned back in his chair.

"Miss Rider, I know I look and sound a bit like a simpleton, but don't let my Kentucky accent fool you. I've started or turned around dozens of careers, which is why Paragon asked me to take over your case."

Foley listed names, dates, and places of some of the artists he had helped out. With each story, Adria found herself paying closer attention.

"Ah. I see you're listening now. So I'll tell you what I see. I see a natural crowd pleaser. You are amazingly even on stage. You can read a crowd better than many people who write better music. And, you're comfortable playing your own modest music. Having talked to Guy, I think you're someone who probably can't manage people and details very well."

Adria started to protest, but Foley held out his hand.

"Let me finish. When you take a band on a tour, you have to be able to do all of those things. When you tour by yourself, you basically just worry about yourself. Does that make sense?"

Adria started to open her mouth to protest then closed it again and just nodded.

242

"I think your previous handlers at Paragon did you a disservice by booking you with a band. Not only did it cost more money, but it was completely superfluous to your ability to be a success. All of which means that you and I and Guy need to sit down and see what we can do about sending you out by yourself to some small, but nice, venues."

When Les finished, he stood and shook her hand and said his goodbyes. Guy hugged her and, to her surprise, Cranston did too.

Chapter 37

Sebastian sat on the edge of his bed. He tried to catch his breath for the third time. After a minute, he decided to lie back down. The phone rang, and he looked at the caller ID. It was familiar, but he couldn't place it right away.

"This is Rachel Farmington. We spoke the other day."

"Sure. What can I do for you?" Sebastian said, noticing an edge in his own voice.

"D.H. and I have been talking, and we were wondering if you really think Duke would see us after all these years."

"I think he would," said Sebastian. "I'm not sure exactly how he'll feel about it right away, but I think the idea would grow on him. You and D.H. seemed pretty set against any kind of reunion."

"We were," came her quiet voice, "but you said something about our kids getting to meet their grandfather. We've been talking a lot about it since then. Duke was hard on his boys, pushed 'em hard you know. Up until Vietnam, there weren't any big problems. Duke was rough on them, like all dads were in those days, but he was still a good father."

"I'm not surprised," said Sebastian.

"We were wondering if you could help us arrange a meeting somehow. D.H. found out that he is getting a bonus from work. Maybe we could fly down for a long weekend."

Sebastian heard some noise on her end of the phone.

"Fox?" Daniel said. "Listen. I owe you an apology for the other night. I shouldn't have yelled at you and hung up the phone."

244

"It's no problem. I was too pushy," said Fox. "When did you want to come out?"

"Maybe the end of the month. Is that too soon? You said Duke was sick."

"He's kind of up and down."

"Do you think he'll let us come?"

"I think so. He was mad when I told him that I'd talked to you, but I know he wishes things were different. Let me check with him and call you back."

"Thanks," the relief was apparent in Daniel's voice.

When Sebastian called Duke, he wasn't sure how to pitch it.

"What can I do for you, Fox?" the old man asked.

"I'm wondering how you would feel about me bringing up some visitors toward the end of the month."

"Let me check my schedule," said Duke dryly. "Okay. I'm clear for a few days at the end of the month. The fish have agreed to take a couple of days off."

Sebastian chuckled then tried to turn things a bit more serious.

"Duke, listen. Daniel called me today."

"Oh," said Duke, all of the bluster going out of him.

"He's been thinking, and he'd like to come and see you."

"Trying to make up with the old man before he dies."

Sebastian hesitated, wanting to get the next part right.

"I don't think he's going to come out to apologize to you, and I don't think he expects an apology from you either. But he does want to see you and have his kids meet you."

Sebastian heard a muffled noise from the other end of the line.

"Duke?"

"I'm here. So he'd bring whole family out?"

"Yes. His wife and his two boys. Carter and Antonio."

245

"Antonio?" came the quiet response.

Sebastian could feel Duke being transported into the distant past.

"I don't know how old they are. Early teens I think."

"I don't know Fox. I don't know if I can do it."

"Sure you can, Duke. Haven't you thought about it before?"

"Of course, a hundred times, but what would I say to him? What do you say to someone who you lost years ago?"

"Well," said Sebastian, trying to think of what he could never have, "Tell him that you're glad to see him. Ask him lots of questions about his kids. Go fishing for a few hours so you don't have to talk at all."

Duke was silent for a few minutes.

"Okay. I'll do it, but only if you come up with them. That way if we run out of stuff to talk about it, you can talk to them."

Three or four more pep talks, over the next couple of weeks, were needed to keep Duke from canceling. Each time there was a new set of worries. Where would they all sleep? How would they get from the airport to Duke's? Should he invite Lilith over?

Sebastian borrowed a van from a friend and picked up the Montana Farmingtons at the airport in Atlanta. Carter must have taken after his mother's family with his dark complexion and dark hair. Daniel and Antonio both looked like Duke.

When the old drive came into sight, Sebastian thought Daniel might cry.

The kids looked around, but didn't seem to sense the same magic that Daniel was seeing. As he drove up, Sebastian could see Duke standing on the porch. As the van emptied, the old man slowly came off the porch toward them. After a moment, Duke and Daniel were running toward each other.

They hugged and cried, their tears falling onto the same gravel driveway where Daniel had scraped his knees as a boy and where they had fought about Vietnam all those years ago.

Sebastian heard whispered apologies. Rachel and the boys crowded around, moved by Daniel's emotions. Sebastian stayed by the car the whole time. Duke's glistening eyes caught Sebastian from across the way, and the old man mouthed a "thank you." Sebastian gave a quick nod of acknowledgment and then busied himself with the luggage.

Duke made biscuits and eggs, showing off his new kitchen. Rachel and the boys laughed as Duke told stories about Daniel's childhood.

"So here were Antonio and Daniel standing next to the lake, naked as a couple of jaybirds, and when Winnie asks 'em what they are doing, they tell her 'What do you mean what are we doing? We're washing our clothes in the lake.'"

Sebastian laughed along with the rest of them.

Antonio, who'd been silent, pushed away from the table.

"Hey, Grandpa. Dad's been telling us about the lake. Can you show us how to tie some flies that'll work out here?"

"Sure. Just let me clean up."

"I'll do it," said Sebastian and Rachel at the same time. They smiled at each other.

"We'll take care of it," said Sebastian. "You Farmington boys go fish."

They trouped out with Duke leading them to the shed. Bits of their conversation wafted across the lawn and through the open window, where Sebastian rinsed the dishes, and Rachel loaded them into Duke's new dishwasher.

Rachel spoke first. "I never thought I'd see this day."

"It was a long time coming."

"A very long time. You don't know how many times when I was first dating Daniel that he said he'd never have kids. He said he didn't want to screw it up like Duke had."

The scrape of dishes filled up the kitchen as the two of them watched out the window as the fishermen skirted the lake. Daniel immediately made for some rocks that he seemed to know. Duke walked with the boys, pointing out likely spots for them to try.

Lilith, Calvin, and their twin girls Mia and Carrie came to breakfast the next day.

"Mia and Carrie, this is your Uncle Daniel and Aunt Rachel. And these are your cousins, Carter and Antonio," said Lilith.

Daniel scooped up Mia, and she hollered as he swung her high into the air, and back down onto his knee.

"Daniel, you'll scare her," said Lilith severely.

"Oh, she won't break," he said, a taunting smile on his face. "Will you Mia?"

"I don't think so, Uncle Daniel," said the girl, aware that she was the center of attention.

Lilith fussed some more, but soon it was Carrie who was asking to be swung by Uncle Daniel. Breakfast was served, and after a polite interval, Calvin and Lilith were bundled the protesting girls into the car. Both girls had their faces pressed against the back window as they waved furiously to their newfound relatives. This was in stark contrast to their mother who sat stone-faced in the front seat.

Rachel and Sebastian volunteered for the dishes again, and the Farmington boys put up no fight, making straight away for the shed.

"What an amazing weekend," said Rachel once the two near strangers were alone again with the dishes. "Daniel cried last night. He wishes he had come back years ago."

"Well, he's back now."

"He's back, but he's wondering how long they really have. He says he's never seen his father look so bad."

"There's not a lot that he can do about the past. Those choices were made a long time ago, and all he can do is deal with the present."

"The present is nice enough," she said, her eyes going to the lake.

Rachel put her hand on Sebastian's arm. He looked and saw the tears in her eyes.

"Really. Thank you so much," she said.

"You're welcome. I have to admit that I did it more for Duke than for Daniel."

"And Daniel did it for the kids."

"Which just goes to show that a perfect motive isn't always necessary for success."

Chapter 38

The hills near Avellino, Italy. September 1943.

Duke rolled off the boulder, tugging at Maria, just as
another shot cracked the top of the boulder. Maria's dead eyes
stared back at him. Still in shock, Duke realized that he had left
his rifle back at the creek.

Without hesitating, he began to crawl toward the spring.
A searching fire came in his direction, and he heard bullets pass
close by him a couple of times. He slid over the bank,
scrambled through the spring, caught up his rifle and went up
the far bank just as a shot clipped a branch nearby.

Duke threw a hasty shot over his shoulder and pushed
into the brush. Herman gave him a small wave from the top of
the barn.

Tears flowed down Duke's face as he thought of Maria.
Maria was dead because of his carelessness as surely as if he'd
fired the gun himself. The peacefulness of the cool morning
had lulled him into thinking he was safe, and now, an innocent
young girl was dead.

He would never be careless again.

Duke saw a patch of grey and fired, instantly rolling
over a few feet as gunshots crashed all around him. Three extra
ammo clips rattled around in his pockets reassuringly. He could
hear movement, but didn't see any point in giving away his
position. Instead, he focused his aim on an opening in the
bushes, three feet off the ground. When a patch of grey filled it,
Duke squeezed the trigger and heard a grunt. A German

toppled down by the spring. As the man tried to crawl away, Duke fired a shot into his back and another into his head. How many Germans were there?

Suddenly, they came in a rush. Two made a feint directly in front of him then dove for the bushes. Duke looked to his left and saw a German lining up a shot on him. Duke moved, but someone else shot the soldier before he could shoot Duke.

Duke felt, rather than saw, the Germans to his right. One of them was already falling under Herman's gun, and Duke swung that way and fired from where he lay. The shot pounded the body of a huge man, who threw up his arms and spun around only to be hit by Herman's next shot. A shot from across the creek ricocheted off the roof top. Duke saw Herman drop off the side of the barn and land below before ducking around the corner.

The two on the right were down. On his left, two or three guns continued to fire in his direction. Three left? Suddenly, the man on his left reared up and Duke's gun echoed the shot that took the German in the back.

Looking down the hill, Duke saw Tony.

Duke heard a whizzing sound and saw that one of the Germans had tossed a grenade. Duke rolled to his right, dropped into a shallow dip in the farmland floor, and flattened out as best he could. The concussion was loud, and Duke felt a searing pain along his left calf. Duke spotted a rock wall to his right and crawled toward it.

Once behind it, he yelled to Herman.

"Tony's back there so don't shoot him," Duke yelled.

"I figured that's who that was," Herman said, "Where's Maria?"

Duke was silent for a minute. He could see Rosa's face at a window and he wondered if she had heard Maria's name.

"She's dead, Herman," Duke said, his voice breaking.

251

Herman swore.

"I'm sorry, Duke."

Suddenly Tony fired once, twice, three times. A German stumbled out of the brush then they were all firing. When they stopped, the only noise was the sound of a retreating soldier, crashing through the bush in a desperate rush away from the farm.

When they went back for Maria, Duke fell on his knees in tears. Tony cursed. Herman just stood there, his face masked behind a stony exterior. Duke handed his rifle to Tony, and picked Maria up in his arms. She felt like a doll as he carried her down to the house.

Rosa saw Maria's body and ran to meet them. She was screaming and asking questions. Tony didn't know what to tell her other than the Germans had killed her.

Duke set her on the floor in the house, and Rosa collapsed on her cousin's body sobbing. After a few minutes, she jumped to her feet and came at Duke, beating on his chest and screaming at him. Duke just stood and took it as she slapped his face. Drawn back by grief, she moved away from Duke and knelt by Maria.

"Get everything ready to move," Duke said.

"What about Maria?" Tony asked.

"We'll leave her in the barn or in the house, wherever Rosa wants her. We don't have time to bury her, at least one German got away, and he'll be back with more men."

Duke went out to the barn to be alone. He retched into the hay and fell on his face in the barn repeating "I killed her" over and over again. After twenty minutes, he composed himself.

Back at the house, he found Herman on the front stoop with their packs ready to go. When Rosa came out, she spat at Duke and started to go after him again. Tony wrestled with

Rosa until she collapsed onto his shoulder. He whispered to her in Italian, and they walked out the front door.

Duke walked to where Maria lay on the floor of the living room and looked down at her. No tears came now. He was all out.

"I'm sorry," he said one last time.

Rosa led them though the hills. At the crossroads, the three men left her and headed toward Avellino. They found a half-burned house to take shelter in that night. Duke risked a fire just before dusk figuring that it would be unseen. The fire was small, just enough to heat their K-rations and have a warm meal.

In the morning, Duke's leg was worse, and he struggled to keep up with Herman's lead. Coming around a corner, they ran full tilt into a German patrol. In seconds, there were bullets flying from all directions. Duke felt a tremendous wallop on his right leg, the same one that the bear had broken, and knew without a doubt that it was broken again.

Tony, Herman, and Duke fired back and retreated as best they could. Yells in the distance told them that the area was crowded with the enemy. Herman rigged a makeshift splint and got his arm under Duke's shoulder. Tony led off, trying to find a way out. Behind them they heard more shouts. They kept moving until a river blocked their way.

Looking west along the river, Tony could see that there was firing between two lines.

"Our guys are down there. All we have to do is get past this German position, and we'll be home free."

"All we have to do is dodge, what, five thousand Germans?" Herman asked.

"Now who's the optimist?" said Duke through gritted teeth.

They worked down river, but quickly realized that the Germans were packed thick on both sides of the river while the American position was further downstream.

"We'll float down," Duke said, remembering his encounter with the bear.

"We'll get shot by both sides. Besides, your leg will get beat up," said Herman.

"Forget my leg. I want to live, and we don't have a choice. Here come our kraut friends."

Dusk had turned to darkness, and now they could see lights coming through the woods towards their position. Edging into the cold water, they slung their packs in front of them to use for flotation. The current swept them quickly away from their pursuers. Duke successfully fought the urge to pass out, but nothing could stop the pain.

The first German spotted them after a quarter of a mile, but couldn't bring his rifle to bear in time. As they reached the dividing line between camps, the Germans opened fire. Duke prayed for the bullets to miss. Finally in the no-man's land between the two armies, they began shouting that they were with the 509th. One shot sounded from the American side before someone in authority ordered a halt. Herman and Tony dragged themselves onto shore. Tony pulled Duke out as he floundered, unable to push off on his bad leg. They were met with ready weapons.

"The password is Winter Wardrobe," yelled Tony angrily.

"Put your hands up. Every German knows that password by now," one soldier yelled.

Tony obliged.

"My leg is broke," said Duke while he sat there.

Duke's splint had partially snapped, and the leg was pointed awkwardly to one side. Herman gingerly tried to straighten it. A medic came forward and began to help Herman, and the whole group moved back further away from the reach of the German snipers.

Tony and Herman were put back on active duty the next day while Duke was evacuated to the rear. The doctors there told him his leg was too badly broken for him to return to action. The army decided that he would return to Fort Benning to train paratroopers once his leg was healed. In the hospital, a letter found him and for the first time in weeks, he smiled.

"Dear Duke,

I just received your note about Frank, and it made me cry.

It seems like everybody knows someone who has died. I don't go to the dances anymore. I just can't stop thinking about Frank and you and the other boys I've known. Mary's Sergeant Casey is missing, and she is beside herself with worry.

They say that the men that come home from the war are changed. They don't talk or laugh as much as they did before they left. I don't care. I'll be waiting for you, Duke. No matter what this war has done to you, I'll be waiting for you.

Your Southern Love,

Winnie"

Chapter 39

Monday morning, Duke led them out to Winnie and Antonio's graves. Having Daniel along brought fresh emotions to the surface. Rachel stood clutching Daniel's hand and brushing tears off his cheek.

Duke remembered the previous time they had been here, burying Winnie together. It was also the last time they had spoken. Death had brought them close for at least a moment.

"Did your dad tell you about the funeral we had for his mom?" Duke asked the boys.

Antonio and Carter shook their head. Daniel turned his head and smiled beneath the tears.

"After the ceremony, your dad and I filled in the grave. Just the two of us with a couple of shovels," Duke said.

"What about when you buried Uncle Antonio?"

The boy's voice sounded odd and Duke wondered if it was from standing in front of a tombstone that had his name on it.

"Yes," said Daniel, before Duke could answer. "We did the same thing for Antonio. Mom – my mom – went back to the house because it was just too much for her."

Duke saw Daniel stiffen and wondered if this was the moment he had dreaded all weekend – the moment when the old hurts would surface, but Daniel regained his composure.

"It helped us deal with the grief of losing them," he said finally and left it there.

Duke walked toward Daniel, wanting to hug him, wanting him to know how much he cared, but something was wrong. All of a sudden, Duke fell against Sebastian and hit the ground.

"Duke!" he heard the shouts, far away.

They turned him on his back and he tried to speak, but it was just a gurgle. He was lying on his grave, but he wasn't quite dead. For some reason that seemed funny to him, and he let out another gurgle that was supposed to be a laugh.

He passed out and when he came to, there was a terrible smell, and he realized that he had tubes in his nose. All around him was a familiar sea of hospital green, and he wondered for a moment if they'd buried him alive. The curtain was pulled back, and a nurse looked at his flickering eyelids before going to get a doctor. Breathing seemed like the hardest thing he'd ever tried. A nurse gave him a shot and everything faded.

The next time Duke woke up, Daniel was waiting for him. He reached his hand out to Duke. The old man tried to speak, but it came out more like a croak.

"Don't talk right now, Dad, just rest."

A tear sprang out of Duke's eye when Daniel called him Dad and not Duke. Daniel squeezed Duke's hand, and Duke squeezed back. He reached for a glass of water near the bed and realized he had a tube going into his arm.

Daniel brought the sterile, plastic cup to his lips and helped him take a drink. There was still a tube down his throat, and he longed to yank it out.

"Heart?"

It was all he could get out.

Daniel nodded. "It's a class IV heart attack."

Duke knew the term. His second had been a class four. "Smoke?"

Daniel looked confused for a minute.

"You want a cigar? You're crazy."

"Is it bad?" Duke mumbled, the half formed words barely making it past his dying lips.

Daniel tried a half smile and nodded his head. Duke closed his eyes. He had always wondered what it would feel like at the end. It was different from how he thought it would be.

The door opened, and a nurse came in.

She touched her hand to his forehead then checked his IV, all the while calling him Mr. Farmington and giving him a solemn smile.

"Hot," he said, realizing that he was even though he was naked under his hospital gown.

The nurse nodded and took his temperature. He felt suddenly ashamed and helpless.

When she left, Daniel sat on the edge of the bed and spelled it out for him. The heart attack had damaged his body because of lack of blood flow. Some organs were shutting down. There would be a lot of pain and then the end would come. Daniel said it without emotion, delivering the news the way that Duke would want to hear it.

"Sorrieeeeeee," the word came out of his mouth with a funny twist.

"It's okay. At least we got to see you."

"Lil?"

Daniel disappeared and reappeared with Lilith at his side. Her eyes were red, and the tears began to flow again when she saw him.

"Sorrrr," he croaked.

She cried some more and put her head on his chest.

"I'm sorry too. Why? Why did you wait so long to try to make things right?"

Daniel tried to stop her.

"No. Daniel, you were gone. You were safe in Montana away from him."

258

Shaking her head, Lilith stormed out of the room.

Duke cried because he was helpless, because his daughter hated him, and because he deserved it.

"Dad," Daniel tried to soothe him.

Everything went black for Duke. When he came to again, the room was full. Rachel and the kids had joined Daniel and Sebastian. Sebastian sat across the room from him. The cute nurse stood behind him talking to Rachel.

Duke made a motion and a hoarse croaking sound. Daniel helped him with water, and Duke barely croaked out again the word, "Fox."

Sebastian moved over and sat by him. Duke waited, trying to get enough air. He didn't know what to say.

"My friend," Duke finally managed.

Sebastian squeezed his hand.

"You're my best friend," said the writer.

Duke nodded, sighed, and closed his eyes. Rachel moved to the bed and held the hand of this old man who she had hated for so long. Daniel told his sons that it was time for them to leave. Antonio got up to go, but Carter wouldn't move.

"I'm staying with Grandpa."

There were tears in his eyes. Daniel started to argue with him then acquiesced and let them both stay.

"They say that it's not going to be very long. Do you want me to have them remove the tubes?" Sebastian asked with a soft and weepy voice.

Duke nodded, blinked his eyes and squeezed his hand. Sebastian squeezed back.

The nurse came into the room and hung a bag on the rack that lead to his arm. She gently removed the other tubes. For a few minutes, Duke could smell again. When the nurse left, Sebastian pulled one of Duke's cigars from his pocket. He placed it in Duke's mouth and held it there. The old taste filtered through Duke and then he remembered no more.

Sebastian sat watching Duke. He was unconscious now. The morphine drip the nurse had set up had taken away the pain. Duke's chest rose and fell. Everyone else sat transfixed.

The breathing pattern became more ragged and unsteady.

Each breath seemed to be Duke's last, until finally, one of them was.

Adria flew out for the funeral providing moral support for Sebastian who wasn't sure what to say. A minister assisted Sebastian and read a passage from Psalms. When the casket had been lowered into the grave, each attendee was given a flower to drop onto the casket. The family stood to one side and shook hands and exchanged tearful hugs. To Sebastian's amazement, Adria broke down and cried – huge, anguished sobs. Sebastian held her, feeling her wail echo through his chest meeting both his pain and fears in that place.

"It'll be okay," he whispered into her hair.

As the crowd thinned, Lilith took her leave. She hadn't spoken to Sebastian since Duke had died, and Calvin had merely looked at Sebastian with helplessness.

Daniel, Antonio, and Carter joined Sebastian, each one putting on a pair of work gloves and picking up a shovel. After a few shovelfuls of dirt, Sebastian took his coat off and set it on a chair. Antonio and Carter were soon worn down while Daniel and Sebastian continued. The pastor, who had been watching as he spoke to the last of the mourners, took up one of the shovels that the boys had dropped and wordlessly joined the men.

Finally, quietly, Adria took up the other one.

"Adria, you don't need to do this," said Sebastian.

"Oh, shut up, and move out of the way. I loved him as much as you did, Mr. Fox."

When they were done, Daniel surveyed their handiwork and smiled at the group.

"Thanks. Duke would have liked it."

Rachel had a surprise as well. While they were shoveling, she had gone to the car and returned with a bottle of honey mead.

A writer, a happy couple, a movie star, two underage boys, and a minister who had never tasted alcohol in his life stood with Styrofoam cups raised in a toast on that cold morning.

"To Duke," said Sebastian, "We'll miss your biscuits, mead, and the smell of a good cigar."

"To Duke!" they shouted.

Chapter 40

Adria was tired of Kansas. She had grown up in Colorado with its mountain views and had moved to California for the ocean. No matter how long she stayed in Kansas, she would never get used to the horizon that seemed to stretch out forever without a break.

The concerts were getting more difficult, too. As the cold rolled in, people stayed home and were reluctant to venture out. The ones who did come out drank more against the winter cold, making for a less pleasant crowd.

"Only play coffeehouses in the winter," she said aloud as she primped in front of the mirror. She winced as she realized she was talking to herself again. Her one woman show made the setup was simpler than ever, but also opened the door for the loneliness. Last night she had let a guy buy her drinks after her last show, desperate to have someone to talk to, face to face.

"I was just flirting a little," she said, arguing with the face in the mirror. "Nothing happened, and it's none of Sebastian's business whom I talk to."

Adria had barely talked to Sebastian the past couple of weeks. Between his schedule and hers, there hadn't been a lot of time. In fact, she realized, she had talked to Cranston Newberry far more than Sebastian. Cranston's first couple of calls had been a discussion about Adria playing *Johnny's Beach House* on New Year's Eve, but the last two times, Cranston had called just to talk. A glance at the mirror told her that the crimson flush was back.

"What?" she said to the mirror angrily.

She found the cell phone in her purse and called Sebastian's cell. There was no answer. His home phone was next and she was rewarded with Petey's cheerful voice.

"Hi, Adria. How is your new tour going? Sebastian told me you were busy."

"It's going okay, Petey. Is Sebastian there?"

There was a silence, and Adria could hear some background noise on Petey's end of the phone.

"Uh. You just missed him. He's running some errands," Petey said in a strained voice.

"Is everything okay out there?" Adria asked.

"I suppose," said Petey, "Sebastian's been moody, not too talkative."

Sort of like you right now, thought Adria. What in the world was happening? Was she getting suspicious for no reason or was there something going on with Sebastian and Petey?

"Okay, Petey. Do you know if he's going to be in later?"

"I think so," asked Petey.

"Good. I'll call him."

Adria hung up her cell phone and dropped down on her knees, with her head on the edge of the cream and brown comforter.

"Don't cry. Don't cry," she admonished herself.

Thunder rolled, and she was drenched by the time she made it to the car. When she turned the key in the ignition, Adria was greeted by a breakup song as the radio came to life. She bawled all the way to the bar then sat in the car trying to do something with her makeup. Lightning flashed, and her makeup job was undone by a downpour that caught her in the last fifteen yards of asphalt.

Adria got set up and went and talked to the manager. When she was part way back to the front, she passed a couple, and the man was saying, "She looks like a wet rat to me. More like a cheap imitation of the great Adria Rider."

His companion's response was met with laughter, and Adria looked for something to crawl under. She was mortified, and any bit of self-confidence that remained was completely drained by the time she took her seat to play.

From there it was simply one disaster after another. A string broke on the second song, and Adria forgot the words on the fourth and fifth songs. A heckler let her have it after that. She was about to shut him up with a comment about "that's what happens when you grow up drinking Missouri moonshine," but moonshine reminded her of Duke. When the set was done, she hurried to the refuge of a bathroom stall. After a few minutes, Adria washed the streaked makeup off her face, leaving her red-rimmed eyes as the only reminder of her tears.

She found the manager waiting in the hall to talk to her.

"Look," said the manager. "I don't want to sound mean, but if you're not up for this, why don't you just take the rest of the night off."

"Oh, I'm okay," said Adria, trying to be professional. "There were just a couple of hiccups."

"No, really," said the manager, handing her half of what she was supposed to get for the night, in cash.

Speechless, Adria took the money and shoved it in her pocket. She unplugged her guitar and put it in her case and gathered up her CD display. Her face felt hot as she pushed out into the cold and rain. Behind her she heard a smattering of applause at her departure.

Every light was red on the way back the hotel. When she got there, she noticed for the first time how dank and musty the room smelled.

Adria's cell phone rang and she found a surprised Sebastian on the other end.

"Oh. You're there," he said, "I was just going to leave you a message that I was going to bed early and would talk to you tomorrow. I thought you'd be doing a show."

"Well, I got off early tonight. I had a rough night, and the manager was short on cash so I just did the one set. I started thinking about Duke and lost it."

"I'm sorry. I've been thinking about Duke a lot, too," said Sebastian.

"Petey mentioned you had something going on. Is it Duke's story?"

"Yeah. I've got two problems. One is that, when we started, he didn't want his family to know his story. He wanted me to have a copy and wanted a copy sent off to Italy. All of that was fine, except now, I think he'd want Daniel to know about it."

"Well, is there a problem with telling Daniel?"

"I don't know. I don't like to go back on my word."

"Duke's dead, Sebastian. He'll never know."

"I know, but I've always given whoever I wrote about the opportunity to read what I wrote before publishing it. I don't want anyone to think badly of Duke. The war was so awful. There was so much death and so many things going on."

Where was his spark? Adria wondered. He sounded like he'd lost his best friend, and maybe he had.

"Sebastian, cheer up. Like you always say, it'll work out."

"I wish it would, but there are just so many things going on."

"Why don't you come out and see me? We could take a break and go away for a long weekend. Just the two of us and a jacuzzi."

Her idea was greeted by silence.

"Adria, I've been thinking that maybe we ought to take a break from each other. I just feel like I'm in over my head with you."

"What do you mean? Have I treated you like we weren't equals?"

"No. You've been great. It's just the expectations of where we're going. When I started all of this, I was just looking for a date."

"So now that there is some sort of possible commitment, you're ready to run. What are you afraid of? Are you afraid that I'm going to dump you because you're not an actor? You're real. You care about important things. Do you think I would throw that away because you don't have an Oscar?"

"No. I just don't think I can give you what you want in life. You're running around making it to the top, and I'm in Georgia, with an alcoholic roommate, and a whole set of issues to deal with here."

"So bring Pops out to California. We'll let him room with Winston. I don't understand why you're doing this."

Adria heard the near wail in her voice, but couldn't do anything to stop herself.

"It's not that simple. I just need some time to work things out."

"So you've made your choice then," Adria said.

"It's not a choice. It's just what's going on right now."

"That's not what you said at Disneyland. You said you didn't believe in reasons, just in choices. So you've decided to not choose me," she said weeping openly.

"Adria, I'm so sorry. I didn't ever mean to hurt you. I still love you."

"Oh, don't even start with that BS. If you loved me, then we wouldn't be having this conversation. Instead of ignoring my phone calls, you'd be showing up with flowers and

266

trying to cheer me up, not tearing my heart out from a thousand miles away."

"I don't know what to say, Adria."

"I think you've said enough."

Adria hung up the phone and hurled it across the room where it bounced off the wall. She fell to her knees and sobbed.

"Why, why, why?" she cried, but there was no answer.

Chapter 41

Sebastian was surrounded in his office by boxes. The latest was labeled "Donaldson to Higgins." He took the biography of Wendell Higgins out of the box and leafed through it. The favorite parts made him smile, a tortured phrase made him cringe, and the entire process killed another hour in his now boring life.

Breaking up had been the right thing to do. Even if Adria hated him right now, the pain would be better in one big dose rather than a series of inevitable, little doses down the road. Her photo, sitting on the window sill of his office, mocked him and told him he was full of it.

Another box was pushed into the corner of the office as the cleanup continued. From the far room, he heard the front door open, and the voices of Petey and Pops.

"Knock, Knock," said Petey as she gently pushed open his office door.

"Tsk, tsk," she said. "It's Christmas morning, Sebastian. You're supposed to be getting the kitchen ready for breakfast, not working on your office."

"I've got to get it ready before I leave on the first."

"It's not like anyone is keeping up with what you're doing between now and then, Sebastian."

"I guess not."

He knew his tone of voice was harsh, but he had neither the energy nor the desire to change how he was feeling, Christmas morning or not.

Petey's face took on such a look of sadness that he sighed audibly.

"Okay. I give up," he said.

She smiled and helped him to his feet.

"Merry Christmas, Sebastian."

Petey kissed him on the cheek, and they walked back to the kitchen arm in arm.

"Are you two dating now?" said Pops, "The last thing I remember, Sebastian was sleeping with that actress lady."

"I wasn't sleeping with her, Pops."

"Well, you should have been sleeping with her," replied the older man. "I would have been sleeping with her. She's hot."

Embarrassed, Sebastian yelled at Pops.

The old man looked hurt and glanced at Sebastian while talking to himself, "Just because he wasn't smart enough to sleep with her, he's trying to wreck my Christmas."

"Sebastian," admonished Petey, "It's Christmas. Try to be nice."

Sebastian moved between Pops and the TV.

"I'm sorry, Pops. Merry Christmas."

"Merry Christmas, yourself. Now get out of the way," said the old man.

They sat around the kitchen table eating pancakes and eggs, a Christmas tradition. Pops received a predictable set of presents.

"Beer and more beer! Thanks, guys."

Petey got a series of earrings from Sebastian, and Sebastian got a gift card to a book store from her. Pops hadn't gotten them anything, but they had expected that.

"Well, it's been a good year, hasn't it? What are you guys thankful for?" said Petey.

"Hooters has been good," said Pops.

"That's it Pops? Well, I got to go to the Bahamas, and I had another fun year with my two favorite men," said Petey.

"You need to get out more if we're your two favorites," said Pops.

"Ain't that the truth," said Sebastian.

He sat there silently after that, remembering why he hated this time of year and hoping in vain that Petey would skip over him.

He sighed. "Well, I got older, that's always good."

"You can do better than that," said Petey.

"Okay. It was a good year with Adria, even if it's over," he said. "Are you happy?"

"Not really," she said, "Not when I see that look on your face."

Sebastian slid out of his chair and stalked down the hall. He commenced packing another box, fairly throwing things in. The scraping of dishes disappeared into the hum of the dishwasher warning Sebastian that he was about to get scolded again by Petey. Behind him, the office door re-opened, and he prepared himself for an onslaught that didn't come.

"I'm sorry, Sebastian," she said.

He held himself still for a minute.

"It's not like I had any choice. I should have ended it after the first date. There would be no memories of Disney, her place, finding her in this office, or drinking with Duke. There wouldn't be memories of her everywhere to haunt me. I could have had my date, and we both could've gotten on with our lives without all of the hassle."

"There was a lot of good in all that hassle."

"And some bad, too," he said defensively. "Watching her crying at Duke's grave like that. I couldn't put her through that pain again."

270

He went silent, staring into the past at the cool fall morning – the crunching of the shovels, the smell of dirt, and Adria's wails caused him to shudder.

"Is it so bad that she loved Duke? Did you really save her any tears?"

Sebastian finished packing the box, writing on it with long, aggravated strokes. When he finished, he stood and turned to Petey.

"What exactly did you want me to do?"

"I don't know, Sebastian. I mean it. I just know that it would have been nice to have her here at Christmas or to know that you were with her instead of with me and Pops."

"What did you want me to do?" he demanded again, this time within an inch of her face.

"I want you to be happy. Even if only for a little while," she whispered softly.

Sebastian really wept for the first time. He had held it back all of these months, making decisions, but refusing to really face the end. Petey gathered him into her arms, but he was wishing that they were different arms, and a different figure, and long hair that tickled his nose.

He wished he was smelling the ocean and hearing the waves.

"It's not too late, Sebastian," Petey smiled at him, hopefully.

"It is, actually. She's dating someone else."

"She is not. Not this soon," Petey said.

"Petey, it's all over the tabloids. There's a picture of her with this producer, walking through a restaurant holding hands."

"I'm sorry."

"It's not your fault, Petey. I knew when I shot for the moon that I'd probably end up looking like a fool. This way she gets to make me the bad guy and move on with her life."

271

"And you?"

He stared out the window feeling the chill of winter as it descended.

"I guess I get the memories of her, instead of vice versa. I get to follow my dreams and move into my mountain cabin and retire early."

"You could stay here for a while longer?"

He smiled grimly, "No thanks, Petey. Not unless you're having second thoughts."

"No," she said, "I'm good. I'll take care of Pops, although I will miss my best friend."

"I'll miss you, too, Petey."

A few days later, Sebastian rose for the last time in his house.

Inside his office, Sebastian stacked the boxes near the door where they could be easily moved when the time came. After twenty minutes of heavy lifting, he had to take a break. In the bottom drawer of the desk, he found the padded mailer envelope. It was packed and marked with a California address. He would mail it on his way out of town.

The finality of it all felt like a crushing weight, and Sebastian physically struggled out of the chair. He picked up the last of his new books and placed it carefully on the blotter in the center of the desk.

With an oversized duffle draped over his shoulder, he met Petey in the kitchen. She sat in "her" chair at the table. It was a table they had shared many memories over -- her interview to work with Pops, several Christmas breakfasts, and the heartbreak of unwelcome news.

He realized that he didn't want to leave just yet.

Instead, he wanted to sit down beside Petey and laugh at something she had to say or maybe have an argument about Pops. The chair beckoned, but he worried he'd lose his nerve if he sat down so he dropped his bag on the chair and leaned over to hug Petey.

"I'm off," he said.

Petey stood and hugged Sebastian again, her tears wetting his shirt. He had known that this morning would be rough for all of them.

"I'll walk you out," she said. "Have you said goodbye to Pops, yet?"

"No," he said, staring at the ground. "Although we talked about it a while back."

Pops was propped up in his chair, wearing only a pair of boxers as usual. Petey muted the TV, and Pops started to protest until he saw the bag in Sebastian's hand.

"Finally leaving me," the old man said.

"Pops."

"I'm just joking around. I'd be dead now if it wasn't for you, Sebastian."

Sebastian choked up a bit, as the old man continued.

"I know I'm a pain in the butt a lot of the time, and you've put up with more than anyone I've ever met. I don't rightly know what I'll do without you."

Pops shook Sebastian's hand as firmly as he could. His bloodshot eyes were filled with tears, but none escaped. The three of them walked outside, and Sebastian put the duffle in the passenger seat of his car. Petey launched herself at him one more time, nearly suffocating him.

"Take care of yourself, too, Sebastian," she said.

"Good bye, Petey. Thanks for being my friend."

Sebastian took a look around the yard, putting the picture of the house solidly into his mind. He climbed into the car and pulled out of his driveway without looking back.

Chapter 42

Adria could already feel the jet lag setting in and she wasn't even off of the plane back from the Bahamas yet. Cranston had whisked her away after her sold out New Year's Eve show at *Johnny's Beach House*. She had known that he had something planned because he had asked her to keep the week open. Without her knowledge, Cranston had arranged for Mary to pick up Winston and take him to her place for the week.

Adria had found out a lot about Cranston during a whole week of lounging on the beach, dancing and drinking at night, and soaking in the jacuzzi.

For one thing, Cranston was rich. She hadn't realized the number of clubs that he had his hands in. *Johnny's Beach House* was his baby, but she was starting to realize just how many people and places he seemed to control.

Cranston was also scared of planes, and he squeezed her hand as a solid bump greeted them as they landed in LAX. This was followed by the shrill reversal of the engines. This final flight had gone through Atlanta, and it had made Adria wonder about Sebastian again. Adria and Cranston's outbound flight to Los Angeles had been delayed, and Cranston had chosen at that moment to try to wow her with his sense of humor. Where Sebastian had a natural comedic flair and a gift of words, Cranston's jokes had been predictable, and occasionally crass.

He is holding my hand, though, thought Adria. He hasn't left me because he can't handle the commitment or the lifestyle or whatever Sebastian's problem is. She sighed as she realized that she was still trapped by Sebastian.

"Is everything okay, Adie?"

Cranston thought it was cute to cut her name to Adie, but it was just another reminder of his faulty judgment as far as Adria was concerned.

"I'm fine, Cranston. How are you holding up?"

"Fine. Now that this deathtrap is safely on the ground."

They parted at the gate, and she waded through the parking lot until she found where Mary had left Adria's car. After picking up Winston from Mary's house and recounting her weekend, she made the drive to the beach.

She slept late, waking to find Winston sitting quietly nearby looking at her with simple, trusting anticipation. At first she just lay there and reached her hand out tentatively to pet him, but he hopped up on the bed with her and barked loudly in her face.

"Okay, boy. Let me wake up a little bit then we'll go do that thing you like," she said.

He thumped his way to the door and waited while she made a cup of coffee and sorted through the bevy of mail. Among the New Year's fliers offering carpet cleaning and hyping sales, she came across a manila envelope and froze. She knew Sebastian's handwriting well and felt her heart beat faster. Winston barked at her from the front door, and she set the package on the far corner of the table.

"Okay, Winston."

The smell of her beach hit her squarely in the face, and she drank it while paying scant attention to the dog. Winston ran off with something in his mouth. After a minute, Adria followed. The dog waited for her, dropping the faded orange tennis ball at her feet once she caught up with him.

She threw Sebastian's last gift into the water, and Winston splashed into the water with a happy bark. Adria hurled the ball again with all her might, this time sending it past the first set of waves and out near the break where the surfers played. For a moment, it seemed the ball would disappear forever. At the last moment, a hopeful wave caught it and pulled it toward the shore, a small orange surfer riding a morning wave home.

Adria collapsed on the sand, the tears coming in buckets.

Her vision blurred as her hair dropped around her, and she tried to see through the saline spray. The ocean pounded out its loud rhythm and at last she heard the steps of her forgotten Winston. With a dull thud, the grungy tennis ball rolled across the sand and settled at her feet.

"You don't give up, do you?" she said.

She took the ball again and threw it the direction of the trailer.

"I'll race you, you old dog," she said and began to run. Winston loving this new game raced far ahead of her then off to one side to grab the ball. Adria continued her run, and soon, it was an all-out sprint for the trailer. Winston took the stairs three at a time, stood on the deck, and barked out his victory cry.

Adria kicked off her sandy tennis shoes, pushed open the door, and turned toward the mail on the table. Sebastian's envelope beckoned her. She tore it open and peeked inside.

Adria turned the envelope and tumbled the two black skeleton keys onto the table.

There was nothing else in the envelope besides the keys to Sebastian's mountain abode. No note. No card. A distracted walk to the coffee pot did nothing to calm or enlighten her. There were no more tears. She had left them all on the beach. All she could think of now was her weekend at the cabin with Sebastian.

It was an opening, she decided. A chance for her to do something. His cell phone gave an out of range message, and the house phone had been disconnected. She stood looking at the table, his words echoing in her mind.

"I can't give you what you want," he had said the last time they had talked. He wasn't choosing not to give it to her. He couldn't, but she hadn't listened.

"Oh no," she said staring back down at the keys of death. "No, no, no."

Her suitcase was still packed from the night before, and she threw it in the car and bounced off down the gravel drive toward the gate. Delta had the next flight out of LA, and Adria just made the gate. Landing in Atlanta, she found a rental car and drove to the house in Marietta. She pulled into the driveway, relieved to see Sebastian's mustang framed in the cold January night.

She parked and walked across the yard, wondering for the first time how this all would look if this was just Sebastian's way of getting her attention. The keys rattled on their ring in her hand as she crossed to the front door. Her face blushed and anger filtered through her muscles. Sebastian had called for her, and she had run across the country on the first plane like a desperate child.

Petey answered the door and looked down at the keys, a worried look on her face.

"Where did you get those?"

"In the mail. I don't know when they came. They just came in the mail. Is he here?"

"No. He's there. At the cabin," Petey said gesturing vaguely at the keys.

"Is he okay?" Adria asked.

Petey looked at her, hesitating.

"Is he dying?" Adria asked, her anguish coming through loud and clear.

Petey's face was sad, "Come on in. You look like you're going to collapse."

They sat down in the kitchen.

"Yes, he's dying," Petey said.

The shock nearly made Adria fall out of her chair.

"I told him that he should just tell you the truth, but he didn't want to do that. He was afraid that it would just hurt you more and make you feel trapped," Petey said.

"How long has he been gone and what is wrong?"

"It's some kind of cancer."

"Why didn't he tell me?"

"He thought he was protecting you," Petey said. "When the cancer first hit, he used to tell me that he'd love to sit across the table from you and talk, just to see what you were really like. Sebastian wanted to make you laugh and be remembered by a beautiful woman. For a while there, his health got better, but after Duke's funeral, it took a turn for the worse."

"I saw his car, and thought that he might be here," Adria said, as if that changed anything.

"He gave me the car, the house, and left enough money for me to take care of Pops. After that he left and drove up to the mountains. I just stopped crying yesterday," Petey said.

"We've got to do something," Adria said finally.

"He's calling out to you, at least. We'll drive up in the morning," Petey said.

Adria nodded still in shock. She bedded down in the guest room, but lay awake. There would be no happy ending for her. After a couple of sleepless hours, she went into his office.

A solitary book sat on the desk, *Sebastian Fox – Personal Biographer to the Non-Stars.*

Adria smiled at the title despite her mood and took the book back to bed with her. Flipping toward the back, she found a chapter entitled, *The Happiest Six Months of My Life.* He had

278

written it all down there. Well, not quite all of it, but the highlights at least. Starting at the beginning, she began to read. In the middle of his college years, she fell asleep.

In the morning, the girls took Adria's rental car. They were silent as they wound their way into the hills. Petey had a map and gave occasional directions, but otherwise they kept their thoughts to themselves.

The gate at the bottom of the cabin drive swung wide under the keys. Adria jumped back in and sped up the hillside. The first thing she noticed was that there was no car in the driveway. Sebastian's stuff was piled in the cabin, but there was no sign of the writer.

"The waterfall," said Adria and started for the back door of the cabin. She remembered his words about wanting to die there. Unseen from the front, clear tire tracks led down the path toward the waterfall. As they rounded a bend, they saw his new KIA near the shack.

Inside, they could see a figure lying on a cot.

"Sebastian," Adria cried as she ran.

There was no answer except the peaceful flow of the waterfall.

Chapter 43

Adria stood frozen for a minute. Emotions pounded uncontrollably through her body. Sadness, anger, pity, pain. Petey ran past her and yanked the door open, and ran to his side.

"He's alive!" Petey yelled.

Adria burst through the door to the smell of urine and sweat. Sebastian's breathing was ragged, and his face looked thin and pinched.

"Sebastian. Sebastian, it's Adria."

There was no answer from the unconscious figure, other than a small fit of coughing. Adria knelt on the floor and cradled him against her chest.

"He's burning up," she said to Petey.

He was lying half in and half out of the sleeping bag, and Petey pulled it the rest of the way off to try to cool him down.

"How can he be this hot when it's so cold out here?"

"It's a fever. It wouldn't matter where he was."

Petey grabbed a shirt off the floor and opened a bottle of water from the meagerly stocked shelves. She doused the shirt and passed it to Adria.

"Start with his wrists and the backs of his knees then we'll do his neck and forehead. It will cool him down slowly."

Adria did as Petey told her. A look of grim determination settled onto her face as she worked. Meanwhile, Petey looked around the cabin and saw a calendar with a couple of days checked off, five days had gone by since it was last marked.

"He must have gotten sick right after he got here."

"This isn't working," said Adria. "We've got to get him to a hospital."

His car keys sat on the shelf by the bed.

"Let's get him into his car," Petey suggested.

Petey hooked her arms under Sebastian's while Adria grabbed his legs. They half carried, half dragged the writer the fifteen feet to the Kia and wrestled him into a semi-seated position in the back. Adria crawled in next to him and cradled his head as he slumped to the side.

"Hang on, Sebastian. Just hang on," she said through the sniffles.

Petey turned the car around and zoomed past the house and down the road. One frantic conversation with a gas station attendant, and they were on their way to a local hospital.

At the nurse's station, there was a line of people waiting to talk to the gray-haired attendant who was making sure that forms were checked and double checked. Petey pushed her way to the front.

"Please, I have a friend who is unconscious out in my car. I need someone to help him."

The woman stopped what she was doing and pushed a call button.

"Vernon, we've got a 422."

Looking back at Petey, she said, "Vern will be here in just a second, honey."

She went back to her paperwork without another thought.

Vern appeared and moved quickly to where the girls were standing.

"My friend is unconscious. He's out in the car."

"Has your friend been taking drugs?" asked Vern.

"No. He doesn't do drugs. He's got cancer, and he's been living alone so no one really knows what's been going on."

She led Vern to the car.

Vern knew his business and soon he was wheeling Sebastian into the ER and out of the girls's view. Adria felt the whole world crashing down on her, and the only person who ever seemed to be able to calm her fears was hidden behind two double doors, fighting for his life.

Time seemed to drag as they waited with a sense of dread both hoping for and fearing each time the ER doors opened and a doctor or nurse stepped out looking for a family.

"I'm looking for the family of Sebastian Fox," said a doctor in a green coat.

They both stood and approached him.

"He doesn't have a family, but we're his friends."

"I'm Doctor Gordon. Why don't you come with me?"

"Is he okay?" blurted out Adria, almost bursting into tears again.

"He's stable, for now," said Dr. Gordon calmly. "Let's talk in a room down the hall."

They walked down the corridor with its white linoleum floors, annoying incandescent lighting, and overpowering antiseptic smell. He led them to a room labeled "Family Waiting Room #3." The doctor sat in a chair by the door and the girls took seats opposite him.

"Your friend has severe pneumonia. We've got him sedated for now and on an IV of antibiotics."

Adria began to cry softly and felt Petey grab her hand under the table. They clutched each other tightly as the doctor continued.

"We've sedated him so he won't fight the ventilator or the IV."

"Is he going to be okay?" Adria asked.

"He's stable now, and we're monitoring him. The short term prognosis will depend on if he responds to the antibiotics. If he does, he should be stable in a few days. Can you tell me how long he's been sick?"

"Months," said Petey, without really thinking.

"Months?" said the doctor. "That's odd, pneumonia usually only takes a few weeks to really come on. Does he have any other conditions? AIDS, history of heart attacks, or any other illnesses?"

The two girls stared at each other. "You tell him, Petey, you know it better than me."

"He's got cancer. About a year and a half ago, he started feeling sick and went to the doctor."

"Where was he getting treatment?"

"Somewhere in Atlanta. I'm not really sure where though. I think the doctor's name was Jackson."

The doctor scribbled notes.

"I'll get an oncologist here at the hospital to take a look at him as well, but for now we have to fight the pneumonia. It's really taken hold. Now, there's something else I need to talk to you about. What was Sebastian's living situation when you found him? I ask because he seems to have been wearing the same clothes for a long time."

Petey took a deep breath. "Before Christmas, Sebastian moved up here to the mountains. He was feeling worse and thought the end was coming. That's what he said."

She glanced at Adria, who shook her head in disbelief, still shocked by the information overload that had started yesterday.

"When did he move to the mountains?"

"He had moved up here a while back. Last week, we think, he moved out of his cabin to a little shack. It is near a waterfall on some property he owns. When he found out that he had cancer, he decided that he wanted to die there."

Tears trickled down Petey's face this time.

"Well, he almost got his wish," said Dr. Gordon. "If you hadn't found him, he probably would be dead by now. We can talk some more tomorrow and call around to see if we can find out where he was treated."

"When can we see him?"

He looked at his watch. "Well, he's only been on the antibiotics for an hour. One of you can probably go in and see him for a couple of minutes right now. He's unconscious, and we'll probably keep him that way until morning. Later we'll start to bring him out of it slowly."

The girls nodded.

Petey tapped Adria on the arm, "You go."

Adria nodded, not wanting to argue with Petey.

The doctor led her to the door of the ICU.

"Are you going to be okay?" he asked Adria.

"I don't know," said Adria.

Inside she was thinking. It's not real. It's just a movie. Just act like everything is okay. They entered the room, walking past cordoned off beds. Adria caught glimpses of people hooked to machines and tried to avert her eyes. She focused on the doctor's shoulder till he came to a stop in front of a bed.

Sebastian's color looked better than it had at the cabin, but it was a shock to see tubes running into his body.

"Can I touch him?" she asked Doctor Gordon who was scanning a chart.

"Yes. He won't go anywhere."

"Sebastian," she said, stroking his hand. "It's Adria. I know you can't hear me, but I'm here, and I'll be here when you wake up. I'm not going anywhere."

"Okay. It's time," said the Doctor.

Adria leaned over and kissed Sebastian on the forehead, amazed at how much cooler he was than an hour ago.

"How is he?" Petey asked as Adria crumpled into her arms.

After a minute, Adria got control of herself.

"He's better," she said, "he's got tubes coming out all over, but he looks better. He's got to get better Petey."

"I know," Petey said, "He will."

284

Chapter 44

Sebastian shivered his way through another cold night. Death waited to claim him, and he spent his few waking moments repeating the twenty-third Psalm in his head. He listened to the waterfall and wondered when his weak and tired lungs would draw their last breath. His lungs began to burn, and his whole body shuddered.

He pulled the sleeping bag tighter around himself and began to drift. The night and his sleeping seemed unending. The waterfall was the constant. From time to time, he heard the edge of a song being sung by Adria's soft voice. The singing faded and he found himself alone, and lucid in the shack on his property.

He felt fear. It wasn't a fear of death, but a fear that death would be long and painful. Sebastian tried to stand and crashed to the floor. It took all of the energy that he had just to get back on the bed.

"I miss you," he said to the smiling picture of Adria. She was standing in front of Sleeping Beauty's castle at Disneyland. The chills shook his body like an earthquake and made his teeth chatter. His lungs ached, and his eyes burned like white-hot fire.

Darkness brought another level of cold that seemed to grab him, pulling him until he didn't know if he was alive or dead.

He must be dead.

Suddenly, it was quiet, and warm. There was a poking sensation then it was silent for a long time. In his dreams, he was holding Adria's hand, but she kept going away. He tried to talk to her, but nothing came out.

Sebastian's eyes opened with a start then closed slowly as the room seemed to wobble. Adria really was holding his hand so perhaps it hadn't all been a dream.

"Sebastian, can you hear me? Am I going crazy or did you just open your eyes?"

His eyes tried again and found a tired looking Adria, staring back at him. There were traces of tears in her eyes. She knew.

"Hi," she said, offering him a sad, angelic smile.

Sebastian tried to answer, but couldn't.

Adria released his hand, reached behind him, and summoned a metallic voice.

"Mr. Fox is awake," she said, excitedly.

She took her place at his side.

"It's good to see you again. Awake that is. I've been seeing you asleep for a while."

Sebastian gave her hand a squeeze, but his mouth didn't seem to be working.

He managed to croak out, "When?" despite the tube that was running down his throat.

"When did you get here? Or when is it?"

Sebastian felt himself smile at her babble and just as quickly felt tears come to his eyes.

She wiped them away. "You're going to be okay. I'm going to take care of you. As for when, it's January twelfth. You've been in the hospital for a week. We almost lost you, a couple of times."

This time, the tears were in her eyes.

The door opened, and a nurse named Crystal came in, with Petey on her heels.

"He's awake!" Petey nearly yelled it.

286

"Okay, ladies. Give me some room," said Crystal, staring at the chart.

"Mr. Fox," she said, looking him over. "You've got a feeding tube in right now which we will get removed. Don't pull on anything or try to stand up, okay?"

Sebastian croaked out an "Okay."

"And don't try to talk, sweetie," said Crystal, who was ten years younger than Sebastian. "Just nod, and I'll keep the questions to yes or no. Once we get the tube out, you'll be able to talk a little, but mostly, you need to sleep while the drugs get out of your system. Okay?"

Doctor Gordon came by the next day to talk to Sebastian. The nurse had removed the tube, but Sebastian's throat was too raw to do much talking.

"Well, Mr. Fox, it's a pleasure to finally meet you," said Doctor Gordon.

"Call me Sebastian," Sebastian said in a quiet voice.

"Okay, Sebastian. I hope you've thanked these ladies. They saved your life, and now I'm going to ask them to leave for a few minutes so we can talk."

At first, neither girl moved, but under the doctor's withering gaze, they rose.

"No," said Sebastian, "They can stay."

"Very well," said the doctor.

"You had severe pneumonia when you came in, probably due to some lingering infection in your lungs which was exacerbated by exposure up on the mountain."

Sebastian felt a chill roll through his body as he thought back to the shack.

"Your respiratory system has been weakened by your cancer. I talked to our oncologist, Dr. Kimlin, about your case, and he's going to contact your doctor in Atlanta to discuss treatment options."

"Will it matter? I've been getting worse. My grandfather died from lung disease, and my dad was always sick too," said Sebastian.

Dr. Gordon shrugged.

"Your friend Petey filled me in on your father's and grandfather's deaths. While they died when they were about the same age that you are, that's where the similarities end. Your family history may help a physician cover all the bases, but with all the changes in treatments in the last fifty years, the range of outcomes is quite a bit more hopeful than it used to be."

Sebastian felt numb as the information settled in.

"You haven't been treating this very aggressively, and Atlanta is probably not the best place to live given its pollution level. A change of treatment and geography might have a positive impact."

"How about the beach?" Adria suggested helpfully.

"The beach is okay," said the doctor eyeing her, "although a dryer climate might be better. The biggest thing is to stay away from the smog and haze, and let the doctors do their job. Questions?"

Sebastian shook his head.

"Good. I'll check back on you tomorrow."

The doctor left, and Petey decided to follow him. Adria looked at Sebastian.

"I'm tired," he said.

"I know," she replied, "Sleep. I'll be here."

Adria leaned over and kissed him. He wrapped his arms around her neck and held her there for a minute. She rose, smiled, and made her way to the door.

"Adria?" he said.

She turned back to him.

"Thanks."

"You're welcome, Mr. Fox."

When Sebastian woke up, he saw that Adria was slumped in one chair with her feet up on a second chair. She was partially covered by a thin, useless looking hospital blanket. He wondered when she had last slept in a real bed.

He pushed the call button for a nurse. When the door opened, Adria stirred and sat up. Sebastian asked the nurse for a cup of water which she provided. After the nurse was gone, Sebastian and Adria sat quietly while she held his hand.

"I was so worried," Adria said softly.

"I know. I'm sorry."

"You don't have to be sorry for being sick," she said.

After a moment, she looked at him, "Why didn't you tell me?"

Even in the dimness of the room, Sebastian could see the moistness in her eyes. He thought through the past few months.

"I wanted to. I just didn't want to see you sad again, the way that you were at Duke's funeral. When we buried Duke, it dawned on me that my funeral was right around the corner. I didn't want you to have to watch me die a slow painful death."

"So you thought you'd make me happy by breaking up with me and dying in the place where we had our best memory?" she asked.

"Doesn't make much sense, does it?" Sebastian said.

"Not really."

A few minutes of silence passed between them. Sebastian stared into space, and Adria sat wrapped in her own thoughts.

"If I'd gotten sick," Adria said, "what would you have done?"

"Dropped everything and come to see you."

"Moved to California, driven me back and forth to the doctors, taken my dog for walks."

"Probably," he said grudgingly.

"But you didn't think that I'd do the same for you? You knew you'd do the right thing, but you didn't think I would do the right thing."

"Adria," he said, reaching out for her.

"I'm not done," she said. "Do you think you're a stronger person than I am? Or do you think that I'm so shallow that I'd somehow cast you aside because you were sick?"

"I didn't mean anything like that. I just didn't want to hurt you."

"Well, you did."

"I'm sorry. I won't do it again."

Adria laughed.

"Oh, yes you will."

"What do mean?" he asked, confused.

"People who spend their lives together always hurt each other, at least a little. You think you stalked me? You have no idea what it's like to be stalked, but you will if you try to get away from me again."

"You sound like you've got it all figured out."

"Well, I've had a lot of time to think while you were relaxing in your coma, just lying there doing nothing, leaving me alone to worry."

"We don't even know how long I have," he protested quietly.

"I'll take what I can get," she said. "I'll take you for a week, a month, a year, or however long we've got. We can elope. That's what Hollywood starlets are supposed to do anyway. You can travel with me when I act, and I'll just play local shows when I want to sing."

"The doctor said it might not be the best for me to be near the ocean all the time."

"So we'll get a second place in Palm Springs or maybe a first place. They've got great doctors, good dry air, and it's close enough to LA that I can fly out there when I need to. On top of that you'll have a new clientele for your biographies."

290

"Just you and me?"

"And Winston and maybe a couple of kids."

"Palm Springs," he said with a happy sigh.

For the first time since he could remember, Sebastian didn't feel alone.

Afterword

First a note about the battle scenes. The timeframes and general locations of the battles are real and correct. However, the details of the battles, units, and terrain are fiction to paint a picture of the war that Duke lived through.

Duke and the others are all fictional characters based on nothing more than the types of men who fought and gave much of their bodies, minds, and souls during World War II.

May we honor their memories and their sacrifice.

Along with my immediate family who I noted in my dedication, I would like to thank all of those who read not only *The Biographer*, but earlier novels and fragments that were the first canvasses.

Many members of the Lee and Ostby clans as well as Aaron, David, and Josh provided incredible amounts of encouragement and feedback.

I wouldn't have completed this work without all of you.

Acknowledgements

Cover Design by James, GoOnWrite.Com

Author Photo by Melodie Purcell
AngelWingsPhotography.Com

293